WHERE NO GODS HAVE GONE BEFORE

OLA AND THE NAVIGATOR

ISBN Softcover   978-1-956998-22-1

To order additional copies of this book, contact:
Bookwhip
1-855-339-3589
https://www.bookwhip.com

This book is dedicated to one of the
most amazing humans I have ever had
the honor of knowing and loving . . .

Ola . . . 1936 – 2021.

The Navigator asked me if I would write the dedication for this book that he and Ola co-created and I immediately said yes!

You see, Ola was my person, my friend, my mom, my hero, and oh, so much more. I felt really honored for this opportunity, but it was turning into a serious problem keeping my dedication to one page. How was I going to write about this totally amazing person without creating a whole new book? A few weeks went by and I remembered a post I had done for her birthday. Right then, I knew that I had already written it. Truthfully, it would take a whole book, and probably more, but this will have to do for now.

November 19, 2021post

Just went to mom's page to wish her Happy Birthday and found this from a previous birthday/Earth Incarnation Day! I have been sitting in bed thinking of some of the things I'd like to say to her right now and I think this says it . . .

Nov. 19th, 2019 post

"Happy ~ Happy Earth Incarnation Day to one of the most amazing people I know on this planet. You are my soul-sister, fellow traveler, best friend, mom, hero, and everything in between. We have been thru sooooo much together, more than most people even understand - some good, some bad, some crazy, some we'd like to forget and some we will never forget, but thru it all you have been there, unfailingly. One of the things I appreciate, being a challenging person, is that you always, always loved me and never made me feel like I should be different. (You "Saw" me) You always followed your truth and that allowed me to know that I could follow my truth. We may not always see eye to eye, but I will always have your back, as you have always had mine!

You are truly a priceless gem in this world, and one I treasure to infinity and beyond. Thank you, mom, for everything you are and everything you have done. I love you!"

There are no more Earth Incarnation Days for her and I, and that will someday not hurt as bad as it does right now, but she is hanging out with the Home Team and I know she is celebrating, feeling good, and getting everyone organized for our next grand adventure

The last conversations that I had with Ola, she asked me "How did you find me?"

I said "Mom, I always find you, wherever you are!"
She looked at me, and with a slight grin, she said "Yes, yes you do!"
I told her that I always will
and she said "Promise?"
Oh, hell yeah lady, I promise!

Thank you, my dear, dear friend, for never following where the path may have led, but always going where there was no path and leaving a heck of a trail for us to follow.

CONTENTS

PREFACE

Warning: The contents of this book may be hazardous to your continued pleasure in experiencing reality as it now exists for you! Proceed with caution!

Most assuredly, you may find the material contained in these messages detrimental to your mental and emotional well-being if it does not pertain to you. There are only a handful who will vibrate to the feelings that will be expressed. You must decide!

If the title and contents have drawn you to this book and you are quivering with excitement and if you are feeling great relief that the feelings which have been haunting you are finally being addressed in printed form . . . . then . . . . and only then . . . should you continue to read. This book is for you!

We would like to list a few of the feelings which have been surfacing in the consciousness of those who have called forth this information at this time. First, we would again warn you who are continuing to read out of curiosity or denial . . . but do not feel an instant identification with this material . . . that any further reading will only reinforce fear and denial which is being created on this planet at accelerated rates at this time.

Our purpose in writing this book is to allow certain entities the opportunity to identify their feelings as legitimate and to know that they are not alone. This undertaking at this time was an agreement of ages ago and certain ones will immediately understand that this is a call to them to allow those ancient energies to emerge in their consciousness and thereby create their reality for the realization of their beingness.

Our intent is not to birth anymore fear! This is why we caution you . . . because, in truth, only you create fear within you from the beliefs which you hold on to tenaciously . . . regardless of what is presented to you from within your own self or what is presented to your experience. Since you operate much as a computer, you are programmed to vibrate at the fear level whenever any revelation is made that is other than the accepted "religious", political, or social views which you received from your ancestors.

However, there are a few at this time who are realizing that there is more! That "more" will be discussed in the other chapters as given. So, with "much ado about nothing", we would continue with our list. If the following feelings are personal and private to you, then we would suggest that this book is written for you and by you and through you.

A list of feelings peculiar to certain ones for whom this book is written:

1. The "accepted" definitions of "God" no longer hold the awe, respect, fear, or worship that they may have had in the past.

2. You feel connected to a living force or whatever you wish to call it, which is creating everything exterior to you and within you. More amazing . . . You feel that this force is you!

3. You would describe the power and feeling of this force as "All That Is" and "Love" is beginning to have a new meaning for you. Connecting and identifying with this force, feels like "Heaven" and disconnectedness or separation feels like "Hell"!

4. Now, the next feelings are kind of sticky-wicky. You really are finding out that you don't even know how to separate yourself anymore. The feelings that are emerging from within you are forcing you to view everything as the same thing . . . only in different guises. In other words, evil characters are seeming like

they are just other "You's" dressed in Halloween costumes trying to scare good characters.

5. You can remember how much fun this play acting has been . . . all the tension, emotions, and unexpected crises . . . . but! This is a big "but"! You are tiring of the game!

6. Of course, this is causing a dilemma within you. You don't even like to look at this feeling. It feels like . . . well, let's see . . . "If I don't know myself as this opposed to that, then there must not be a me". If I am no longer "good" as opposed to "bad", then I don't exist!"

7. If you are feeling that this is no longer a valid way to establish individuality, then you are wondering what could possibly replace your experience of duality.

8. Here's the paradox! You feel more of an individual than ever you could imagine and at the same time know yourself as "All That Is". Whoaaaaa . . . . can this be? Sure! Maybe this describes what you are really knowing within of what you came to this planet at this time to realize. We're talking "integration" here and reconciling of dualities . . . a new creation!

9. "So, this is the unknown! Great? But, what about all of the teaching that says that I'm merely returning back to the Source through many dimensions and levels and joining the ocean of all Beingness? Isn't that the highest teaching?" Really now! Does this excite you? Tell the truth! You are asking, "What purpose does it serve to have gained all this feeling of control in an individual focus if I'm just to surrender it and go back into nothingness?"

10. This feeling is one of excitement about what it would be like to take all this sovereignty that you have gained in this body . . . in union with your knowingness of yourself as "All That Is" . . . and explore further creative possibilities. Can you believe that you're really contemplating this?

11. There is the gnawing feeling that this may be "heresy"! After all, what could be more wonderful than attaining the pure consciousness of the Source of all that is . . . twelfth dimension or white light or whatever it's called?

12. Look, you don't even feel excited about "Cities of Light". Sure, you think that would be wonderful and of course, that's the next level of evolution for mankind to explore, but! This is another big "but"! You want to know if there is more than that! You've read and listened to speaking about other planets and their more advanced and perfect societies and you recognize that mankind needs models for their benefit, but! That doesn't feel like what you are seeking. How can that be?

13. As one who realizes that each individual creates his or her own reality, you know that the games of victims and victimizers are only illusions . . . plays . . . that have allowed experiences in form and structure. You feel that none of these games are interesting anymore. When the questions of environment come up, you feel both the side of the owl and the side of the logger. Politics just convinces you further that both sides of every issue are valid. Each person's view is a valid reality. In other words, you know that there is no absolute truth which can hold your attention long enough to let you join a side and play the games. Basically, you have not found a path or a plan for further creation. This feeling is frustrating, is it not?

14. All those who seem of like mind with you about the need for change and something new . . . all of them seem to have a single focus and intent to create their truth. You've read much material and explored many of these plans. In fact, you are probably a walking encyclopedia of information about the New Age Movement. You feverishly consume any writing or speaking that may give you a clue as to why you're here. All of the information that you have gathered still has you asking, "What then"? Can you really trust your own feeling about the more that you desire? Could it be that the strong desire within you . . . is your path?

15. There is a feeling that feels like home to you and this is the one! Remember the feeling you get when you hear the words . . . "To boldly go where no one has gone before" . . . "Beyond the Beyond" . . . beyond time, beyond space, beyond enlightenment, beyond ascension . . . Beyond anything known to man or "God" . . . the "unknown"! Now! Feel this! This feeling excites you! This is what you want to do . . . Explore new territory and create new dimensions that don't even exist now and never have existed before because they aren't in the memory of "All That Is" yet! So, the motto . . . . . "Do not follow where the path may lead. Go instead where there is no path and leave a trail". . . . best describes your true feeling. Creation is ongoing . . . Never ending!

16. And, finally, is there a deep yearning within to find others who feel the same as you about all of these hidden feelings? Yes, there is and this is the strongest! You know that nothing that you have attained or could attain in your personal spiritual growth means anything to you without love and that means others. So, your heart calls out, "Where in the hell are you?".

We have not listed all that you are feeling, but we know that you will recognize many of your innermost feelings in this list. Good news! So will others!

Now is the time to validate these feelings within you through your own sovereignty and be prepared to merge with others who carry this same vibration. The call is going out now through this writing. You designed the plan in eons past to explore the "Unknown" and you decided the time when you would join up with each other on this planet and prepare for the journey. Now is that time! This is the Gathering!

FOREWORD

"Last Call"!!! This "Earth Time-Space Station" is about to close!

Now c'mon, you must have known that temporary facilities like ours have precise "dates and times of operations", right? Unless maybe, you've been so caught up in all the festivities and sideshows we provide here that you weren't paying attention to the time whizzing by? Yeah, that happens a lot, especially to new folks. You can get so overwhelmed by all the music, the bright lights, side shows and cast of characters that you don't notice the signs posted all around the place about our new hours of operation and the phasing out of so many of our attractions.

Well, in any case…sorry, tough luck, but the truth is that everything here is rapidly wearing down around us! Now that doesn't necessarily mean that it's all "Doom and Gloom" from here on. Nope, you can still look on the bright side of things…after all, it's a big Universe, right?

And so, there's some big adventures for the boldest, bravest and most loving souls…lots of other dimensions and "realities" to explore! Speaking of which, did you see that huge object in the sky over yonder? No…? Well, that's okay, "they're" there, trust us and they are carrying a vibration of extreme importance to the "Ending of Time" as you've known it!

As a matter of fact, these "Galactic Crusaders" are our "kinfolks," and they go all the way back with us to "No Beginning" and all the way forward into "No Ending"! Which is why we're talking about them now, because "they" transmitted the information in this book to us over a period of 4 years (1989-1992), to be brought forward at this time period in the form of this intrepid "Travelers Guidebook: To Boldly Go Where No Gods Have Gone Before"!

Kind of an unusual subject matter, isn't it? But hey, you did indicate that you are still looking for more festivities and excitement, right? And if you're still here after reading that crazy Preface… (I mean, what kind of crazy authors tell their potential readers that "reading our Book may be hazardous to your "well-being" here?). Strange "Business Minds" that's for sure, but maybe they're speaking from personal experience! Because a lot of the subject matter that is in these pages may be new territory for you and you may find yourself "outside your personal comfort zones" as far what "is reality" and what is "crazy or not true"! This is a very "normal response" to subject matters that are unfamiliar to you, but it is also a very strong motivation to begin learning about new aspects of "Reality"!

There have been many Books, Movies and TV Specials that are covering a great amount of the subject matters that are found in the chapters of our Book. I was amazed by the new ideas that were covered in the 2015 Science Channel's episode of "Through the Wormhole" called, "Do We Live in A Matrix?" starring Morgan Freeman in which he asked, "are we players in the greatest Video game ever…a Universe created by someone or something else? If so, then this should free us to take risks and live life to its fullest."

There were also a lot of shows and interviews with scientists and well-known researchers concerning "whether or not we all are living in a Simulation?" When Elon Musk was asked this question at an appearance on stage, he replied that in his view, "the chances are billions to one that we are NOT living in a Simulation!" So, if our third Dimension is a "simulation", what are we "the humans who are unconsciously being tested here", in training for and who is observing us and looking out for our safety?

Well, an efficient "Guidebook" will give you valuable information in its Table of Contents to prepare you for the directions taken in the Book, and this book shines brightly from the first chapter through the last. The first "inspired" Chapter 1 was written by Ola and gives our readers the most beautiful and important information they will need to begin their most important journey! And you will know it when you read it, so don't worry. It's all "Good News"!

Love triumphs and the "End is only the Beginning of the Adventures Beyond"!

And, as to the purpose for "us being in this world and unconsciously being trained while growing a new view of reality", Ola's first channeled message to our family was: "You are not surrounded by dangerous potential events, but rather by an army of Beings who will guide and direct you in the ways you should go!" This was further emphasized as we learned more about the nature of this world and our role as "conscious beings" with these words: "You are not in the world; the world is in your Consciousness. Your view of "reality" can create forces that are opposing, and you must experience them. You are more powerful than you know!"

The messages in these chapters are a road map of sorts for those people who are seeking a great evolutionary leap in the consciousness of humankind at a critical juncture in the history of our planet and the universe. And what is being revealed here in the messages of this Book are the true pictures of our reality and our potential to "grow out of a temporary human only experience" and into a new view of "our own consciousness as being birthed in the elemental force of the Big Bang" from which all things were created!

This is why Chapter One is so important for you to understand, because all creation, everything that "is" originates in Love! We're talking about the Source of "all that IS" and your individuality was derived from that intense desire, your life Source is that energy of love and no greater Love can be shared with others than a full participation in this union upon this plane!

This is a Knowingness of "Oneness"…a "Christ"… the hope of humankind!

CHAPTER 1

"IN THE BEGINNING . . . . ."

Now, we need to establish an understanding at the very beginning of this chapter. Truthfully, we will be describing many things that are indescribable! Got that? We will use words to convey to your conscious awareness certain models which will allow you to envision for yourself what you call the "Past" and the "Future". However, realize . . . that there are truly no words to describe any of this. However, it is knowable.

Your imagination and intuition must come into play now for this to impact you as you have planned. Imagination and intuition have created all. . . seen and unseen! Anything created first existed in a mind as a thought of an object or event and then through desire for the experience of the object or event, it was created.

Whoooaaa. . . I better slow down a bit and make sure you've got this! Nothing, right now, is more important for you to grasp than the understanding of what we've just said! Think about it! Take anything that exists in a reality. . . any event or any object. . . and contemplate its creation in a linear fashion.

First, there was the thought of an idea of an event or an object. Second, either desire was present or it wasn't. If desire was present to realize the event or object through experience of it, then an intenseness set in and third . . . action was initiated to bring it into manifestation or materialization. First, the thought of an idea . . . second, the desire to realize the event or object of that thought . . . third, the action necessary for the creation of the object . . . in that order. Thought . . . . Desire . . . . Action.

See, there really is no mystery concerning creation. It is simple. It always has been. We needed to get that straight because this chapter is going to involve the beginning of everything that is known. Of course, we will begin with the "Source" of all creation. Now, right away let's get something else understood. We will be referring to the "Source" by many names . . . "God", "The Force", "All That Is", "I Am". You may use any words that best describe this to you. Your own words which describe your feeling about this concept . . . . will resonate within you as truth. This is what we desire . . . Intensely!

"In the beginning" . . . . . before there was anything . . . there was only darkness . . . which really isn't anything because darkness is the absence of anything and light is, obviously, the presence of something.

Basically, science says the same thing. They have concluded that all creation was derived from an area of darkness in which a sudden "Big Bang" materialized. In fact, they theorize that this area of the "big bang" is where every seen and unseen universe and all within the universes . . . first appeared. With modern technology, they declare that they are looking back into the past and viewing this happening. Of course, they are viewing light.

You should really be getting into this about now. Are you on to something? Darkness . . . nothing. Light . . . something. Science is now confirming an event which was created in your distant past. What was this event?

Imagine that you are in this vast area of darkness and imagine that this area is really a gigantic mind or brain. All of a sudden, you observe a tremendous explosion of light! Of course, you would be blinded but when you recovered, you would have the realization that you had just witnessed a synapse. The dictionary defines a synapse as . . . "the point of contact between adjacent neurons where nerve impulses are transmitted from one to the other".

Just suppose that was what the "big bang" really was and that this nerve impulse contained all of the consciousness and energy that would ever be needed to materialize and manifest all ideas of events and objects that could ever be imagined. Could that thought have been the first thought of an idea that formed all of creation? Yes, it could have been and we would like for you to stay with that image to help facilitate knowingness within you of what we are saying.

What was that thought? It was . . . . "I Am!". "I Am!" was the first thought. Now, stretch yourself a little bit here to imagine what that felt like for the "Source Of All That Is" to be aware of existence. Remember, however, that at this point, it is only a thought.

Actually, none of this that we are describing could have been linear because there was no time or space. So, we're really speaking "simultaneously". Okay? Simultaneously, there existed an intense desire to know fully and completely this thought of "I Am". This intense desire was "Love". Now, we are speaking of a divine love . . . a love which has always been the motivation for all action. So, our definition of "Love" is . . . "desire to know "I Am". All creation . . . all creation . . . originates in "Love".

This is what motivates you and has always motivated you and will always motivate you because you are the means of realization of the thought . . . . "I Am". You are the manifestation and materialization of "I Am". Myriads and multitudinous forms and structures have been created to consume all that that thought includes, but none so perfect as you . . . a specialized focus of "All That Is" which reflects back to "All That Is" the realization of "I Am".

Contemplate your own knowingness. Every thought, every desire, every action you have had or ever will have has been exactly the same . . . . for the exploration of knowing you and it is through exploring and experiencing all of your possibilities and probabilities that you come to know yourself fully.

All your adventures are merely a reflection back to the inner source of yourself and then you have the realization of "you". All creations in your reality are mirrors for you. All material things and all people go to make up an objective reality that acts as a mirror in which you can subjectively see your reflection and know yourself. How else can you see? How else can you know? You are unable to view yourself except through a mirror.

The mirror through which you view yourself in the dimension where you are now is dusty and tarnished and only reflects a distorted picture of yourself. You have been exploring yourself as a separate individualization of the whole and thereby, limited. Another possibility created from infinite possibilities, but one in which you are not able to see that "Love" of yourself always is your motivation same as "All That Is". The feeling . . . the vibration of "Love" is your source. Your individuality was derived from that "I Am" . . an intense desire . . . a feeling of "Love".

The energy of that love was the action that brought about creation. For you see, that intense desire created action . . . and you are the manifestation that action created.

Before we get too far ahead of the story, let's go back to the Source and the beginning thought of "I Am". A myriad of forms and shapes and events immediately presented themselves to the mind of "All That Is". Now, when we say myriad, you must know that this is beyond your capacity to imagine, but we will use this as a model anyway. Infinite possibilities for these forms and events unfolding forever . . . may help you to envision this a little better.

As the imagining grew more vivid and in greater detail, the "Source" felt an increasing desire to allow the manifestation of them for the realization of it all. You know that many times your dreaming and visualization of adventures and roles and certain objects can become so real that your desire to see them in actuality . . . in form and structure . . . is overwhelming. At these times, you feel an intense and focused desire for them. Nothing will do you but that you must become the image you visualize yourself as being and you proceed to create the events or objects that will give you the experience of that identity. This is what compels you forward through time each and every moment.

Much religious and philosophical thought has labeled "desire" as the main evil which permeates man and causes untold misery and pain. Many have tried to eliminate this desire through the denial of certain experiences . . . material objects or legitimate functions of the body and instead, focus on a state of being in which there is no feeling of want or desire or need. How sad!

This cannot be the "will of God" as so many have imagined . . . for the example just given shows that all creation is derived from desire . . . intense desire. Without the vibration of desire . . . Which is love of "I Am" . . . all movement would cease and all creation would disappear. Reason it! Consider what your science knows concerning the nature of reality . . . it is all vibration . . . all energy . . . all movement. Nuclear physics . . . quantum mechanics . . . In their search for the building material of mass, have discovered what? That there is no mass . . . no solidity . . . only a continual perpetual flow of movement . . . energy! E = MC squared . . . Einstein's theory of relativity says that energy equals mass and mass equals energy!

This realization manifested on your plane in 1905 from a man called Einstein when he published his revolutionary paper. Heard of him? Heard of his formula? Ever wonder where all of the miraculous wonderful technology that you use every day was derived from? This formula! This realization! And much more is being created by those in certain circles who have realized that all of the creation sensed by your five senses are merely patterns appearing in a sea of energy. "Light is nothing but rapidly alternating electromagnetic fields traveling through space in the form of waves." (1) ("The Tao of Physics" by Fritjof Capra)

So Albert Einstein, at the turn of this century, introduced new thoughts. Do you know what they were? Look them up? They have revolutionized your earth technologically but they have not influenced your mass consciousness yet. The average citizen lives each day in total ignorance of the structure of physical reality. In fact, the information coming to your world recently from extraterrestrials has been known on this planet by your scientific community for almost 100 years, but because of the control exercised by those in power, you think this material is "new".

It's not new! It's just that this information . . . this light . . . has not impacted your consciousness. Why was this realization kept from you? Why have you not wanted to know what Einstein discovered? One little word . . . . change! Change! Yes, everyone and everything would change if this information was common knowledge. Remember that we said this as you read on further, because you will feel a resistance to knowing this and you will feel a vibration of dread or fear. As you begin to allow this information to enter your consciousness and you begin to feel certain vibrations, we will address them.

You must know that the incredible knowledge that Einstein shared is not complicated! Oh, but you thought so, didn't you? We will attempt to explain it simply so that you need never be in the dark again. He said that all mass was pure and simply . . . energy. Much confusion has circulated around this simple understanding that energy and mass are different names for the same thing because certain ones did not feel that you were prepared to know this. However, we encourage you to ponder the many ramifications of that thought because we have the utmost confidence in you and your ability to define and image this understanding and draw certain conclusions about the nature of your existence and all other existence.

Realizing that mass and energy are different forms of the same thing, we need to ask the question . . . forms of what? In order to answer this, we need to contemplate this "I Am" thought a little more. We said that this was awareness of existence. Now, it seems that "consciousness" would be a good term to use for this awareness. So, staying with our little model of the synapse or "Big Bang", darkness would represent unconsciousness or no awareness of existence. Light . . . we determined was something and now we can image what that something was . . . Consciousness . . . awareness of existence.

Could this be? Could all creation be but consciousness? But that would mean that everything that has ever been created or existed was the result of awareness of "I Am" which felt intense desire . . . "Love" . . . and the action which followed was merely an expression of that consciousness . . a realization resulting from an awareness of existence.

But, wait a minute! That would mean that everything . . . all creation and its adventures and all knowingness gained from creation does not have the importance or deep meanings which you have given it! You ask, "Are you telling me that there is nothing more significant in all of creation . . . that there is no other purpose than awareness? Can that be all there is?"

Oh, my dears! Don't you see what you have missed? Don't you see why you are considered asleep? In your slumbering, you have thought that you placed so much value on so many things and all the time . . . your awareness of your existence was the "Image of God" that was gifted to you.

Why else would you fight so tenaciously to hold on to what you call "Life" and fear losing it in "Death"? What is "life"? Isn't it your awareness of existence? What do you think "death" to be? Don't you believe that it is the loss of awareness of existence? Feel this!

Sometimes, if you can face the fear of losing something, then you can determine what it is that you really value. Backasswardness is one of the characteristics of the human drama which you have been exploring. It's a good example of humanity's sense of humor. So, we would show you that your fear of dying is nothing but a realization of how much you value your awareness of existence! "Death". . . which you believe is cessation of awareness . . . is your greatest fear. Therefore, life . . . awareness . . . is your greatest treasure.

We do not mean to imply that you are separate from this awareness. You are this awareness! You are "I Am". Your language leaves much to be desired as a means of expressing these concepts but still, we know that you can feel the vibration of our thoughts being conveyed to you in this written format.

Now, what is "life"? What does living consist of from moment to moment? Does it consist of things, houses, jobs, people, etc.? No! . . . because you could lose everything that you possess . . you could lose all of your relationships . . . you could lose health . . . you could lose your acquired image . . . but, you would still have what? Consciousness . . awareness of existence . . . and because "Love". . . desire is so intense, you would still rejoice because you exist. That desire for existence would continue to create and provide and maintain life.

We probably will be talking about this third-dimensional illusion called "death" later on. It does not exist in the context in which you experience it anywhere else in all the universes. However, to help you understand this, we will need to continue our discussion about the first thought . . . "I Am".

So, light manifested everywhere in darkness all at once! That's a big statement! Let's break it down to a simple form. Previously, we have proposed that all is energy and, of course, so has your scientific community.

Just what do they theorize about the nature of physical reality? Do you know? Chances are . . . you don't. Probably, there are several reasons. We will list a few and you can pick and choose which ones apply to you. (1.) You were told and you believed that it was too complicated for you to understand. (2.) You were too busy manipulating and juggling material reality to wonder about its nature. (3.) You were convinced that your pursuit of spiritual reality required you to ignore or deny value in the knowledge of anything physical. (4.) What you had heard and understood about physics made you feel insignificant and impersonal. (5.) You knew that if what they were discovering was true, then your whole belief system about reality would have to change and so would you. (6.) You just haven't had "time".

How are we doing? We feel that we have probably hit all of you by now. Possibly, we will address these excuses before we are finished with this topic. Really, though, doesn't it make sense to find out as much as you can about your existence in this physical reality since you are so desirous of remaining here? Maybe a clearer picture and understanding would afford you more creativity than you now experience. It might even convince you that your love of existence in physicality with a greater expansion of awareness could be your next adventure!

Did you pick up on something that we dropped a little way back? It was very cleverly slipped in to prepare your mind to receive our next discussion. We said that "all of the creation sensed by your five senses are merely patterns appearing in a sea of energy." Very clever of us to interject it before so that we could repeat it. Repetition is a great aid in impressing you with something that we are presenting.

Now, if you haven't already gone ahead of us and realized where this is leading, we will tell you. Consciousness must be energy! Obviously, if consciousness is "All That Is" and energy is "All That Is" . . . . then consciousness is energy! More precisely . . . . "awareitized" energy . . . . meaning, energy that is knowing, cognizant, and informed!

That's exactly the terms used in physics to describe the quantum theory of particles at the subatomic level of physical mass.

CHAPTER 2

THE GODS CREATE HEAVEN AND EARTH

All present. The bell has rung and class is ready to begin.

We are here now to convey to you certain words and symbols that should allow a conscious awareness on your part of "knowingness" which resides in you. We will not give a name for our "presence" and our energy because it is a combination. It has been our decision to share in this and we welcome this opportunity. Thank you very much.

It is a necessary undertaking for the time and period which you are entering and which, in fact, you are already experiencing. Many words have been conveyed by us to all present, many words have been read by you, and many of you have done many things with those words. Many of you have recognized that the words themselves were not the thing which they spoke of but, merely symbols. So, we hope to bring you to a clear awakening and understanding. All that has been spoken to you and all that you have read will become very clear in this process. The meanings that you have attributed . . . the meanings that you have heard that others have attributed will become your very own knowing.

This is a revelation and an understanding like none other that you have received. The time is drawing nigh . . . for there must be a recognition of who you truly are, and what this world truly is, in order to prepare you for the cessation of what you have experienced to this date and the beginning of the "New".

I have introduced to your channel today a re-understanding of her name that was given her. The name is "OLA" . . . and she has not taken it seriously. She found it extremely humorous, as have others, because of the "sounding" to those present. She has not understood because her machine will not register the value. That name is her personal identification of her "knowingness" . . . not her physical form.

"Her name is: "O..L..A"...with "O" standing for Omega and "A" standing for Alpha." That may sound backwards but, in reality, it represents the ending of the old and the beginning of the new, which is her gift and reason for being here. "O" stands for Omega . . . the Ending. The "L" stands for the transition, the middle transition... to the "A". . . the beginning of the adventures beyond.

"OLA" is the center of the word "Solar", which is the "Sun". As will become clear to you from the instructions being passed along, the symbols and words "Sun" . . . "Son" are very significant, because in the "Sun/Son" and from the "Sun/Son" and by the "Sun/Son" are all manifested creation and form derived. You do not understand that now, but hopefully, you will at the end of these sessions . . . begin to understand.

Now, we do not want to frighten you with religious or scientific terms. So, we will be using drawings and symbols as well as words to convey these understandings to you. It is visual because what is being transmitted and received cannot be conveyed in 3 dimensions, even to the drawings. That is why symbols are used . . . to trigger a jumping . . . a spiraling of your knowing to other dimensions. But, it will not be produced in 3 dimensions. You must have more awakening, understanding, and seeing of other dimensions.

However, we will proceed from your fourth dimensional understanding of words and symbols to direct you into a passage and a doorway . . . allowing of the knowingness that is within you.

Now, you have heard many terms, such as the "Knowing within You". You have not understood that, but you have been faithful in allowing yourself to hear, to sense and to feel these words and thereby, you have become conscious of an unknown.

Consciousness of an "unknown", that conscious awareness that there is an unknown, was presented to you to create within you a desire to know . . . to feel . . . to go beyond the "known". Many of you have been frustrated in your attempt. You have felt that the unknown was difficult. You have felt that possibly, it was not for you. Or, you have felt guilty and judged. Do not judge yourself and you will see why that is a foolish undertaking as we proceed in the understanding of "how" you know and "how" you think and "how" you feel. We will begin to separate and divide the third dimensional experience from the new ones which, in reality, are not new for you but, must be relearned from limitation.

That is your value. That is your mission. That is your desire . . . which is, indeed, the mind of God for you.

Now, as I begin . . . do not let your prattling in your mind convince you that you cannot comprehend what you will be hearing. Do not turn off . . . do not phase out on what you are hearing. If you will really and truly remain open to allowing of the vibration and symbols that will appear . . . . to enter your conscious awareness through your senses . . . they will trigger a doorway to your knowingness.

Do not attempt to think sequentially concerning the phases of the understanding that we will present on the board and in our instructions. Do not allow the mind with which you act each day, the brain, to attempt to force you to try and understand what I am saying in the moment because you have anticipated a future or because, from the past, you are trying to integrate it from a past understanding.

Please, realize now . . . that we are in the moment, that this is you, that this is to be received in the moment as you. You cannot take into this moment what you learned in the last ones. You must drop it in order to proceed. A child in growing . . . as you as a child matured . . . as you observe others maturing . . . must lay aside elementary understandings that have served them well at certain stages of growth. If you are tempted to maintain that in your conscious awareness, you could not go to the next level of maturity. Do you understand that this is what stumps maturity in your race? You do not relinquish the childish things, the things that have served you at one time, but will no longer serve you. And therefore, you maintain an immaturity from old thoughts that served you well at that time . . . but, you are fearful of letting go of them.

Imagine a set of stairs. Imagine yourself climbing those stairs, one at a time. The steps that you have taken in childhood . . . the steps you have taken in awakening to this. If you attempted to pick up step one and carry it to step two, you might have a little luck by putting it under one arm but, when you go to step three, then you have both arms full of the things you have felt secure in on step one and two. Step four is a problem . . . you have no more arms to carry anything with. So, I suppose you could balance it on your head . . . that might be an effort you would make.

Picture what I am saying. The understandings that we have brought you, the understandings that have served you in what you call your search . . . will not carry you forward. Leave them alone. Open yourself to new understanding that is a greatly expanded knowing.

I caution you about that because logic . . . reason . . . is something that your brain is programmed to perform and it does it well. But, we are going to shut it down long enough to experience the one mind that is truly operating the brain.

Now, you have not understood much of what I have said but, you have gained a feeling from it and a caution, in certain areas, that you will recall.

I would like to proceed to begin to demonstrate certain understandings. I have decided to begin by telling you "how" you think . . . how you think you think . . . how you think you reason . . . how you think you established the identity that you are struggling so hard to get rid of in order to become greater, which you are.

So, let's begin with an understanding of how all things appear to you in this dimension.

Figure 1   Figure 2

So, a good place to start always is with what you call "God". . . . the "Source", the "Force", the "All That Is". And for the time being, I am going to draw "God" as a circle. . . . . *(figure 1)* for the purpose of demonstration and understanding in third dimension that...God, the Force, All That Is, is all that thinks in the universe.

You, as the individual that you are now, have never thought a thought. Now, I hear many responses to that statement. You believe that you understand what I am saying . . . some of you. You believe that you "think" that you're understanding some of what I am saying and your machines are rapidly working on what I have just said. But, in reality, you do not know what I have said. That will become clear as we go along.

What is "knowing"? Because, to you that involves thinking, which I mentioned. You "think" you know. "Knowing" and "Perceiving". Knowing is what God does. *(Figure 1)*

Perceiving is what you do. What do you perceive and "how" do you perceive? Well, let's get you drawn here. That's you *(Figure 2)* . . . . "Does Knowing" by God, involve information? No. God does not accumulate information, because that would require time. God, "All That Is", does not exist in time. He merely creates the illusion of time for you, here . . . or for him, here . . . whichever. So, you perceive . . . . . God knows.

Now, in some way, you have become consciously aware that there is a difference. And, you have divided it up and most of your confusion proceeds from the fact that you do not know whether you are perceiving as your brain or you are "knowing" from your God-Center. Most of your confusion has proceeded from your uncertainty about which is doing which . . . when. Some of you would say "well, this is good enough". Some of you would question that you ever had "knowingness". And, some of you have had glimpses of this knowing which has made you dissatisfied with this . . . perceiving. So, at this point, we have arrived where you are ready because this confusion . . which is not confusion but, perceived that way by you . . . . . has created desire. All creation is a result of desire. God conceives an idea . . . . . . *(Figure 3)*

I believe that's the way you draw an idea . . .
. . . a light bulb. God had an idea . . . . . .
One . . . . one big idea.

You see, God does not have ideas in time . . . progressively or sequentially. Remember? He's not in time.

So, this one big idea that he had . . . .
encompasses all that has been created or ever will be created . . . exists in

that one idea . . . all the eons, the multiplicity of creations have been but the parts in progression and seeming "time" . . . of that one idea.

That one idea was to express Himself. You have heard it said that He wanted to see Himself. But, He desired.

God desired . . . the idea. We will call it "see". Seeing, He sees the idea, which was one . . . Everything was that one idea unfolding and enfolding. When you have an idea, you see it. Do you not? Within your conscious awareness. You see your idea and, then there proceeds either the desire or no desire to see it expressed. Correct? This is the means of all creation in this dimension.

You see Christmas dinner and gifts under a Christmas tree . . . it is an idea of what you would like to do. The idea is there and the more you see it, the more the desire comes to express what you see. That is the excitement, the joy, the enjoyment . . . that is life as you perceive it.

Because, without the expression . . . there is total complete rest in this circle . . . there is no movement whatsoever . . . . there is no time . . there is no space . . . there are no dimensions . . . there are no facets . . . no focuses. . . no individuals . . . there are no creations and thereby, no expressions coming from desire if all was rest.

The minute the idea is conceived with a desire to express there must be thinking . . . thinking . . . in this rest. Now . . . God cannot think without movement. Therefore, the desire creates thinking which creates movement. Now, there is a projection coming from God . . . From All That Is . . . that is moving. *(Figure 4)*

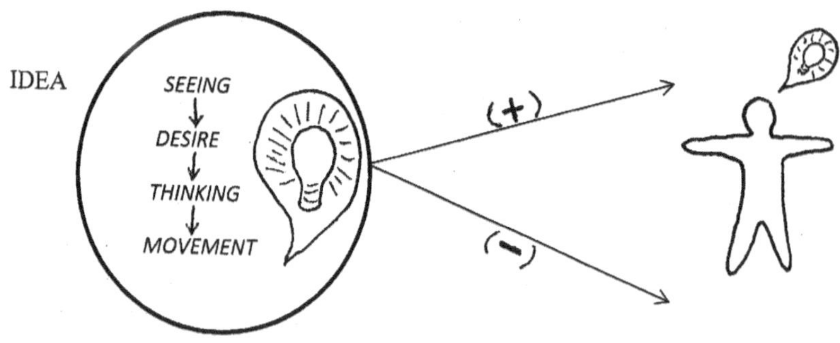

Figure 4

But, if in truth, he is all rest . . . there can be no movement in stillness. Then how does he create motion, time, form, structure . . . creation? God is inseparable. He cannot be divided up into parts. He is total, complete, absolute rest. He doesn't move. Movement means time. All of this total, complete idea that is conceived . . . as we try to explain it to you . . . everything that would ever possibly derive from that idea through thinking . . . exists simultaneously, completely in that one concept, in that one idea. There is nothing that is not there and yet, it never moves. It is never expressed until God thinks.

Everything that derives from that thinking is exactly what is happening right now. Has always happened and always will happen. You . . . "Are the thinking of God" . . . expressed.

So that, God determined to create expression of the idea by dividing light. All expression from God's thinking, which is a result of his desire, is opposites. It is dualities. All form and all structure exists as a result of tension between two electrical charges seeking balance. There is no movement without that.

You have two tanks. *(Figure 5)*

One is filled with air . . . you have an imbalance.

Do you not?

If we open the valve and release . . . you will have an explosion of this . . . air into this tank on the other side.

This into this. . . .

You open up the valve and you send all the air to this side. . . . Do you understand that?

You will have at the same time . . . another inward explosion going in here to receive all of that . . . the empty space. The vacuum will

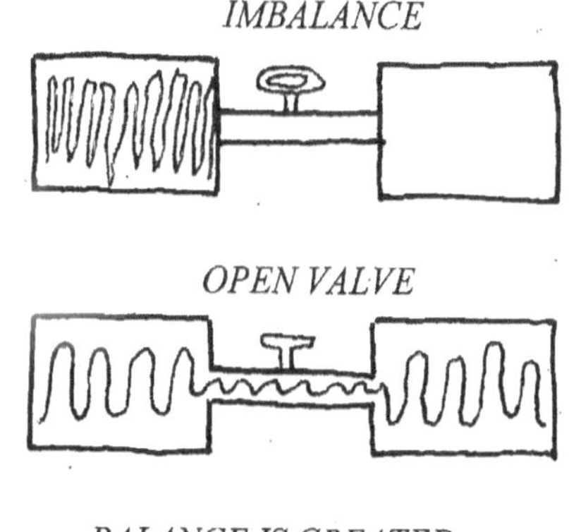

Figure 5

suck in what is over balance. It won't stop until there is absolute balance achieved between these two. There are many principles that demonstrate that to you. Electric batteries...you have an electrical charge from positive and negative poles . . . when it rests . . . when it is equal, it stops . . . it ceases. There is no charge. So, what created movement? Do you see? This is a simple understanding.

Movement was created by an imbalance of electrical charge from one side to the other. *(Figure 6)* Understand . . . not sequentially or logically . . . everything apart from rest . . . .that appears to be motion to you . . . to God . . .to All That Is . . . is this principle right here of imbalance. They are always seeking to balance. Everything in your world is seeking balance. Without this, there is no body . . . no physical body . . . there would be nothing. It is all electrical impulses. It is an electrical universe creation from the splitting of the two because, this simulates motion.

MOVEMENT IS CREATED BY IMBALANCE

Figure 6

Now, a good example that I would like to work with on this . . . is, the house of mirrors. As we go further along in this instruction, you are, indeed, going to see the house of mirrors. It exists in the fourth, fifth, and sixth dimension where you can perceive it. All that geometry you have heard of, spheres and cubes and triangles and crystals . . . is nothing but the house of mirrors that reflects movement to something that has never moved . . . will never move . . . has never separated . . . and yet, it reflects continually, multiplicity in action and reaction. In reality, there is none.

That is the illusion that is spoken of in much of your literature of everything being illusion. Now, you have been taught in the machine's logical understanding that if it is "illusion" that it has no value. That only rest has value. Not so. God desired to think. He desired to create an expression of Himself and his thinking is your experience this moment.

You see, when you come up with an idea over here . . . oh, good . . . you've got an idea. And, that idea is the "Beyond the Beyond". You think that God, back here somewhere in all this rest, conceived this idea that you are thinking right now? Is that correct? But, the thinking of God . . . of His idea, is happening this moment. Because, to think He had to create the tension, that created movement . . . that created space and time.

See, you have deceived yourself into thinking that when you come into this "knowing", and we will get to that "knowing" . . . that you will no longer create anew, in a sense. You will go back into this all-knowing and you will already know everything and that sounds boring. Does it not? The knowing that you are going to experience in this conscious awareness, in this form . . . is God thinking, right then.

Let me see if you followed me. When you perceive "all-knowing", everybody is waiting on this all-knowingness . . . it is going to mean to your mind that you have infinite information, correct? No...no, you will have "all-knowing" . . . not information, not memory. You then have the "knowingness" that you are God thinking.

My goodness! If you could know that, you would be a very powerful being...would you not? Able to experience absolute freedom. If you knew that you were "God", thinking . . . at that moment.

That's what "all-knowing" means. It doesn't mean degrees from universities because you have compiled infinite information. That is not what His knowing is. His "knowing" is the unfolding of His idea in expression. And, you will know yourself as "All That Is" . . . thinking"!

Anything that you think . . . anything you desire to express . . . you will do. You will not abandon all this that God has created because, if you did . . . if all that God has created went back into total rest and no longer did God continue to think . . . what would happen? Do you see? In reality, there was no beginning to this . . . there was no beginning and there will be no ending.

So, what are these two lights? What are these two sources of expression that are coming from God . . . that are creating galaxies, universes, species, mineral, vegetable, animal? What is this? We call it "plus and minus" . . . electrical charges. Well, I've got some new understanding for you. All of the words that you have ever used . . . all of the dualities are expressed by these two lights. ALL.

You see, all is electric. All functions according to opposites . . . dualities. You have heard of seven vibrational levels? There are . . . that this light steps down to arrive at your little world. *(Figure 7)* This is you in your little world. The light that He sends out that creates movement that comes back to Him . . . He sends a positive because He is positive and comes back to Him as negative. Now, stop all mechanical understanding of negative and positive. Because, there are many explanations of negative and positive . . . many facets. Needless to say, they are opposites and I am going to give you a general overall understanding of opposites.

LIGHT SENT OUT TO DENSE MATTER (7LEVELS)

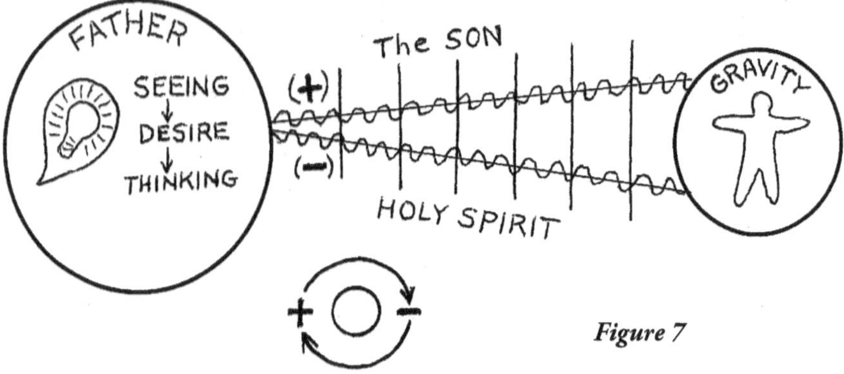

Figure 7

There are two opposites, positive and negative as we have termed them that create all illusion. Because, there is in reality, only one who has never separated and never will.

Jesus Christ was this ray right here. Now, you have your Trinity that you hear about in Christianity? Jesus Christ, the "Son/Sun" was this ray right here, the "plus" . . . "masculine". The Holy Spirit is this one right here, the "negative" . . . the unseen, "negative" . . . "feminine". Without these two, there is nothing. This ray is stepping itself down from expansion, from invisibility, from lightness . . . denser and denser and denser until it arrives at form. That's what the Son did. The Son was the expression of God's thinking in His desire. He was not "God" as you perceive it. He was the expression of God. He did not "Think". What were His words . . . "I can do nothing of myself". He knew what I am telling you. He knew that the expression . . . the electrical motion . . . the thinking all of it . . . was the illusion of one doing all the talking and thinking . . . all the knowing . . . when He said, "I can do nothing of myself. I do what the Father does in me." And, we have for years listened to you interpret that and try to understand it but, that man saw what I am bringing you in these "sessions".

He knew in that form standing there . . . in the forms standing around Him . . . in the trees, the ocean, everything . . . .he knew the principle of the two rays . . . the two lights that God created to simulate motion . . . to create His idea . . . but, that in reality, there was only one mind . . . one thinker . . . one knower . . . one self . . . one consciousness. You have not understood when we have said to you that "You are all one consciousness".

Now, do not proceed too rapidly with me because, we are going to . . . when I complete this little sketch . . . to give you some thought to expand your knowingness about who you are. We will get into this little electrical universe in which you live, and show you how you are nothing but negative and positive charges and, everything you do is nothing but an expression of these two tensions . . . as we showed you between these two boxes . . . seeking rest.

But now, if God is All There Is and He is total rest and He's seeking to create an illusion . . . He has to seek towards a point . . . which is what you call gravity . . . which magnetizes and forces to density, to a center, to mass, to become form . . . physicality. When you study all about levels and dimensions, you are studying of levels and dimensions of vibrations that have been stepped down to the point of actual physical appearance where there is the total separation. This force that comes out . . . is the Son. He separates from the Father. He becomes an expression of God. He says, "I and the Father are one". and, in reality, "I am He, as He is Me". But, he is demonstrating an expression of God dividing Himself. He divided Himself. He sent His "Son" out and it is only through this . . . coming to gravity . . . to form . . . from the Father that He can arrive at the expression of His "One Big Idea".

Remember, "In the Beginning", you were told that God desired to know fully and completely the thought . . . "I Am". So, the Son is the positive force from the Father that separates . . . seeks individuality. Why did God have a Son? He's All That Is. He's everything. Why separate out and create a Son? Why create any Suns in your galaxy? They all represent this Son. This is a principle. This is a principle underlying your world. He desired to express by thinking. That thinking lowered itself down in light until it became dense matter . . . hence you. That is a force to become an individual. It is a force in you that you deal with all the time.

The "I", the ego, the individuality . . . that is not evil. That is one half of God's rays whereby He creates tension and simulates motion where there is none. Because, at the same time, you are continually desiring union, at the same time that you are desiring separation. That is the tension in everything. That is the whole principle behind everything. The Son expressed in materiality said, "I Am the Son of God". He desired individuality from the Father.

Christ was a man like you, who woke up and realized what I am telling you now. He understood that his form and structure . . . what he was here . . . was an expression of God thinking separation. Many individual "I"s . . . complexity of this wonderful idea that can move in what is complete rest . . . but, an illusion is created by this seeming movement. When you have negative and positive fighting back and forth, it looks like movement. We will get into that further, so stay with me.

The Holy Spirit is the desire that wants expansion to encompass all and be in union with all. Is there anyone here who can tell me that they do not experience this tension day in and day out between "self-individualness" and desire for union? Are these two principles within you in everything you do? You can't escape that. That is the whole expression of God's idea.

However, the Christ is the one who wakes up in this and knows who He truly is . . . who is really thinking. Then He is unlimited in His powers. He is no longer confined because He has allowed this knowing into this conscious awareness.

But, understand, all polarities are here, in God's plan. Let's take it further because you will see the Son/Sun. This is only part of what the Son realized. This was only part of why He went to the cross. He was demonstrating the principle of opposites that God created the whole illusion for. For everyone, every bit of energy that proceeds from the Father . . . (and in reality, your Sun gives you everything you have on earth) . . . everything that proceeds reaches a resting point when it reaches its objective and proceeds back to the Father. What happened to your little box when it filled up one side? Didn't it rush back to the other side? It has to! At this point, there is a maturity . . . the energy runs out . . . it has gone to the limit in density . . . now, it turns around and begins to become gaseous . . . light . . . open . . . expansive. It goes back to the Father.

This body that you have was created down until it became dense earth matter . . . which is the core . . . your earth. You were born. All bodies reach a point of maturity where the positive force of growth in density . . . balances and then it begins to die. It goes back. At this point, this body . . . when it dies . . . when it comes to rest . . . the force within it . . . negative and positive are equaled out . . . what happens? Don't you have gas arising from the decaying of the body that goes back up into the clouds and goes back to the Sun from which the elements came? Doesn't it break down into the gaseous elements from which it was formed? That's the Holy Spirit. That is not seen. That is the unseen . . . the invisible that you are always aware of.

You only sense the positive . . . the "physical". You only sense "this" . . . you sense the positive and you call yourself " living" and the frustration is that you cannot see what you're trying to get back to. You cannot perceive God in the physical. You will never perceive the Source that way, you will never find "Him" and prove "Him" to your machine because this body has an imbalance that is set up from the point of rest . . . half had a charge to go to gravity, earth . . . the other to go back to invisibility . . . to lightness . . . to rest in God. That is what you call the "Holy Spirit". Spirit is the unseen energy . . . your body escapes as gas. It creates what you call death.

But, let me tell you something . . . nothing dies . . . nothing dies. Because, the same energy that came and produced the body that goes back . . . dies so it can go back and be reborn again. It gives its life so that new life might be created. Always! And, what you will learn is that all along here to create the illusion . . . you never get above a zero. In reality, because your pluses and minuses are continually exchanging with one another so that the other might live. They just change places. They just recycle. You see, this is desire . . . is the love of God and love is giving. In this whole universe, everything gives its life that new life might be created.

Christ demonstrated that to those who could see . . . who had eyes to see. His death on the cross . . . you've put so many meanings to it . . . it was a symbol . . . it was an understanding of the electrical universe of how God creates the whole illusion. He woke up to the whole comprehensive understanding of the universe and because of that, He gained infinite power. None of this could any longer have any power over Him because He saw and knew Himself to be this. (God thinking "I Am").

This is what you are going to do. This is what we're saying. This is why this must be brought to you and you must understand it, if you must draw it on a piece of paper with these inadequate drawings. You must understand . . . and the next half will even prepare you more to understand...that what is about to happen is going to require you to see the illusion. You have played around with this for a long time.

All that is hidden will be revealed. The knowing of this has been coming in your sciences but, the revealing of it is about to enter your consciousness. In order to stop the machine that is automatically playing through programs, in order to conceive the new that is coming and allow it (which is the knowingness within you). You must see this. Christ studied. He studied but, the seed was within Him the same as it is within you.

We need to take a break from this now.

Greetings! I am Emil, a most Golden Soul, a servant of the Radiant One.

To date, you have discussed many basic concepts that you have possibly heard mentioned . . . maybe not understanding how they related to you in specific terms. That has been the reason for the conversation and dialogue that we have had here.

There was a need, as relayed among us, for a short rest in the acceleration which you have been experiencing for the purpose of allowing some digestion.

I am called a Most Golden Soul because I am coming directly from the Elders and that is the ray that I represent . . . of which I am one of you. You are radiant Beings. You are Light Beings. You have come from a very advanced stage of understanding and you are beginning to recall that. There are so many things that you will be laying aside, as you have already, in order to identify with the new understanding of who you truly are.

Light is a most fascinating subject. It is a subject learned through experiencing, some scientific facts and practical facts, but much of what is going to transpire in the transition of this planet involves light. As you have noticed, we use the word very often. We use it to describe many things and not always does this have a clear understanding in your brain waves because you are not recalling exactly what light is and why it is so important.

You see, the original thought . . . . the original light . . . . conceived, at that time, your existence. You have existed from the beginning. You were there but each soul had the ability to expand itself and become many souls for many purposes in multi-dimensions. I hesitate to go into this because, again, I am only using words and you have many third dimensional concepts that do not fit the picture.

You are part of a larger Soul Group . . . is that a good word . . . that is of the original thought, what is called the "Throne Energy" - thereby much affinity to "Christ". As you have observed, not all entities existing on this plane . . . involved even in the transition . . . are connected with the "Christ". But, the Brotherhood is and the Elders are because that is the plan.

See, I hesitate to say that there was one Soul and then you were created out of that one Soul, because you feel like you've been divided up into little pieces or something. It is difficult for you to understand this. I would like you to understand that you existed from the beginning. You did not get divided into this incarnation. In other words, when you were born as whoever your given name is . . . that was not your beginning of existence. Does everyone understand that clearly?

You have existed for all times. You are the part of the Soul that has agreed to come here in this final period and incarnate as the personality that you are and upon awakening more, you will comprehend just how vast you are . . . just how All-knowing you really are and All-powerful that you really are because you were here when the world was created. You had much to do with that.

But, you have a vast group here that has agreed to something together . . . that is your reality. You are creating it right now this minute and you can have it exactly like you want it. You do not have to seek for it . . . it is in you! That's the "blueprint" that we call it . . . that's the DNA, that you call it. It is in you. It is unfolding and that is why we say it is perfect because the DNA is unfolding. The blueprint is unfolding. The plan . . . the thought from the beginning that was within the Source is unfolding and you have never thwarted it for one minute!

I manifest and share and spread to each one present the Golden Ray of which "I Am." That Golden Ray brings with it the consciousness of the Christ who knows Himself to be one with All...who knew Himself to be All . . . who manifests as All and within All. The Radiant Son . . . the beauty, the Love . . . the Omniscience, the Omnipresence, the Omnipotence, the

Abundance, the Peace, the Harmony of All That Is . . . may it emanate and shine forth from you now in this moment. Thank you.

———∘∘∘)◉(∘∘∘———

Class is back in session.

At this time, we are all present. We are not giving complete understanding of each phase of what we are describing here. So many of the questions that you might have at this point or what you would consider logical consequences that you do not comprehend . . . will be understood in the holographic image that will be derived from these visions. Now, I am going to give you a simplified version that your minds can comprehend because of your own experience . . . to understand the concept of how the idea of motion in time is created when in fact . . . no time, no space, no motion exists . . . merely an expression that God is thinking from rest.

If you think of a house of mirrors *(Figure 8)* . . . mirrors put at angles reflecting images, and perceive that God is standing here in His rest and there are infinite mirrors placed all around Him at angles so that one reflects the other and the other reflects the others. Okay, here you are down here and you're running. God thinks running and all down through, He can observe images and this man proceeds from here and looks down the corridor and he's running. Now, you will have to stretch your imagination.

Time . . . action . . . He thinks running. You look down the mirrors and you see all along someone running all the way down. They seem to be going somewhere. They seem to be moving along down to a point but, you never move do you? You have never left . . . when you stand in front of that mirror and do this . . . somebody down there does that. You run . . . somebody down there runs but, you have never left this space. You tip your hat . . . somebody down there tips their hat. God thinks an "idea" and it is reflected to Him down here through mirrors . . . crystalline, geometric creation of the universe.

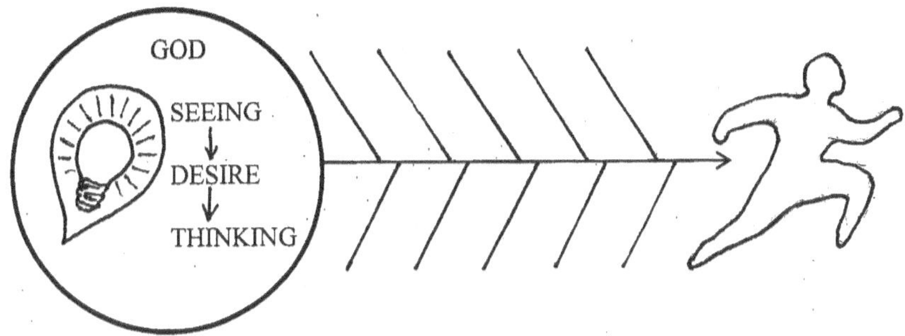

HOUSE OF MIRRORS – (Crystalline, Genetic Structures)

Figure 8

This is you. That is all you are. You are the image in the mirror and that image is created through the two opposites in all things functioning electrically. So, all movement by you . . . all movement by the planets . . . the galaxies . . . the universes . . . time . . . everything apart from this point of rest is an illusion. We are going to get into a further understanding of dimensions .. . a second, third, fourth, and on . . . until you begin to understand that the whole universe is a crystal . . . is angles . . . geometric form that creates the simulation of form, structure and time. All illusion . . . like a house of mirrors.

Many of you are going to have a difficult time permitting that statement . . . allowing that statement. Do not struggle with it. Do not fight it. This is the death of you thinking yourself separate from "All That Is". It is the doorway back to that point of knowingness . . .

"All-knowing" and power. This is the doorway that is opening . . . the same in the understanding of the House of Mirrors.

In order to go through the door . . . the opening of the door does not insure your entrance, there must be desire and a decision of will to enter it and see the reality of all that you have called reality and what you do not understand of what you are beginning to glimpse. You will begin to glimpse because of the words and symbols we bring to you now . . . the total freedom . . . . the total knowing and power that is created when your conscious awareness in this form permits this knowingness to become part of your conscious awareness. You will have mastered the illusion. You do not master it any other way.

Can you feel that it requires that all the value and importance that you place upon this electrical sensed universe that you call "you" . . . is illusion? You will resist that because of the importance that you have placed on the value of that. And, you will perceive it as losing something of value . . . when, in reality, the Son (Christ) told you that it's the key to everything that you desire. The knowing of this in your conscious awareness is the glorifying of yourself and all that you are.

If you will allow this knowingness now from within each one of you now . . . the knowingness is not in these drawings . . . the knowingness is not in the words that I am speaking . . . the knowingness is within you if you will allow it to emerge and blend and come into your conscious awareness . . . even small glimpses of it. You will feel loved and safe and free to go on to comprehend the whole of third dimension.

All entry into the doorway is by . . . Desire. The process that you are experiencing now is for the opportunity to express desire. You are made in the image of God and this is how you function in that image. This is how the mirror image functions the same . . . you see . . . you desire. . . you think it into expression and it becomes for you.

I wanted to complete a quick image because, before I am through, I am going to wipe out the last vestige of hope that you have in your identities. I do not consider this a sad thing that I do.

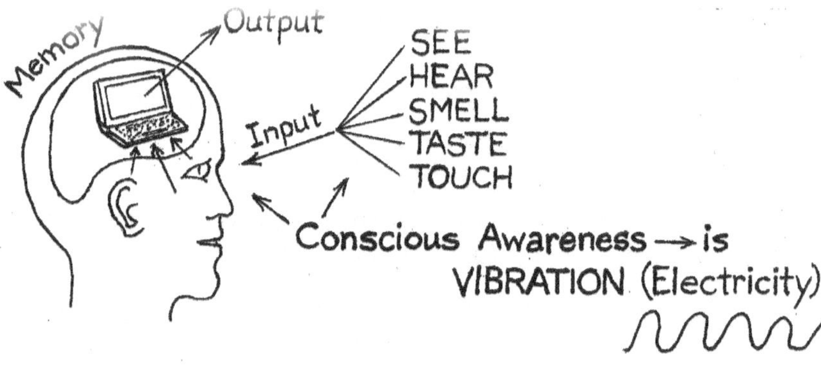

Figure 9

This is not a microwave. Actually, it could be because it heats up from within. This is what you call . . . your brain. Please follow me . . . because

I am going to dispel some illusions that you have concerning who you are. You are desiring to know this.

Let's make a list. How do you perceive? We said you perceived, correct? Through the five senses . . . you see . . . you hear . . . you smell . . . you touch . . . and you taste. So that all of these register through your doorways or openings on your physical body. They all go in and register here. You have different nerve systems and networks within your body. This is where they go and they are logged and they are known . . . what you call "knowing". You also perceive yourself as thinking there. Now, let's find out what you really do.

You've all had science lessons and I'm assuming you remember from our earlier definition (Chapter 1), that all of your "reality" sensed by your 5 senses are merely patterns appearing to you in a sea of vibrating energy. So, that when you see, you are measuring and recording vibration through the eye directly here. Is that correct?

See the computer? This is called output . . . (the monitor) . . . the keyboard is called input for you who have not had courses in this. All information that the computer has is derived from input. Someone puts it in through the keyboard. Now, there are certain programs that were derived from a keyboard that allows this computer to perform different functions which simulates what you call "reasoning". . logical, sequential, deductive, inductive reasoning . . . . this computer does that. This is all your brain is. Hear my words. This is all that your brain is.

You look out of your eyes, you perceive a vibration . . . an electrical wave . . . it is recorded through the eyes, into the brain and you perceive through your brain . . . through this computer . . . what it is that you've just seen. You call it up on the monitor . . . the output . . . and the output tells you what you just saw through deductive, inductive, logical, reasoning. All it did, was take information that had been input previously . . . put it in sequential order and give it back to you. That's all you do every day, in every way.

Now, understand, in your judgment . . . you connote this as bad or good. I am not speaking from a dimension of bad or good. When you begin to understand what I drew there of the illusion, you will understand that judgment ends there. How do you judge an electrical charge? How do you judge any action of the electrical charge when it is God thinking?

All judgment ceases. You will see that. That will dawn on you because you are going to let something else happen up here. We will get to that. You are not hopeless. But, until this registers, you will never allow the other.

You must allow this to register. These are electrical charges recorded through your five senses that are input and output through a machine that works electrically. The computer is an example.

In you, you have eons and generations that programmed your seed. You know those little sperms that you draw *(Figure 10)* with the little eggs that contain what you call genes? DNA's . . . mother . . Grandmother . . . Great grandmother, on down the line. They programmed certain weaknesses, strengths, ideas, emotions, thoughts, feelings . . . all that went into that. And you are so proud of your abilities. They are programs, computer programs in the seed.

You get to this point where you are born and you say, "but I can't do that. I have a weakness. That person has strength." Who was doing their thinking all back there? Whose idea was it? Was it grandma's? No. There is only one thinker. She thought she thought. You think you think but, you compute. You input what your senses tell you and you get out what you perceive and you say, "it's me". The whole image that you form of yourself out here is nothing but an electrical recording from a sensed universe. You have sensed it through your five senses. It was sensed and perceived electrically . . . waves go in and waves come out. And, you believe that that is you.

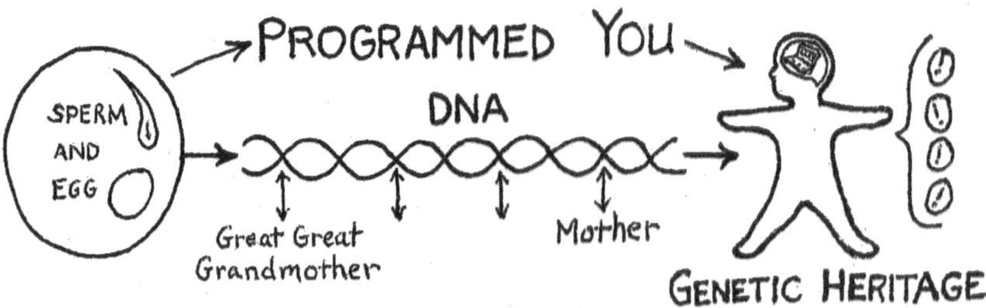

Figure 10

And you are so proud of the things that you think and you're so proud of your ability. And, that's judgment. You can be so down on someone else's judgment and all you're saying is, "my machine is better than yours".

In reality, they are all machines programmed by . . . listen to me . . . this is hard to take . . . there is one mind . . . one thinker . . . one idea . . . and you are merely the expression of that mind.

Somebody told you back here . . . you either heard it with that ear or you saw it with the eye . . "chair" . . . input through the keyboard and output . . . I know chairs now. I have that information stored in my little machine now and I know what a chair is. Aren't you proud of yourself? Some people's machines work better in certain areas than others do, don't they? Certain people have programs that allow them to do fantastic mathematical formulas. It was programmed in somewhere back here and you received it in your genetic heritage and you have this vast ability to make great things but, you have never thought a thought in that machine . . . never. You have merely played the program . . . received the output from a program that was programmed back to you.

Now the difference in you and an animal is that all he does is a program but, his program is not as complicated as yours is. You have developed your program a little bit further because you have developed reason and logic and sequential thinking and the ability to deduct and induct. He cannot do that. The animal cannot do that. He must operate totally by the program in his genes. But, see you programmed yourself back there eons ago to reason . . . to have these abilities. Just as I can put a program in my computer and what do I get? A function . . . an ability that the computer has to do whatever I put into it. It's still electrical. It's still sensed and known through electricity.

See, no "knowing" . . . no knowing has come in here because knowing is not information logged. No thinking has come in here. You go to school and they tell you that 1 + 1 = 2, and that is the basis of much of your experience through the senses. This is logical because there is a logical progression. If 1 + 1 = 2, then 1 + 2 =3 and we can go on. Now, this is what humans were programmed way back there to make that little additional fact known. They have a program in here that allows you to do that. A dog does not. He does not have a program that allows him to add 1 + 1. You have a program and you call it thinking. Teach someone arithmetic . . . you will say . . . think . . . think . . . that means, "check your computer". And how are they teaching . . . senses. Here's one and here's one. You know what two is . . . one . . . two. So, now we have two pencils. All of this is perceived through the senses.

Now, this is elementary but, that's the only way you got any knowledge that you've gotten. When you read a book, you are perceiving and sensing electrically and it's being recorded in this machine. You want to remember it because you see, you have something else you programmed in back here that an animal doesn't have as complicated as you do . . . memory. Remember . . . memory? That's the ability to run back through your files . . . just like your computer has memory . . . and pull up a program or information that was stored there at a certain time.

Many of you have abilities to do things, to know things, to "think" things . . . you call it. Because genetically it was already programmed in. It was there in the gene and when you discover it, you're thrilled. "Gosh, I don't know how I knew to do that. Isn't that wonderful! I'm so smart!" You think you thought it. You think you derived it from this identity that calls itself by name. It was already there in your seed. You made use of a program. It was already there and you pulled it up to use. Every skill . . . every thinking that you've done has been from man's eons and eons of programming this and you have many more skills than the caveman because you have many more files. You have much more sophistication than the caveman because you have more files, that's all you've been doing in your experience here.

The way that you are able to sense and perceive, we call conscious awareness. I want to see some light bulbs going on here shortly. Conscious awareness . . . so, when you see something, hear something, smell something, taste something, touch something . . . you have conscious awareness of it and what is that . . . vibration . . . electricity? That's your conscious awareness. You say, "Somebody is cooking a great cake". You haven't seen it yet. You only smell it. This is a whole science of opposites . . . the electrical charges . . . the light that is touching your nose and when that smell goes in . . . the computer goes . . . bleep . . . bleep . . . and you say, "I know what that smell is because it's logged here in my computer". All of your functions are performed this way.

You call that conscious awareness. You read a book . . . you read words on the book *(Figure 11)* . . . more vibrations . . . your eyes see them . . . the words go in . . . ah, the little computer gets busy. Now, let me tell you something. When you see something or hear something that you don't have a computer program for . . . what do you call that? The unknown. Computers don't like that. They don't like that. They don't like to not find it up here in the machine. Because if you can't find it in the file, and since you are a machine, then how are you going to know how to act? How do you know how to perceive this? How do you know how to judge it? How can you figure out what is going to happen in the future? You need a program to tell you what has already happened in the past and what you can expect as a result of something and therefore you will know how to act in the moment . . . because your machine helps you with that and that's all you are. You are acting from your computer.

Figure 11

A person appears in you sight . . . they're dressed a certain way . . . they look a certain way . . . .they say certain words . . . all vibrations. It goes into your little computer through the senses and it logs up, "I don't like that person. That statement she's making is stupid. I remember". All of your judgments . . . all of what you call knowingness . . . all of what you call intelligence . . . all that is stored in your machines now is so separate and destructive that you are about to wipe out the species. Your computers are programmed to do that. You will do that on an individual basis. You will die. You will reach a point where your body will expend all of the energy that it was given . . . use it all up . . . and go back to where it came from. It is a debit . . . credit proposition. Let me show you something.

You go to the bank. The bank is zero rest. Believe it or not. You go to the bank, there is no motion there . . . it's just you and the bank. The bank's at rest. You want to borrow a thousand dollars. So, you borrow a thousand dollars. *(Figure 12)* Now, you have one thousand dollars plus to your credit. When you went in there you had nothing . . . now you have a thousand dollars. What is over here? You also owe a thousand. You have plused yourself a thousand, and you have minused yourself, in your line of credit, a thousand. It is a debit and credit. And, there's going to be a lot of movement back and forth. As you use this up, you are going to have to pay it back over here.

You have so much energy allotted you in that image and that expression of God thinking and when it runs out it will begin to slowly dissipate. You have got to pay your debt back to the expansiveness from which you came. The sun . . . the sun gave your body life and you will have to pay it back because you will use up all the energy. The minute you were born was when you borrowed the thousand, but you created the debt of a thousand and that is what you call death.

Figure 12

The machine has a life time . . . the circuits . . . there is no energy . . . somebody pulls the cord at some point when you use up your time here. So, I hope I am getting this in because you don't understand why you have a problem with what is called the unknown. Why it doesn't sink in?

There's nowhere for it to go. Haven't we told you that we're developing new electrical currents and avenues in the brain so you can log the new information that is being perceived in your senses? I have to tell you something. There's nothing wrong with this. This was God's idea. It's not . . . "was", it is now! It is now and it is in the future His idea. It is simultaneously past, present, and future and this was the idea of the expression and man was made in His image. He imaged man. It's part of His idea. Every minute you sit here, you are the thinking of God . . . being His thoughts right now. And, this machine is perfect for his plan . . . His idea. It is working. It's evolved and it will continue.

You came here to help this machine evolve into a better machine so that it can function to handle the new that is coming. You are not that machine. You never were. You never will be. Do you remember the mirror down here and the little man? He thought that he was all there was. Now, that was allowed in the idea of God. He could never have thought that if God had not allowed it. But, did God allow it? He thought it! He thought it! He thought what you call evil. He thought negative. What is negative but the opposite of positive that creates all the universes and all expression. He thought and man said, "I'm tired of being like the animal . . . just being totally directed from this knowingness. I want to be my own God. I want to know right and wrong. I want to be me. I want to be me. I want to be separate and be me". Hey, isn't that one of the urges that God had designed in His universe . . . to create density and matter and movement and time and space and creation?

So, He thought it. Now, man had a really developed computer like this, but at that point, man had something else that man is now going to experience in a more expanded way, because this had to be created to include this knowingness. You see, when God looked down those mirrors and saw that little man and that little man said, "I'm All That Is. I'm thinking. I'm knowing. I'm doing my thing. I'm me". That was God thinking. That was God doing that because He knew, that through working on this, that this is necessary. We're going to let Him do this and think . . . "I want to do this. I'm God. I can do anything I want to. I want to try this".

Now, my goal . . . my one big idea . . . that really is already happening because it is all happening simultaneously, anyway . . . is that this little man is going to wake up and see the whole ballgame and know that he has never been anything but "All That Is" . . . know that he has all power and all-knowingness . . . and this little form and structure with a brain that is frail and weak . . . He's got big plans for it. Not you . . . you are not this little form and structure, this machine but, you can operate through this. You can use this machine.

You did not come here to evolve as mankind has. You came from a density out there that had a really difficult time lowering itself down and confining itself to this. You have no intentions of burning up energy and going back in death in this form. You want this form because nothing ever dies and when you understand (we're coming to that) . . . in your conscious awareness . . . when you become conscious of what your consciousness really is . . . who it really is which is what I'm telling you now . . . then we have a new machine . . . a new form . . . a new species.

CHAPTER 3

WOULD THEY LIVE HAPPILY EVER AFTER . . . OR IS THE "NEW AGE" FEELING LIKE A BORING "OLD AGE"?

It is December. Icy cold rain has fallen all night. As you look out of your window, you see frozen, silent shapes. Limbs of ice hang everywhere. How marvelous is this world of winter! Such is the scene of humanity as it is viewed from other worlds.

What has caused the buildup of ice on the branches and trunks of trees? A steady wash of rain water. . . layer upon layer frozen. How? Cold winds have created a change in the elements. . . . water to ice. Same as human form. . . so say other entities from outside space and time.

All thoughts are chosen from a pool . . . a reservoir of supply. Only you choose and give them importance in what you call your life. Years . . . . . of thoughts. Layers upon layers . . . piling up on your human forms. Cold . . . . cold winds of doubt, fear, and guilt have blown over your humanity. You are perceived as frozen, silent shapes by those who visit your planet.

Well, the thawing has begun. Feel it. Life is stirring underneath the solid shapes. Warm winds of passion and love are entering your existence. Bring them on! Let them swirl fiercely around and through you. They will permit the movement of life and limb that has been so long hidden by the transparent hardening of thoughts.

Thoughts chosen to keep you safe. Remember, you thought that you were safe if you never changed. Movement was dangerous. So, you covered yourself in thoughts that would preserve your identity. Isn't that how you preserve things? Freeze them so they don't deteriorate.

So, you have remained in a solid state of immobility . . . . . caressed by winds of fear. The heat is being turned up. Thoughts no longer bring you a sense of security. They are melting back into the pool from which they came. Now, you must choose new ones to understand how to exist in a state of melting.

Before, you just didn't move or cause any vibration that would disturb your frozen state. That way you could be safe and not initiate cracking in your façade of solidity. But, new winds . . . .from a new dimension . . . .are blowing and melting the old forms.

Careful, though. Many are choosing thoughts and calling them new! But, are they using them in a new way? Without winds of fear and doubt? Those winds will freeze any thoughts and leave you still in a solid state.

The movement of currents from other dimensions is going to reveal what is underneath. It is not going to allow solidity to remain. Your choice now is to free yourself from a frozen state into a fluid state that will be unlimited by form and structure.

Beware . . .the new thoughts of the "New Age" can be used by you unknowingly to cover your true self in another casing of words. If the new thoughts bring about a wind of fear . . . . you will discover that you have just added another layer of solidity to your old state and called it new. Illusion . . . .

Call us what you will . . . . unseen entities . . .spacemen and women . . . .angels . . . .future selves. It matters not to us. We exist in a realm of knowingness that all is one. We are portions of that oneness . . . . of you . . . .that have come to help thaw a frozen dimension.

We would like to lovingly, humorously, and quickly bring to your awareness the clever . . . clever manipulation of New Age thoughts by you. We have never doubted your ability to transform new energy into old patterns and proclaim those same patterns as new truth. However, you certainly will get an "A" for the current trends that you are projecting and calling them "New Age".

Obviously, certain ones will vibrate at different speeds while reading this material. The choice of speed is yours. We do not interfere in those choices. Love of you by us is not contingent upon your understanding our vibratory rate of information. You will create the rate of electromagnetic vibration that is best suited to the reality that you are presently creating according to your desires.

There are those, however, who are suspiciously aware of the pitfalls that await them if they receive the enormous amount of material being presented without checking the vibratory rate desired by them. Feel what it is that you want to feel. Align with the thoughts that create that feeling within you. Accept no limitations. You are not an illusion.

Now, that brings us to the reason for this discussion that we wish to have with you . . . .

∞∘≬∘∞

Wait! . . . . . Time has passed and there is movement being detected below the thawing, icy branches! Spring has brought new "winds of change" to the pond and as the ice has thawed, life is again beginning to stir among the creatures who call the pond their home.

Toggle Toad knew that he must meditate today. So, at early dawn he was sitting near the edge of the pond on his favorite lily pad. The sun was only beginning to light up the clear water and sparkle on the dew that had fallen the night before.

Always, he had trouble forming a pyramid shape with his rotund body. He never knew exactly how he was to place his legs, but he was diligent in arranging his shape the best he could. After all, Toggle was a "New Ager" and he knew that his whole day was depending on his observance of this ritual.

Besides, he was perplexed by his feelings of late. Nothing was working as he expected. He'd listened so diligently to the teachers who gathered a small handful of other pond residents around them. They brought such wonderful images of something new for his world.

For eons, all frogs were raised on the story of the prince. Long ago, in the history of this pond, a prince had come to tell his ancestors of their own royalty. How they were victims of a cruel hoax. They were not really as they appeared. In truth, they were all princes of great wealth and freedom. But, "way back when", a curse had been placed on them and they were doomed to survive in the misshapen body of a toad.

With bulging eyes and hoarse voices that sounded more like belches than anything else, they lived each lifetime knowing only the small little pond. Many dreamed of being a prince but, few really believed the legend. The reason it was so hard to believe was because, according to the legend, the maker of all life lived way up in the blue sky and he was the only one who could lift the curse. But, no one had ever seen him. At least, not one of his frog brothers!

On rare occasions, a creature with great wings would swoop down from the sky and land near the world of the pond. They always sang such beautiful songs that all hearts nearby were lifted and happy. This seemed to convince the residents of the pond that truly the Great Maker was in the sky where the winged creatures descended from to visit them.

Everyone believed in the story of the great prince or, so it seemed, until a particularly beautiful winged creature appeared one day. Certain frogs received a message from the angelic beings that proclaimed an end was near for the spell of limitation that kept all frogs grounded and limited to such a small area as their pond.

Ridiculed by most but, believed by a few, these frogs began to exemplify a new way of experience as a frog. They began to jump further than ever a frog had before. Food was not a problem. They always seemed to be satisfied as though full of the daily fare that all the other frogs spent hours acquiring. They just spent their days dancing and acting special.

"Really," said the wise old toads. "Who do they think they are? Delusions . . . . illusions. That's the way of the young who have not the wisdom to understand the responsibility of being a frog. After all, the duty of every frog in this pond is to be the best frog you can be. They will learn that pretending to be something else will bring them to the awful state of poverty."

Well, every frog knew that word. "Poverty" was the dreaded disease. The old ones knew that it had to be stopped before it spread and wiped out the population of their world. So, extreme measures were instituted to convince the deluded frogs that life depended on maintaining the same identity as a frog that had served them well for all the many centuries that the pond had existed.

Toggle had listened to the caution that the old toads spoke. They had been very wise in not attacking the new words and thoughts that were spreading. Instead, they seemed to embrace the validity of them. They just wanted every frog to beware of using the new philosophy to destroy a species that had made a place for itself in the pond's community. They were highly respected by the other members. The pond ran rather smoothly.

Of course, there were those who thought that certain changes were seeping in and needed attention. Many committees had formed to look into the level of the water that seemed to be receding and really unique creatures were disappearing. Oh well, they really hadn't served any purpose. Why get excited? The general consensus was that more care and concern on each one's part would maintain the status quo. At least, more damages could be averted.

Toggle was getting boggled with all these thoughts that were running through his head. How was he to meditate? See, this was his problem. He knew that.

When first he had approached one of these frogs to find out what the message was, he had been very simple in his desires. Now, it seemed as though life was getting more complicated every day.

He hadn't realized then that he would be so affected by their words of a "new something" that was fast approaching their world. At first, he had used his trusty logic to determine if what they were saying was appropriate to his own experience. And, truly, he couldn't argue with them because, it all made such good sense. If you believed in the legends at all, your frog heart beat faster to hear of a time when you would wake up out of the cursed dream and find yourself a prince.

So, he had sought them all out . . . . the frogs channeling the words of the beautiful winged creatures. At first the words brought new excitement to him. He agreed with what they were saying! He found himself knowing within his little heart that they were speaking the truth for him. He embraced those words . . . . repeated them often to others and began to feel different about himself and the reality that surrounded him.

That was one of the teachings that he was so convinced about. "You create your own reality" . . . .was a favorite topic of the messengers. "Change your thoughts and you change your reality"! Golly, he loved that one! For as long as he could remember, he had felt that somehow, somewhere. . . .there was a power that could create anything. Now, he knew that it was in him. "God is within", they said.

Even now, he could still feel the vibration that he had felt upon first hearing that. Someone inside of him agreed totally with that expression. That someone . . . he decided was the being that he truly was, but, had been waiting for, for so long. This was the prince! He was the prince! It was all one and the same . . . . the toad he knew himself to be on the outside and the prince that he was feeling and experiencing from the inside.

What glorious truth! Why hadn't he heard this before? Why had no one ever told him this? His parents hadn't even hinted at this possibility. Why? The old wise ones wouldn't even let anyone speak of this in their presence.

That's when he had to make his big decision. Could he just accept this as his truth and not have any agreement with those that he had respected and looked up to his whole life? Security . . . . safety . . .had always been the prime pursuit of life in this community. To believe the feelings he was having . . . . why that could cause him to lose all that he had ever known as wisdom. He would only have his own knowing from within him.

In the beginning, he tried desperately to convince himself and others that this new understanding only supported the legends that were so revered. Surely, he thought, anyone can see that. But, as time progressed, he became aware that there was more to this new revelation than he was prepared to admit because . . . . he was changing.

His new beliefs and thoughts concerning himself and his reality were changing everything. Nothing was the same anymore. His words no longer convinced him or others. His feelings were different and they were creating an impossible situation for him. He said one thing, but felt another.

It wasn't long before, he knew. "Your thoughts create your reality". He was experiencing a new reality. He was a new creation. He could not even remember . . . anymore . . . how he used to be. His friends and family wanted to assure him of their love for him but, it was getting harder for them because, they no longer felt that Toggle was the same Toggle that they loved. Now, "he is just deluded", they said. "We must give him time to sort things out. Surely, he will return to his old self that we love so dear."

Oh, love! Love! Golly, he didn't quite know how to explain to them the new feelings of love that he had. He tried. He really tried. But, that only made things worse. Because he expressed a love of all frogs equally, they were more alarmed. "Has he forgotten who he is? Doesn't he realize how foolish it is to open yourself in such an unprotected way to others? Wisdom . . . history . . . frog experience . . . . should remind him of the extinction of any creature who does not protect himself by trusting only those who are safe", so they said.

He had pondered over the past days, his own lack of concern for the warnings that were being issued by all family, friends, and wise ones. There was only one conclusion that he kept coming back to . . . . . they have never tried this new way. How do they know that it doesn't work?

Already, he was experiencing a new feeling about himself and his reality was becoming very different. Everything in his reality was only convincing him more of the choice he had made to allow the understanding coming from within. He knew he could not go back . . . . forward was his only choice.

So, here he was . . . this morning . . . confused.

He knew . . . he knew that just meditating was not going to un-confuse him. The feelings that were newly arrived within him didn't always hang around. They came and went and he seemed to have no control over them. "There", he thought. "Finally, I can express what I'm confused about."

This was a questionable step for Toggle. His thinking was, "If I create my reality from my thoughts . . . then, I can't admit any confusion or fear or doubt. That will only ensure more confusion and fear and doubt. This just doesn't help me at all with my problem. Now, I've done it. I've just said "problem" and that is surely going to maintain the reality that I'm experiencing as a "problem."

He forgot his triangular position as he grabbed his head with his feet and shook it back and forth. To someone watching, it looked as if he was trying to shake an object out of his head that didn't belong there.

Let's leave the story there for the time being and perhaps . . . investigate the "tangle" Toggle Toad is "boggled" in . . . . or the "boggle" Toggle Toad is "tangled" in . . . . . .whichever. . . . .

"Boggle", I understand is a game that is played by seeing how many words you can make out of a number of letters that appear on dice in a dish. Please forgive me if it offends you that I would like to borrow the concept for a little game that I wish to play with you.

I will take letters contained in certain words and make more words to help you to better understand. Understand what? I don't even know how to explain the dilemmas that you complain about. So, how do I begin to discuss it with you?

"Understand" would be a good word to start with for now. "Under" implies that it is hidden. Well, that certainly describes the way you feel about certain expressions that are coming to you. So, we can agree that the feeling or vibration that you are feeling concerning many "New Age" teachings is that it is hidden and you must find whatever it is that eludes you.

"Stand" implies a position taken . . . . a specific position. Now, if we put "under" with "stand", I suppose you could mean that you are trying to find the hidden meaning of a specific position taken. Well, maybe that stretches your imagination a little but, it will be a nice starting place.

Based on the above meaning, you can now realize why I said that I don't even know how to explain the dilemma described by the story of Toggle Toad so that you can "understand". In the first place, nothing is really "hidden" that must be uncovered. That is illusion. Second, no position can truly be taken about reality. That is illusion.

Let's concentrate on the first supposition . . . . that nothing is hidden. How many believe that? Do you? Really? No . . . . you don't. You have acquired a belief . . . in your much searching for spiritual truth . . .that you will require more of something in order to unravel the many words written and spoken. You believe that there exists "truth" which if you somehow studiously apply yourself to the study or search for, you will "understand" what you want to know.

So, your days are filled with trying to acquire this nebulous something that you think you lack. Don't you think sometimes, that the words you are hearing are a code that you can't break? If only someone would help you decipher it!

Yes, if you choose to believe it, these truths you want to know, were hidden to protect them from those who were not ready to hear them. Even Christ said, "let those with ears to hear, hear and those with eyes to see, see." Well, are you ready to hear and see the kingdom you've dreamed of for so long?

Now that you are hearing and seeing, why do you not believe that you can see and hear? See, I've got to introduce you to old stuff that you've forgotten . . . your beliefs. I know that you think you've gone way beyond that . . . you know all about beliefs and how they create your reality. You do? Then why are you not creating the realization of all you know?

Don't you realize that the conscious mind that you created for this journey has been trained to only allow thoughts that line up with your belief about you? One of those long held beliefs is that you are going to make progress . . . grow . . . understand more. . . . learn higher truths.

Higher truths and lower truths are a creation of yours. Okay? Get that? You, in your egocentric, conscious mind believe that you are expected to gain access to higher teaching by your diligence. Bear with me a little while. I am uncovering some hidden positions you have assumed . . . ."understanding", you call it.

By the way, don't vibrate too quickly about my use of "egocentric conscious mind". I have many things to say about that in the future. Just slow up and patronize me a little longer with what you consider basic truths that are supposed to be a "given".

I can hear you now, "I've already learned that. I've already uncovered beliefs that I no longer needed . . . that limited me." Like hell you have! Whoops, pardon my language but, I bet that expression just brought out another belief about vulgar use of language.

See? You're riddled with beliefs and you haven't got a clue to just how many or how limiting they are for you. Well, we do. And, it's getting harder and harder for us to relate information to you that you consider "higher". Really, it's a joke. Because you create a reality in which there is higher and lower, we must oblige you as best we can.

That reminds me, I forgot to tell you who I was or better yet . . . who we are because there will be others who wish to speak to you. I'm sort of breaking the ice.

I am energy . . . . same as you. I am unseen by you. I channel my thoughts through an electromagnetic circuitry belonging to another energy presently in human form. I am the Force . . . . generally speaking. I am "Aknom" . . . . . specifically. Pronounce it however you like . . . . names are a problem where I come from but, I know they are important to you.

I love you and your world . . . . same as you. I helped create it . . . . same as you. I have visited it many times in the past to bring light (information) and love (oneness) to those inhabitants who were "seeking" . . . . same as I'm doing now. . .and, same as you are doing now.

My expertise is relating to you from a stand or position that recognizes the patterns that the conscious mind has acquired from the journey in third dimensional "social consciousness". Call me a psychologist, if you like. I am expert at showing you the dilemmas that you create for yourselves. However, I prefer to bring a lighter touch to my conversations. Many . . . . too many . . . .take their realities much, too much . . . .seriously. Just to get you warmed up to the game we're playing . . . . notice that word "seriously". Smack in the middle are the letters . . . I . . . . O . . . . U. . . see? That's what happens when you take something seriously . . . . "guilt". Got it? Fun, isn't it?

So, we will now continue with the revelations and understandings in Chapter 2.

Now, within you, you have heard that there is "all-knowingness". That you are "All That Is". That God dwells within you. It is all there. How many of you are conscious of that? Your machine knows it because it has recorded the electrical impulses of the speaking of that. You've heard it and you've allowed it and you've recorded it because you all picked genetic bodies that had a program in it that would allow you to do that. Not all are genetically evolved enough to allow this information, but you picked bodies that would be. So, you heard it. You recorded it in the machine. You are using electricity . . . vibration because that's all this is.

Now, you all must be puzzled at this point. "How do I get out of the machine? How do I get anything but more machine?" There is . . . this will be another lesson . . . there is nothing but a big Zero and rest at the center of everything. Every particle . . . because remember, I drew you God and said He created this projection out here. The truth is it all spiraled and popped out within Him. It never went anywhere. It is all within the same as He . . . All-knowing, The Force, The Source, "All That Is" . . . is in every particle in this room . . . is in every cell in your body.

There would be no form or structure if that rest did not exist there to operate with the negative and positive. This force is going on all the time. You talk about your electro-magnetic fields. What is it? Everything functions from a center and you have a field that emanates from you that creates your form and the tension between this negative and positive holds your form together. Because, what is the negative and positive? Lots of things. *(Figure 13)* We've already called it the Son and the Holy Spirit, but it is also matter and space. So, you have a tension here between the space outside your skin and the skin which you call your matter. . . the body you call matter. There is a tension . . . pressure. This is a field around you that is a parameter . . . a boundary so that this field is your field. So, you have your little circle around you that keeps your body.

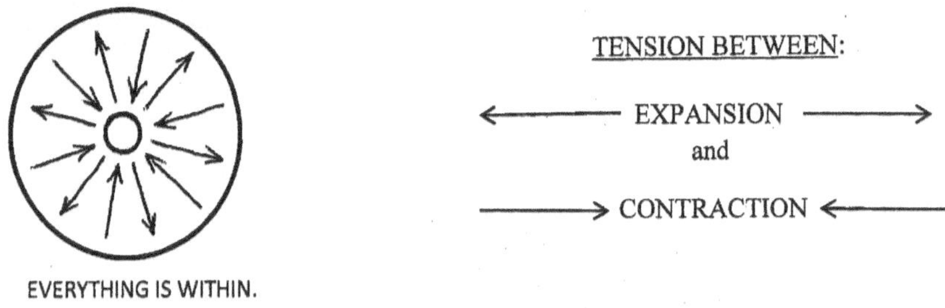

Figure 13

One part of that is always striving for rest in the center . . . gravity. One part is always striving for rest in the spiritual . . . the invisible. You create and feel that tension all the time until the knowingness reveals what it really is.

Everything operates from a center. You have a sun . . . you have planets orbiting . . . you have another sun that is greater than your solar system orbit . . . so forth and so on. Go down to the minutest particle of your body and you will find an orbit of a center that is "All That Is". Go to the highest central sun and you will find "All That Is".

It is creating through the projection of electricity . . . the sense of an image of itself, Its own thinking. God is thinking.

Now, we have to go back. I am just giving you previews so we don't lose you.

Conscious awareness. When you go to sleep, are you conscious? Yes, you are. You are never unconscious. You are not aware of your senses. You have shut them off and thereby, you have shut down this computer, but you are conscious. You do not perceive through the electrical impulses in your sleep, but you are never unconscious. You have conscious awareness in your sleep of other dimensions, parts and realities of yourself. You study, you learn and involve yourself in many activities which you later create here to have conscious awareness of them.

You become consciously aware of other realms and dimensions and aspects of yourself but, you are not sensing them through the five senses. Your machine shut down. Now, what is it you desire? You are desiring to be awake in the sleep or that other area of consciousness. Right now, you are only remembering conscious awareness of your senses. What is the door that is opening . . . between these two . . . your "Knowingness" and your "Computer" . . . because everything is within you?

So when you understand what I began to teach you in the beginning, that All-knowing . . . Desire . . . Mind . . . Will . . is in the one central "All That Is" and that is who is everything in the illusion. Everything that you are doing and thinking and expressing are His thoughts . . . His expression. It is not Him. It is not the All-Mind. It's a reflection . . . an expression . . . an illusion that is created. The thought is not the thing itself . . . is it? You are "Him" . . . what I am calling "Him" . . . what you insist on separating out . . . you are that Mind.

In reality, this is what we've been telling you. You are creating the illusion. You are thinking the thoughts. It cannot be otherwise, but you don't have conscious awareness of that. You're trying to . . . because we've told you the words and you've felt the vibrations and you want that. Good! Because, what did I tell you? You see . . . you desire . . . you think it into reality. You are at the point of intense desire and you felt somehow that this was wrong . . . the fact that you wanted so much to be done with this machine and you wanted so much to realize what was being said . . . you wanted so much to experience! "Why can't I"? and, there is a total judgment of yourself and disgust with the situation.

You've been revving up *(Figure 14)* . . . revving up . . . getting more intense . . . building more energy . . . vibrating faster, sometimes through anger. Whatever. Because you're going to open that door through desire and thinking who you really are.

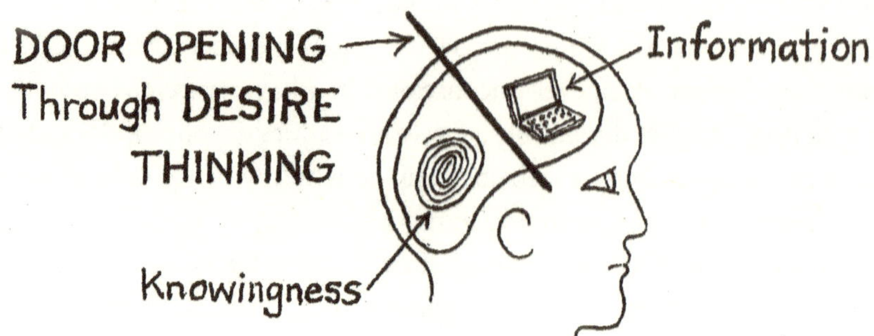

Figure 14

That is at the center of you and all that is created around you is emanating from the center of "All That Is" and, in reality, in this room with every center that is present here . . . there is no separation. The center of you is "All That Is". The center of you is "All That Is". The center of you is "All That Is" (points to individuals in the room). Now, let me tell you something. If the sun came out there and reflected through this window glass onto the floor, would you see maybe, five, six, seven, spots of light from the sun?

Yes. The curtain, the rod, the window panes, etc. would divide it and you would have maybe six or seven pools of light out here on the floor. But, how many lights are there in reality? One . . . because there is only one sun and there is only one light reflected down here. Now, when it came through this grid here, you saw spots of it, and you can't put them together. You would have to remove this window, so there would be a clear reflection and then what do you know? You know that there is only one light and in this room, I look at you and you see separate centers that I drew you . . . separate Gods in every one of you here. You're seeing through a grid, as it should be, but you're moving into an electrical situation here where your senses, you . . . will be able to see through the grid. You won't see but one being in this room . . . in absolute stillness with all power.

That is what is going through the doorway . . . that consciousness. The doorway is in you. The inner being and the conscious awareness . . . the human is the only creation ever created whereby they could be unified. Your consciousness will be able to be aware of "All That Is" at any moment. This is knowingness (points to the spiral), this is information (points to the computer). *(Figure 14)*

Now let me warn you . . . What many of you do not realize. This knowingness in you . . . according to your own plans, is surfacing more and more and more. Your machine does not recognize it. Your machine says, "That's unknown". And, every time that consciousness rises up to become conscious, your machine labels it because it has to put it in a program. It has to run through there to see "what is this?"And, it is labeling the unknown, the All-knowing mind . . . many things that it is not . . . because it is the Knowing Consciousness seeking to emerge so that you can be consciously aware of it . . . the same as you are the sense world.

Whatever you will or whatever you think . . . you will do. If you want to experience the sense world, you will. If you want the consciousness of All-knowing, you will become that. Wherever you focus your awareness, you will be able to be conscious of whatever you choose to be. You will be able to be consciously aware of the electrical system that operates behind this . . . if you choose. Whatever you choose, is what God does.

I want to show you something. Every one of you in this room have a knowingness inside of you that doesn't want to earn anything. Doesn't want to work to earn a dime. It doesn't want to work to earn anybody's love or approval. It doesn't want to expend any energy to do anything. What is that? What is that? That's the knowingness. The knowingness of itself. Not information about itself, mind you, which is all you have in the machine. The knowingness of itself . . . of itself as completely at rest.

How have you labeled that feeling and that knowingness? What have you done to it? Have you judged it? Has it annoyed you? Have you been ashamed of it? Have you tried to hide it? Have you called it all kinds of things and has it worried you? Have you failed to allow it to emerge in your conscious awareness? Yes . . . because, your senses tell you that that doesn't fit into this "sense world" that has been created. Do you feel what I am talking about?

Listen to me. That is the All-knowing mind of God that you are. And what is it that is happening on this dimension . . . on this earth . . . that everybody has labeled and given you all kind of information about? This is it! All that is hidden will be revealed! You will be known as you are known. You are going into another dimension. You will be All-knowing.

You're waiting for something. It's been happening to you! The vibration that we've brought. You see, the way that you're going to allow this... is by speeding up... everything is speeding up. You cannot not allow it. Why are some not going on? Why have we said to you that there's a choice being made "not to" and there is a choice being made "to go on"? What is this? Good people . . . bad people? What? No. It's who allows this to emerge.

You can forget all your words. We've tried to teach you the feeling . . . knowingness within you. If you do not allow this (points to the computer) to merge with this (points to knowingness) . . . . . so that it becomes consciously aware of that that you truly are at your center . . . you cannot stand the vibrations that are coming because you are still in this illusion. And, that's okay. That's okay. But, if the desire is becoming more intense and more intense . . . check out the All-knowing Mind that is within you.

Let me ... "Is there not a vibration and knowingness in you . . . has it not always been there . . . of wanting to just give...to give Love... without judgment. What have you done to that? The machine has all kinds of programs about that. Danger! God, you see that printed across the computer now. "If I give this to you, I don't have it". Oh, my goodness! Remember the little illusion? Remember? It's all illusion. There is nothing to gain or to lose. That is all illusion. The positive and negative . . . that's all part of the illusion. As long as you function that way, you are not allowing what I drew you on the board . . . that is what you are. If you are "All That Is", please tell me how you can have a knowingness of losing anything? Didn't you think that this knowingness that is emerging is a knowingness of abundance?

Did you think that you were going to log some kind of information that we were bringing to you . . . that you could put into this computer and therefore, in this new that is coming . . . you would know how to act just like you knew how to act before, when you logged information and the computer told you "how to act" when something happened? No! No... that's not it!

Feel what I am saying. It is a"Being"! It's the only "Being" in existence that is going to emerge in your conscious awareness and that Being is "All That Is". Those feelings that you have had all these years . . . that natural knowingness within you, that is going to push and push. And it is going to drive some people to kill, some people to destroy. Because fear . . . from the computer is going to tell them that they can't allow that knowingness. "I'm going to shoot my employer because he took something away from me". Why? Why? Because we've got an imbalance here. The imbalance is going to force a huge rush throughout those little tubes . . . it's going to explode and seek that restful state of All-knowingness.

You are no longer judge. That knowingness within . . . you haven't looked at it. You haven't looked at it. It's scared the hell out of you at times . . . it seemed weak at times. It doesn't fit into this sense universe. This sense universe is an illusion. You are what I showed you in the beginning . . . you are the Mind of God and to become consciously aware of that consciousness that is God, is going to be from within.

Have we not told you that and have we not told you that it's always been there? That you cannot even exist without it. But you desired experience. You closed that door deliberately. That was the plan. But, you are bringing this little creature here . . . there . . . there . . . there . . (points around the room again) . . . into a new dimension of experience. You don't want to lose that species . . . that's the idea that must continue on . . . the creation of God. That is why you desire to be here, because you are God desiring your creation.

So, you took one of these little forms and you've been working on it. You may not stay with it. But, you can reform it at any time you want to. We do, by our will because we know that our will is the only will. Our mind is the only mind. Our love is the only love. Our consciousness is the only consciousness.

You see, you will never be . . . One . . . As long as every one of you in this room is operating on this machine because everybody has a different machine. Everyone in here has a different genetic program and you will never be able to see the light as one through this machine. That is the grid that divides the light. But, you don't have to do anything to allow this. You just choose. It's your will. You don't have to make this happen. It's going to happen. If you can't handle it, you won't be here. You'll go where it's not happening because you can't deal with that yet. That's okay. There can be no judgment because there is only one mind deciding who goes where and who does what.

But suppose you have this intense desire within you? Are you crazy? Is this good or bad? Is this right or wrong? Should I go with it or shouldn't I? That's irrelevant. You can have only one desire at any time. And, that's the desire of "All That Is" as He thinks you into existence every moment because, you . . . flash on and off every second because everything comes to a zero. The minute you flash on . . . you flash off. The minute there is a positive image of you . . . there is a negative one that cancels you out because you don't exist. But, for a split second there . . . you created the illusion that there was something there when there really wasn't and you are living in that illusion.

There are many more places to go where no man has gone, much plans for this species. And, you may not want to be involved. There are many, many thoughts which are only one thought. Whatever you desire is what God is thinking in the moment for you . . . indeed, what you are thinking for you. This becomes the criteria . . . the movement, spontaneity . . . no storing of information . . . spontaneity, because the minute you do something, God has thought it and you are that thinking. As if there were infinite electrical currents in God's brain and here you are, one of them . . . here's somebody over here and over here . . . and you wake up and you're this little person inside of this brain and you see these electrical lights going off . . . it's God thinking and you're it . . . you're being it.

There is nothing to do if the desire is there. The intenseness of that desire is such that you're "thinking". Now, the words that we've brought you . . . the message that I'm applying here is to get you "thinking it" . . . allowing the "imaging of it" to be created in your reality. The desire within you will indicate the direction . . . what is drawn out, and how much can be contained.

Please, concentrate. Think and allow your thinking to go wherever it wants to go because it doesn't exist anyway. I have really given you food for thought. Your machine is going to work overtime, but it doesn't matter because the seeing is here and it is emerging. It is emerging. You are not going to do it by concentrating. This is what is coming for this planet. This is "It" that everybody is waiting on. It is the emergence of the evolution of the species of man of conscious knowing . . . conscious awareness of Himself as knowing Himself as "All That Is".

Now, what I have told you is who you really are and who you really are already exists within you right now and you know it. You've felt it, but you have allowed the machine to judge it and you've been afraid to allow it emergence. This is the Fear that we spoke of and the Love that would divide the species because they were going to have no choice if they feared the feelings that were arising within them . . . if they resisted it. If you resist it for whatever reason . . . it is going to create imbalance within your physical, emotional and mental bodies that will not allow you to go on.

Now, I am not creating fear by telling you this because, I have prefaced everything by telling you that whatever you do . . . there is only one person doing it. The illusion will be in you if you think you're missing out and that's okay. That's okay because there are always more adventures in creation and since you have the right to do whatever you want, you will . . . you will.

Okay, I have more. This will have to be assimilated and we will have to let you know when the time is ready for more. It will take several "sessions" to complete.

CHAPTER 4

PARADISE IS A LIMITATION

Suppose . . . Imagine . . . you are God. You have vast space . . . vast space. How do you know who you are? You are "what" in comparison to "what"? If there is no other, you have no reflection. You have no way of seeing yourself and knowing who you are. If you're the only one that "Is", you will never know yourself. Can you put yourself in that frame of mind . . . of being "All That Is" . . . the only one of your kind? Contemplate it.

So God, in order to see Himself and know Himself . . . remember the first thought . . . He contemplated Himself, same as you would if you were the only one around. You would say "What am I"?

Welcome to our plane. Would you like to come in and sit down? We have a table set for you. Let us dine together. You are beginning to know the wonder of oneness and multi-levels. Who would you like to have seated next to you at the table that you can have a conversation with?

Audience: Aknom.

I salute you, brothers and sisters of the stars! I am Monka, the strong one! Very forceful! I love to hand it out! Information is my game! You have described me. You have requested me, have you not? Let's get on with it.

<u>Audience</u>: Okay, Aknom left off with our beliefs and being . . . . . .

<u>Monka</u>: That was another entity that you have exhausted! Why do you think they have brought the strong one in? You are getting a reputation. That is why I am here.

<u>Audience</u>: We go through them, boy!

<u>Monka</u>: Okay, you wanted to hear some more about "beliefs" . . . . but you must feel the futility of so much listening to hear the same things repeated.

<u>Audience</u>: We do.

Monka: I have listened and watched many of you reading and reading, hearing and asking questions, figure it out . . . playing the "information game". Oh, there are many entities who will come here and give you many stories to satisfy you, so that you can continue to play the "game". They have their reasons for doing this. But, I believe I'm sensing energy here now that's saying . . . . "I'm done with that"!

Now what happens if you have perceived yourself as a being who must put responsibility on others to create for you and that other person, namely me, in this case . . . tells you, "Nope, gotta do it yourself!" At that moment, you are going to make a decision to continue in that identity of shifting responsibility . . . and the first thing you will do is say, "Ohhhhhhh,,,, woe is me. I can't do it".

Do you understand a viewpoint of yourself that is phony . . . illusion: shadows of the reality of the glorious being that you are? That beingness that we discuss has been telling you and talking to you and whispering to you for many years . . . of how glorious you are . . . how glorious everything is! But, you have a belief system that says, "Whatever that is, just does not understand and does not have a clear picture of what I go through. If you only understood, you wouldn't say all those nice things."

Okay. Must admit, that I am merely trying to create a tone here of understanding of how you function. It is not complicated. You have a belief system that says that "it must be complicated because the more complicated it is, the more intelligent that I am. If it's simple, God, that must mean that I'm an ignorant person. I don't want to appear ignorant. So, I must appear complicated."

Many belief systems! Put them in your lagoon, in your garbage dump! That's where they belong! Well, what happens when an illusion is no more "your illusion" . . . what do you see?

Audience: Reality!

<u>Monka</u>: Right. So that is all we are concerned with here . . . is that correct? All we are concerned with here now is reality and I am reality . . . same as you. Good! Well, wait a minute! What are we going to talk about? We can talk about doing whatever we want to do. All on this plane seem to find that a very interesting subject . . . attractive.

<u>Audience</u>: Yeah, that's always a good one.

<u>Monka</u>: But, wouldn't you know . . . it's all wearing down, isn't it?

<u>Audience</u>: You don't want to do the same things you thought you wanted to do.

<u>Monka</u>: All wearing down. Bet you thought that was just you, didn't you? Whole planet is . . . yep, planet is feeling it. You are beginning to get in touch with a vibrational level that will survive. You know it's like many old serials on TV and movies . . . one of the big cracks in the earth when there's an earthquake and you're standing over here . . . this part's getting ready to totally disappear and be demolished . . . all of a sudden he jumps across the chasm and he's on the other side. Correct?

Yes, this physical world as you know it, is wonderful . . . it's beautiful, but it is a limitation of the first order. First, within your consciousness you will feel the first waves . . . the wavy disappearance of identity. Emotionally disappearing . . . typical responses . . . old hat . . . don't remember them. Physical dominion out there . . . all around you . . . wavy . . . fading in and out. Opening between dimensions . . . going to begin to look like a ragged old curtain with holes in it . . . thin material.

You know what thin material looks like when it gets old and the threads begin to come out of it? It's thin . . . fabric . . . the fabric of the physical universe is wearing thin! Holes coming in it! You're not going to have any desire to patch it up. Hmmmm, know what you're going to want to do? You're going to run up to those little holes and try to peek through! Okay, this is long awaited . . . long awaited for this to happen. Planned on it. But, you know what . . . you think this is going to be a big deal?

<u>Audience</u>: That's pretty big, but I don't think that's going to be all.

<u>Monka</u>: As they say . . . "You ain't seen nothin' yet, baby"! No. No. But you've got to take those glasses off that color everything. Sunglasses that make everything dark . . . colored . . . got to take them off. Lotta light coming to this planet . . . lotta light. Did you know that? Not going to need sunglasses. You're going to be able to look right at it. That's what is showing you the holes in the fabric. That's what is making the fabric look so thin. Know what I mean? Lotta light coming through it!

You just don't know what in the hell to call it yet. You don't know where to put it when you see it and you feel it and you talk about it. That's all well and good and all you're doing . . . God bless your souls . . . is trying to find these boxes to put it in so you can relate to it. Right? My God, what's the purpose of all this if I don't know how to talk about it and relate to it? We've got to talk about this vibration stuff . . . this energy here.

You haven't known, in that limited dimension of mind, what to do with this energy. You've identified with that creation that had an identity in this dimension. But, if you're going to "be", you're going to be "All That Is", you're going to experience this energy. You're going to know it and I'm going to tell you something else . . . you're going to control it. You see, we can get all this worked up and get it all to the right place . . . but, you're going to have control over this body, that is energy . . . just by your thoughts. In the act of being who you are, you will have control over all energy . . . the elements.

So, you can't just keep on being dumb! You've got to start... realizing who you are! You're the "God of All That Is" and you created these human bodies to contain yourselves and you maintain this through energy . . . vibration. Now, I can't get into all this stuff about feeling vibration. Now, this is legitimate . . . it's legitimate. But, by God, I want you to be that vibration! Do you know what I mean?

This energy is going to vibrate faster within your bodies . . . physically. Got that? You know that! You know what we're doing to these little cells and you know what they're doing to themselves. Okay? The emotional body is not going to be eliminated. The mental body that we deal with . . . with the apparatus and all that stuff . . . is not going to be done away with either. You see? We're going to wind these three people up . . . mental, emotional, and physical. Like one of those little gadgets that you look through?

Audience: Yeah . . . a kaleidoscope.

Monka: And you turn it and you turn it and little pieces of glass just fall in place and patterns form? Yeah, we've got all these patterns in these three bodies. We're going to put them in this little thing . . . okay . . . and shake them all up and turn them. Got it? We're going to give you new patterns. You've got new patterns of vibrations that are going to become the source from which you relate to everything.

The Navigator: This is part of what's happening with the "light" coming in?

Monka: Right, it is . . . and why aren't you happy with your other patterns? Because they don't work! They don't work!

They've served you well for a long time. Served you well. But, you understand, the astronauts trained by the government, NASA . . . they go through some tough shit. Am I right? Ever seen those little gadgets that they put them in and turn them around and around and around . . . so they can function and not lose their equilibrium? Well, you have created an elaborate one. Do you understand that? It's turning around and you're supposed to get out of this contraption and be standing on your feet.

Audience: We're astronauts in training?

Monka: Yep! Sometime you should look into that stuff. Check out those experiences they go through. Check out the . . . oh what the hell is the word . . . the phases of training that they must go through to become an astronaut? There's a lot of good stuff in that. But, that little gadget is very disorienting because there's no up or down. You must understand that those that love you will go to any lengths to pull every damn prop . . . that you have used . . . out from under you, till you are left with nothing . . . Ha, Ha, Ha . . . nothing but God!

Audience: (laughter) Oh . . . that's a horrible place to be! Thank you.

Monka: Isn't that absurd? That's absurd, isn't it? My God, what a job that we have! It's the pits!

Audience: Now . . . well, I'll be damned! All the Zen masters . . . that's all they were ever doing, wasn't it? Are you the Zen master that I've been working with all these years?

Monka: My friend, you've worked with many Zen masters. They're all the same. They're all One . . . there was never a Zen master that has ever lived that tried to help another soul. Do you think I'm trying to help you? Now you're getting very close to who I am. I'm not Monka! You wanted me to be Monka. That's why I said I was Monka! But, I'm not. However, I have come from the east.

Audience: I thought so!

Monka: But you are no longer identified with that teaching. Am I correct?

Audience: I was, big time, for a long time.

Monka: Correct! You are discarding it? You see it was only half the truth! Why did Christ not become a Zen master if it was all the truth? He was a Master, correct? And he taught, did he not? Did anyone understand him? I will let you feel this . . . discover for yourself what is to be discovered here.

The Navigator: Well, Zen masters threw all the beliefs out. Threw everything out! They didn't have the knowingness of love and union.

<u>Monka</u>: They knew much about the Oneness . . . the Oneness . . . everything but, nothing about the new creation of God . . . where His heart dwells.

<u>The Navigator</u>: They just wanted to melt back into the Source.

<u>Monka</u>: The Oneness of everything . . . What is the new creation? What was it that the apostle Paul saw that flipped him over 180 degrees?

<u>The Navigator</u>: The God/Man.

<u>Monka</u>: The one new man! There have been many ways to describe . . . others that have talked about it . . . one new man! A new Creation! That knowledge was not to be given until Christ came!

Get out of the past with Zen . . . Chung Foo . . . whoever. Oneness . . . Yes, Yes! But that Oneness has created the most magnificent plan whereby He took this crummy thing . . . this body that you think is so pretty . . . and it crumbles and is raising it to glorious heights to become the container of Himself. Many of them . . . Many of them.

That is the heart of God. Never before . . . God is going to divide Himself. He's going to have a Son who will contain all that He is. Let me give you an example that I have used. Okay . . . . we've all used it. What the hell! Take biology? Remember that text book picture of a cell dividing? One nucleus becomes two nuclei? Two cells!

One the parent . . . one the child. One the Father . . . one the Son. You think that's big? You are it! You are it! All that you are . . . everything that you are . . . is it! Now . . . Now. You are it! All of it! All . . . . all of creation is envious of you . . . if I may borrow a human term . . . because you are the heir of God. He remembered! Christ remembered . . . He was the first of many! Do you think that we teach Christ consciousness because it sounds good to you? He knew and He said, "I wish for you to come to know the love the Father and I share".

Christ went in front of a bunch of Jewish priests that the name of God was so sacred that no one was allowed to say it. Did you know that? Day after day, He walked in front of them and said the name . . . the sacred name that they weren't allowed to utter . . . about Himself! "I Am".

Generations of Jews could not speak that name and Christ, a carpenter's son . . . looked like everybody else . . . just walked around and people followed . . . and He said "I Am". "I Am". He discovered this was the way. I mean, He studied everything that the rabbis could give Him and He went to the East and studied everything that the eastern guys had given Him and He came back. He had exhausted everything but, that that was in Him . . . that had guided Him . . . all the time to absorb all that and go to the east and absorb all that . . .was telling Him who He was. Had to get both sides of the picture. God said over here in the Hebrew . . . "Behold I do a new thing". Goes over here in the east . . . finds out that half and puts the two together and says, "I'm It! I'm It!" Saw the picture. "I Am".

Now, you can read all that New Testament that you want to and you won't find one place where He tried to convince another soul of who He was. He was convinced. That's all it took. When He was convinced, He created a reality that was a total expression of that . . . complete, total expression. Did you know that?

<u>Audience</u>: Yeah . . .

<u>Monka</u>: But you know . . . you're looking for an easy route or something tricky here. Can I tell you something? You've got it easier than He did, because for one thing, times are changed. There is no more restriction and limitation that He faced. He was the first one who put it together and He was the first one to know. First of many more to come! They had blueprints. "Behold . . . forget all those things past . . . I'm doing a new thing!" Got it? He did it! Christ was the first one.

You know, your Bible has letters that Paul wrote to the people he was talking to, and he told them,"You're joint heirs with Christ". Let me ask you something . . . what is an heir?

<u>Answer</u>: Someone who inherits when a parent dies.

<u>Monka</u>: When they're dead? Why did He tell them they were joint heirs? Was God going to die? Wait a minute! As long as Christ is sitting on the right hand of the Father and you're on the left . . . and I don't know all that . . . remember you studied all that? But, you're with God, right? That's

all you can see. Get back with God. Okay, hey, that's the Source. So, why are you an heir? Is God going to die? Now listen, you're joint heirs with Christ . . . meaning you're an heir and He's an heir. You're heirs of the Father. But the Son doesn't need to inherit as long as He's with the Father.

Audience: He's already got it.

Monka: He's leaving the Father! Remember what I told you . . . separating from the Father. Son's going to go out and become a Father. Joint heirs with Christ. Everything that belongs to the Father is now becoming the new Son's.

The Navigator: Wow, I didn't know that's what that meant!

Monka: Take it with you! You know that parable about the prodigal son that you like so much? You read all those parables and you think that they're just about you on this earth . . . humanity. No . . . remember that He's describing that the kingdom of God is like this. That's wherever God reigns and rules. That covers a big territory, right? Do you know why He told that parable?

The Father had two sons. One of them went to the pits with the pigs, right? One of them stayed there. Well, He's talking about His whole creation. He had to help those guys who stayed behind, you know? He had to give His little parable to teach everybody. Got it?

"You know, don't get your feelings hurt. You've always had me and everything I have." You know, you've got to read these parables differently . . . learn a lot from them.

Yeah, lot of wonderful things there. Lot of vision there to inspire and lift you up, but I'll tell you something . . . All of it will make you feel something that none of this teaching will do, because this has been in you from the beginning to do.

Magnificent plan! Magnificent plan! Glorious! Never before! You know, you study in your history books about the "Big Bang" and the planets and the nebula and the galaxies and the whole thing and you're so proud of yourselves in this dimension because of what you can see and know. That's wonderful but . . . God has a greater plan.

Hey! You've got to get tired after a while . . . same stuff! He's going to do something new! There is no limit to macro. There is no limit to micro. Don't put any limits anywhere!

God is All That Is! The Source that created everything is as small as the atom and the atom is as immense as the God of All That Is!

Pause

For God so loved His Son. You know that love. You are that love. The energy . . . vibration . . . from the knowingness within me could not come through when I left you.

Words are not necessary. I suppose you do not think anything as wondrous as that could come through a foul mouth entity such as me?

<u>The Navigator</u>: No, I thought it could.

<u>Monka</u>: It can . . . but I have been a beautiful mirror as you are . . . for this evening and I will be back! Okay? Truly magnificent! Always know it! Own it! Christ did! Own it! It belongs to you! It is you!

Okay . . . okay. I'm going to leave you now. I salute you. I'll be back.

CHAPTER 5

AS BELOW . . . . SO ABOVE

Always remember: "You are known. You are loved". I am your brother named Wonton. You need to be awakened to your true embodiment. You will be! Prepare yourselves to receive understanding and knowledge. Now, your heart has told you that you want to go "Home". Then go! Do not feel that you must wait. That is a mental game that you are playing. You are capable of consciously relying upon your own desires. We are aware of your struggles, but we must wait for you many times to know your own desires. Come "Home"! Does that sound difficult? Well, this may make it even more difficult for you. You are already Home! Does this help? I thought you needed a little loosening up there, so I thought I would help you.

The World is in your consciousness. You allow a negative force into your world. You created it. You create your own reality. You are not In the World.

All things exist in God. If you polarize to a negative thought or vibration, you create it and you must experience what you create. You are more powerful than you know. You have seen the negative force outside of yourself, is that objective? The objective truth is that "all things" exist in God. Your view of reality can create forces that are opposing and you will experience them. Consciousness creates through energy

The question you've all had is . . . why did the negative exist in your reality?

Because all things exist in God. When you create judgement, right and wrong, negative and positive, then you must experience that. What

I am saying is that your consciousness can embrace all things in love. Neither express good or bad. You just express love. If you have difficulty with this, then observe why your mind struggles to maintain a position in your consciousness and yet you need only observe the battle. You do not have to participate in it.

A consciousness without judgement is the place that you need to be, because there is absolute reality. Right and wrong, good and bad, negative and positive is a creation of the Gods in this dimension to reflect all possibilities. But you are going home. Remember? You are going back where you remember only love without judgement. Don't you know that when you say something is good, you have created the bad? Don't you know that God only exists as oneness in a consciousness that has aligned itself with no polarities?

But you are riddled with the "polarities of your mind". You have decided what will be "good", so you have decided what will be "bad". It will still be a riddle if you do not understand that "polarity" is part of this world. You "can't take it with you"!

The "image" was created to reflect that (polarity). You have been taught that all thought embraced with emotion will manifest. This has been spoken and taught to humanity in this dimension. Your prophets have decreed that bad must be punished and good must triumph. The only problem with this is that every religion has its own good and bad. That leads to wars of confusion. Allah has predicted and declared through his prophets that anyone opposing him will be doomed and anyone following him will be rewarded. Christ followers say that everyone who doesn't follow him will go to hell and anyone who does will go to heaven. All believe they are right and good! So they have created bad and destruction in this world. We do not interfere with creations of this world. We choose to protect and redeem those souls who are able to find love in their hearts regardless of the creations of religious tyrants. Don't you feel that? Don't you desire that? You wanted that. You chose a journey that would put you right in the middle. You thought you could handle that. You have! Know this. Put it to rest.

Okay, you are progressing very well with our little talk tonight. You have heard many new concepts. Good! We must break down some barriers in order to introduce you to new truths for you. This has been an exercise in expanding consciousness and you are feeling the energy level, but you must allow this to rest with you. I am always with you and am available for consultation. Did I say that right?

The Navigator: That's right.

Wonton: You are unique. Your mission is unique. But very serious. Very important. But do not forget in your desire to know your mission, the love of yourself. The needs for yourself are most important. I wish to share my thoughts of love for you that you might feel and know the love that you have for yourself. Do not put that second because that is the creative force behind all things. That is God! The "I Am" within you. Allow it! Experience it! Be it! In doing that, you will know me and all of God. Goodnight.

The Navigator: Goodnight!

------◦◦◦❮◉❯◦◦◦------

Feel the absence of all tension. Feel the zero of All-Knowingness. Be that center within you where "I Am That I Am" is present.

Within that center you can see the red masses of the burning suns. You can see the spiraling galaxies against a background of darkness. You can see the stars. You can see the nucleus within the atom. You can see the fight between the forces that exist. You can see the fields of energy that spiral and radiate within your vision of the eye. (I) . . . with the eye (I). These are all emanations from the center of you.

You are all that you see. You are All-Knowing . . . aware of the vastness within which you dwell.

Return slowly to the focus that is present within this room to receive further symbols that trigger the knowingness that you have just entered.

We are all present. Again, we are a group that is involved within you from the blueprint that exists for those here. We know that since our last visit, you have experienced many things. Words are not necessary . . . they have been personal and individual. Words have not described it . . . words have merely been an attempt for your machines to understand the energy acceleration and the knowingness from the center that is emerging from each one of you.

We will continue tonight to expand on what was brought before. We feel that time has been well spent in your own thoughts that have spiraled from the ones that were delivered here.

Pictures from within your "eye within" have emerged to give you a feeling and understanding that is allowing you to go forward and to eliminate unnecessary debris. So we will continue.

In our last discussions, we've called this *(Figure 15)* . . . "All That Is". This is the positive . . . . it is also the Zero. We understood that all out here was created by opposites . . . negatives and positives. We called it "God" . . . "All That Is" . . . the "Zero" . . . the rest that is in everything. We are going to expand on that Zero and understand more how that exists in all things.

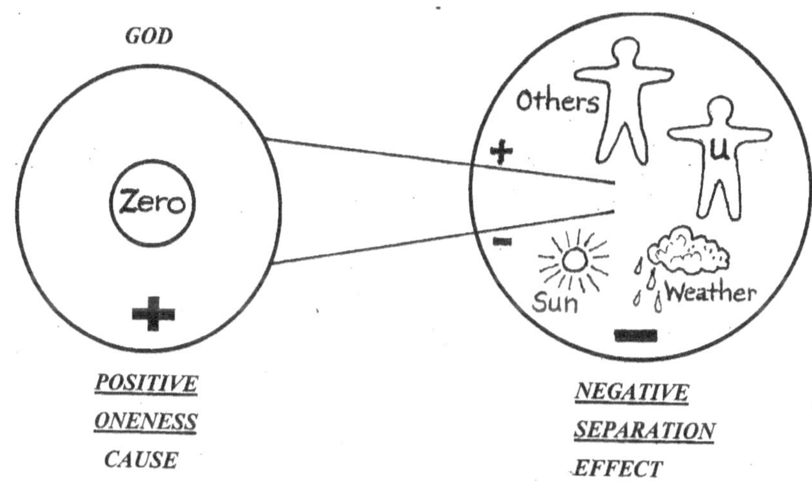

Figure 15

In the two rays that we referred to as the positive and negative, all of "this", "you" . . . are created. A simulation, an illusion, an expression of the thinking of "All That Is". There is a need now to understand that all of this that is created by the negative and positive forces, the opposites within, all things . . . you, your bodies, the universes that are created in a simulation of motion and time through the interplay between these two charges, are in reality, the negative. *(Figure 15)* They are the negative to God's positive. This is the opposite of God in that sense. This is the positive. This is what exists. This is a negative, so that all that you have experienced in this body and all that is experienced here . . . everything . . .

is negative . . . the opposite of the truth. This is Separation . . . this is Oneness. Oneness is the positive. Separation is the negative, the opposite of Oneness. In this negative, there is the semblance of multiplicity created through the separation of these two rays of God's splitting.

Now, there is something else that we must enter into that will be, in part, a continuation that will reveal more of this. Everything, apart from zero . . . the center that is God, is "Effect". This is the only "Cause" that exists. So that, within this negative effect here, you have believed . . . and, this was the illusion . . . that you caused "things". And, you have looked at others and said "That is the effect" of what you caused, whether it has been material, emotional, or physical. You have believed, in your separation, that you could be the cause of something . . . physical, mental, or emotional. That was the illusion. That is the fun. That was necessary.

Hear what I mean. You many times, believed that you caused things to happen. You create . . . you are the creator of events, situations, products that you produce, work, thoughts, and ideas, so forth. You have thought that you were the cause. But, more than that, your universe and your world became stuck in the concept that everything outside itself causes what happens to you. You have thought that heat, sun, fire makes you hot. You have thought that cold makes you cold.

You have thought that you were being affected and that others like you are the cause of things happening to you. Whether it is the elements, rain, clouds, sun, flowers, vegetables that you eat, whatever . . . you have thought that "It" is a cause, same as you are a cause. You have thought . . . and this is the illusion of these two . . . that you lived in a universe of cause and effect. Is that correct?

When in reality, what we have brought you in our last discussion and what we will elaborate on now is that neither you nor anything in this negative "Effect" has ever caused anything. It is all the "Effect" of one "Cause" . . . the "Thinking of God".

This is a very liberating and freeing understanding. This is what we introduced at our last session, that we are aware that your machines have been working overtime with because, we approached the thought with you last time that, "you have never thought a thought . . . you've been the effect of one thinker". Now, that was hard. That was scary. But, we brought you the clear, expanded understanding of that. That's what we have been saying all along. I am sure you recognized it.

We are aware that many of these programs that we brought you were designed for the machine because you are existing in "Effect" and we've been telling you that you were the "Cause" . . . you were the "All That Is", you were the one mind . . . the one consciousness. What we approached and what is "Happening" and the area that you are approaching, the "Newness" that is coming . . . is when this "You" wakes up and realizes that it has never caused anything in that separation . . . it has merely been the "Effect" created by the one Cause, the one Mind, the one Self.

This was difficult because this meant that you were a puppet, possibly? That you were a nothing! We even told you that you don't really exist because science can show you that you don't. It's merely illusion and it is more illusion than you know because we have not gone into the science of how the illusion is created through mass, density, positive and negative electricity and magnetism, and mirrors. Remember the house of mirrors? You thought you were running here when in reality, God was thinking running and it was reflected out here in your physical density.

What does that tell you? God was the cause of everything. This one mind, this one consciousness, which we have told you that you really are . . . has been the cause of everything that you have ever said, done, thought, or felt. Was that difficult for your machines? Do not tell me it wasn't! Do not tell me it wasn't! Because we are going to investigate that little machine and how it has played with you since then and maybe enlighten you a little more.

We're changing positions . . . identities. This (the negative) is where you've been identified. You've been looking for "This" (the positive), for union . . . for God. But, we are bringing you the thought, because you are preparing for the emergence of this that will begin to look at all this differently from the way you've been looking at it . You see?

God has been out there. God has been somewhere. You've been trying to get back to Him. But, you are going to change places in this opening and this consciousness and this new that is emerging. You will begin to see yourself from the "Cause" . . . the center of all Effect. So, do not try to imagine or reason your machine's contemplation of this because, it will see it as frightening when, in fact, it is absolute freedom . . . to be and know yourself as the Cause of all things, seen and unseen.

Remember`. . ."Cause" . . . "Effect". This is called the plus, the positive, all that exists in reality. This Effect is called the negative. So we still see the opposites existing. They do not exist within the center. There are no opposites within the center. There is just the positive . . . all-Knowing, all Loving, all-Peace, "All That Is," that has caused everything, that is the Cause of everything.

You in your sleep state have thought that you caused your problems, that you caused your good times, you caused your smartness, you caused your dumbness. That other people around you . . . organizations, elements, whatever, were working on you to cause what was happening in your life. Begin to contemplate . . . as you truly will when this thinking is seen . . . a feeling begins to emerge, as you realize that you are the cause of all of this.

This (the positive) is the only reality. This (the negative) has been created for fun, for enjoyment, for adventure . . . to express all potential in the thinking of God. You see, your scientists do not recognize what they see yet, within the atom that causes all this play between the two forces. They do not understand what bonds them. They do not understand the unified principle of electricity, of magnetism, of strong and weak forces. They are seeking this "The Unified Field". The Unified Field is the thought of "All That Is"! Every mass that they perceive that is made up of these subatomic particles . . . do you know what that is? It is called "coagulated thought". And, they search and they see the effect of this thought. They see the effect of the bond. They see the effect of the charge between these two and they call them different things. They call them atoms, electrons, protons, electric and positive and negative charges, magnetism, weak force, strong force . . . they call it many things within that subatomic particle which cannot be seen with your visibility.

What is it? You know! You are being told. It is the "thinking of God". It is "God thinking"! So, when you appear as you do here, with all your thoughts and what you are in your body which is pulling from all these electromagnetic principles . . . What are you? What is holding all of it together? What is the Glue? It is coagulated thought!

They are looking for particles. They are looking for some kind of force. The Force is the thinking of God. This "Effect" becomes the thought.

It is the consciousness and the thought of God that creates all form and structure. It is the desire of God. It is the love of God, because all His thoughts emanated from His desire and love, and they create everything. So that all of "This" is coagulated thought, created by love.

You've heard these expressions, but you have not understood them, and in the realm that your scientists are not able to go into . . . they merely measure the effect of all this. They have not seen any of this that they tell you of, because it cannot be seen. Remember? This cannot be seen as it returns back to the Father. It is the invisible . . . the unknowable. And you, as a species, do not have the vibratory level of vision and sound and so forth, in order to view . . . to view the invisible. But, you are approaching that now. That is what is happening.

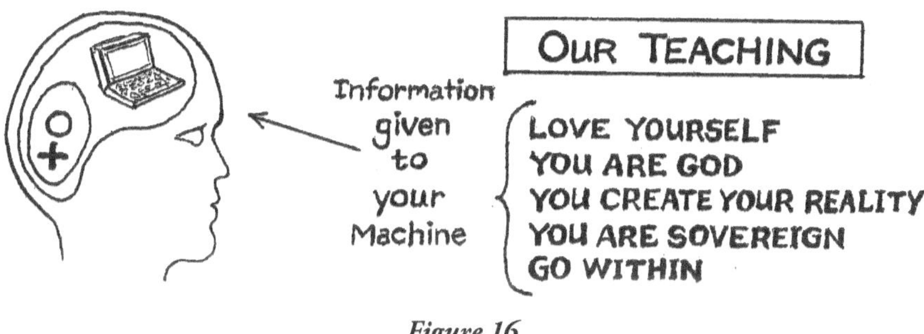

Figure 16

Let's illustrate. *(Figure 16)* Am I improving with each drawing . . . possibly but not particularly? Does this look more like you?

Remember, we spoke last time of your little machine, your computer that sits up front and then the consciousness emerging right back here? We have brought you many teachings. We told you "Love yourself". We told you "You are God". We told you "You create your reality". We told you "You are sovereign". We told you "Go within". Recognize those? What was that spoken to? Does the zero, the plus . . . the one consciousness of God need to know this?

This was information. This is a perspective . . . this was for perceiving. This was for preparing you for something. It was all given to the machine. It was a new program for your computers. All of this! Everything we taught you was a new program for your computers! Let the weight of that descend within you. Know that.

Why did we do this? Because, the human species had evolved, or remained in a position of evolution . . . being controlled entirely by forces from outside. "All cause dwells outside of me." We hear that all the time and you have said it many, many times. "You are not the master of your fate or the Captain of your ship", somebody else was. Something else was . . . outside of you. And, all of your experience has been to maintain, derive, rationalize some kind of control. But, it has put you in tension and conflict with everything outside of yourself, as well as this that was in you.

Now, consider what we did here. It is clever and it works, to a point. This (*Figure 16* - list of teachings) is not this (*Figure 16* – brain). This list of teachings is not for the brain portion of "New Consciousness" coming in. This is not the knowingness, the consciousness, the one mind you are entering because the consciousness, the one mind, the "New" you are entering is real. It is "It"! It is "All That Is"! It "Is"! This (**Figure 16**) is information that you have logged in your computers that has created a new perspective on everything in this effect world.

All of these that we taught you said basically, one thing . . . "Go within". We have been teaching the human species, with which you have experimented in your incarnation . . . okay, quit trying to love the whole world. Just love yourself. Look at yourself. Get to know yourself. Feel yourself and allow yourself. You are God. That's a big one. We've had a hard time getting that one over and convincing you that God was not out there in the sky sitting on a throne, but that "He" was you. That one is in your computer and it still has problems in many human beings on this Earth.

"You create your own reality". Now, that was extremely important because that said, "Take responsibility". Become the cause. Cease to view everything as the effect. Begin to realize yourself as the cause in this dimension. So, you had to go within and you began to get a new perspective . . . "I'm causing everything". That's good! The computer logged that in.

"You are sovereign". Oh, good! That works well because nothing and no one is greater than you or has control over you. You are sovereign. Where? Within yourself! So all of this has been for the purpose of focusing you within . . . to get the machine turned around because, you know what? Your machine is what we call "brainwashing". Do you understand?

Now, your world of social consciousness has created "brainwashing" to serve their purposes. There is no one alive in this world that is not "brainwashed". Do you understand me? And, we must work against this continually. We are the ones that have problems with "brainwashing". There is no one in this world, on this earth that really has the problem of combating "brainwashing". All you do is change programs in the brain that is taught to believe whatever the program says is true.

And when we said that, "You create your own reality", we were trying to get you to foul this little machine up and to get you to understand that everything out there was a creation of whatever you said it was. . . whatever you thought it was. You're the "Brain" . . . "Washing" the machine. You were changing brains. You see? Because you've been taught that everything else was in charge . . . but you!

I don't care what philosophy, I don't care what religion, I don't care what government, I don't care what social consciousness, what ethnic group you belong to or what race of people you are, what history you have had . . . it is all programs in the computer. You can't get more programmed than a DNA. You can't get more programmed than a brain that processes and records electrically, impulses . . . and never thinks a thought but records and spits it out like a computer.

If you join this church, you're going to get their program. if you join that church, you're going to get its program. Now, this church says that that church is "brainwashing" its members because they don't see that of course, "our" program is the reality. "This is the way reality is". "What I say, is reality". What are we talking? Disks, programs, information logged. Every one of them has a history. Every one of them has a philosophy . . . religions, governments, ethnic groups. Check out your Arabs and your Jews. Check out the DNA; check out their history . . . check out the programs. If you're born an Arab, you have a program and all of life will be perceived through that program. But, if you are an Arab and you convert to Judaism, God forbid . . . you've been "brainwashed".

It is a clever manipulation in social consciousness, by the powers-to-be. Do you understand? This controls you. This is your greatest fear. So that when the consciousness of "All That Is" begins to emerge, what does your machine do, because it's programmed to throw up a danger signal, that there's a possibility of "Brainwashing". That's the biggest fear of all. It is that "I won't perceive reality the way I'm supposed to. I will become deluded about what is reality".

The powers-to-be, who control this earth, knew this time was coming. They knew that this machine was about to be joined with this consciousness. "Now, we've got to put something there, that every time the machine approaches awakening to this consciousness, coming out of sleep . . . We've got to have a danger signal there to stop it, so it will go back to sleep." Now, I'm talking about a "feeling" that has been created.

So, when you hear . . . "The problem is within us" . . . you love this, it sounds great and it begins to put focus within you. But, we're entering another time here. We're not just logging in information in this program. We're about to approach our "Awakening". We're approaching . . . "This" is emerging. You don't let it. It is! This is the "second coming". It is happening.

Now, what does your machine say? "Is this reality"? Danger means, "I must find a safe place." Where is the safe place? Where is the safe place in the machine? Where is the little place that you can go back and fit in and everything is "known" and you can anticipate the future and you don't make any waves and you are acceptable?

You've got to be careful . . . because in your religions and countries . . . when they cross the line and get into someone else's "brainwashing", they're not acceptable. So, the joke on everybody is that everybody has to be careful, even in social consciousness, about crossing the line. You have your own . . . you have your own.

What has been going on since our last discussion, is the little game that is played here, that every one of you have felt, that every one of you have a different one . . . it's personal. Don't even try to describe it, because it takes over and it says, "Danger!" I don't know how many of you know this but, your DNA was tampered with long, long years ago. This little game was put into the program for when this time came, to prevent you from going through that door. You were genetically kept as laborers and slaves of the controlling groups all these years.

So, you have a DNA, a genetic inheritance of this little program . . . this little game. It's not even your own. You inherited it . . . each one of you. And, you can feel it. You can feel it, because . . . I say feeling because you don't even need words, you've done it so many times it's so automatic . . .

it's "You" . . . you think, at that moment. It becomes you. You become that machine. You identify with those feelings and you believe that is you.

But I want to ask you something. Has this been a little difficult since we introduced it? Have you been trying to reason and rationalize why this flag popped up there? It doesn't make any sense. What's it doing there? You've been buying this "new" for a long time. You've been buying all the predictions. You've said, "I believe that. I can feel that. I know that's coming. What is that fear doing there now when "this" is coming? Where did it come from?" Now, feel what I am talking about because it is something that goes all the way back, since your birth, through your childhood, through adolescence, through your years and it always raises its ugly head when you get close to allowing the emergence and the awakening . . .this combination. It has always raised its ugly head and caused you to back off and put this off until a later time. I believe that since our last discussion that it is more evident than it ever has been that . . . that fear is not you . . . that this is a genetic program that scares you off of this "Awakening".

You were genetically programmed in the beginning by a race that took over control. Neanderthal was the man that was absolutely programmed through evolution to become this human, the "Christed Being". But, a controlling race of people who populated this earth, took Neanderthal man, sped him up a little bit but genetically removed this possibility from them, placed in that little program that wouldn't allow it and began to have workers and slaves to help them create whatever they wanted to on this earth. They had a ruling class of people.

Your scientists have been looking for a gap between Neanderthal and Cro-magnum. There is none. They were genetically programmed by the ruling party - that are still ruling your earth, still have workers. It's just that now they have programs that say, "I'm free. I'm free". Sometime figure out how free you are. Figure out how all the efforts of this world . . . who really benefits by them. It is not the average human . . . he is a worker. He is a slave.

So, we have all this time watched and seen the experiences of the flag. Did you get caught up in it? Did you feel that old feeling that comes back at that time and says, "What if this isn't true? What if all this they've been telling me isn't going to happen? What if it's not true?" Now, listen carefully.

You see, it triggers in you a mechanism that says, "If this is not true then I've been deceived, I've been "brainwashed". And what does your little program tell you about "brainwashing"? It means that, "I'm not a free thinker. I'm not thinking for myself." What in social consciousness is the worst thing that you can do, in your "freedom" . . . in your "independence"? It is to not think for yourself, even when you've been thinking all this yourself. "Maybe I'm not thinking this?" Now, that should give you a hint, because you're not. You never have. You all are "brainwashed". Always have been.

You have recorded in the human species, all of the experiences of this "effect world" in this dimension that created the negative and the positive. It is recorded now. It never has to be repeated in the next adventures because you have the recording. You know what happens in those incidences, don't you? So, man goes to the "Beyond The Beyond" and never has to repeat them, because he has experienced those. He's tired of those. You're tired of that negative and positive. You're tired of it because you're God "thinking" and God is tired of it. He is ready for a new experience. The human species has got beautiful designs. He is ready to go to the next stage for the human species but we've got to get them to resolve this little thing. That's what you're doing. You are allowing this. That is the only thing that resolves it, 'tis the knowingness, the seeing of the reality behind what you perceive as the forces struggling . . . when, in reality, there is only One and you are it.

Man wakes up . . . the machine wakes up. He doesn't lose his machine. Okay? The human species . . . the whole body is a machine that has been designed by you as a tool. You will not lose this little machine. Now, you will enlarge the capacity of this machine to hold information for the new adventure . . . new recordings. But, there is one difference now, a very important difference. This computer will know that it is a machine functioning as God and that's going to make a big difference. This new capacity that is being plugged into this old computer is going to allow you to know that. Your senses will be increased in vibration (we're going to get into that) . . . they are going to see more, hear more, etc. They have a whole new range coming for them and they're going to record the experience of that. But, all of it is going to be because the One Mind is controlling the machine instead of the machine, supposedly, controlling the One Mind. Believe me . . . that is a difference.

You are feeling this emergence . . . every time you feel the strong push of this emerging with glimpses, feelings, and vibrations. You're feeling this also in what appears to you (as has been taught in many realities on this earth) a deep, dark night, a deep valley, an abyss, a hole, a chasm that you have to jump across because you have to let go of your identity as a machine and allow this. Now, it should be dawning on you by now, as you've contemplated your notes and the taped records . . . that this that you have always known yourself as, is going to cease to have control and is going to relinquish control . . . yield . . . sacrifice . . . whatever you want to call it to this one consciousness. Did you perceive that from what we're talking about because we're getting close to the flag now . . . the feeling . . . the feeling.

The machine cannot perceive anything but your 5 senses . . . your third dimensional world. It is perceiving this information within third dimension. This is third dimension. It is perceiving it. It does not see the other but, you all know deep within . . . there is the relinquishing of the identity here and the assuming of this identity and the machine cannot comprehend this paradox. It believes that it loses and that something other than itself . . . takes over.

It perceives everything in separation. The machine perceives the automatic recording that it is doing in the brain as one thing and the consciousness of the All-knowingness of God as a separate thing. As long as the Machine perceives these as separate, it cannot understand anything but, the letting go of this and letting something other than it . . . take-over, because, that is separation. Is it not?

The information we've been bringing you, and we will continue later with more . . . was a very advanced understanding in order to help you with the danger flags and the machine. You see, the advanced understanding that we brought you was . . . that there is only one mind, one thinker . . . one consciousness . . . one self that has ever caused anything . . . that has ever created anything or thought anything and that's who you truly are. Now, the machine will always see itself separate from that. It will always perceive two. Do you understand? In reality, there is only one and there never has been but one.

I would like to take a break at this time. We will return later with some more important information. But now, Wonton will conclude our subject of "As Below . . . So Above".

Now is the time for all good men and women to come to the aid of their world. Wonton speaks!

I like that! But, I would also like to hear your speak of the things that are on your hearts since our last meeting. You are considering some truths which have been revealed in the past, but you have not enjoyed the "knowing" of them. Open your consciousness to receive greater truths that have been known for many ages of your earth time.

I am trying to convey an awareness that is in your consciousness that you do not believe that you can experience, but you can! All knowingness. All knowingness. That is a very peaceful place. All knowingness doesn't involve separation of anything. Difficult, isn't it? This is not a teaching that can be recorded. This involves allowing, that must be experienced by you. Now, you have progressed as far as the written word will take you. The spoken word is limiting also. So do not hold in your mind a desire or an image of words that will carry you to this place.

Question: You're saying that there's nothing involving our minds that can get us to where we're going? There's no words or teaching that can open it up?

Wonton: Right!

Question: So . . . . it's just simply "allowing"?

Wonton: Being the Source of all things! Which you are! Why did you have no questions? Perhaps you already were perceiving that words would not aid you in your desire? Now, don't be disappointed. We can still communicate. We can still share, but do not expect me to give you something that only you can give yourself. The love that you have is a powerful creative force that will take you anywhere you want to go. You have felt that. You have known that. Consciously release and direct that energy. Now, I imagine that some of your minds have kicked in about now. Am I right? So, who would like to play the mind game?

<u>Navigator:</u> Well, mine kicked in when you said to release and direct that energy. How do you do that?

<u>Wonton:</u> Who asks that question . . . . your mind? What did your consciousness tell you . . . what did your consciousness observe? Was your consciousness without feeling or understanding about itself as the Source?

<u>Navigator:</u> No . . . it was observing my mind, but yes, I felt something.

<u>Wonton:</u> But perhaps your mind wanted to be the center of attention as you focused on it in your observation. But your consciousness knows itself as the Source and it does not need instructions on how to be itself, does it? And it just "is" . . . so, do not contemplate "isness" with the mind. "Isness" is a word and when I say a word I separate it from what it really is. Be it! Allow it! That's the best we can do with words. Your consciousness is that mind. Your consciousness is the word. Your consciousness is all things. You have wanted to locate God in you, in your body. Remove that limitation and experience and feel the unlimitedness of consciousness. You mind is a focus of consciousness in this world. A limitation which you impose. If you place that limitation and focus on your consciousness, you can also remove it. How do you do that?

<u>Navigator:</u> By focusing into your consciousness . . . into its own dimension.

<u>Wonton:</u> How did the "Is" create the universe . . . is it possible that He did it because He wanted to?

<u>Navigator:</u> Desire?

<u>Wonton:</u> Ahhhh....that's not an easy word for you, is it? Why? Perhaps because you've always experienced that "wanting and desire" are wrong. It is "selfish" to want something for yourself, isn't it? Maybe it is good and better to help others obtain their desires?

Navigator: Right . . . . that's closer to the ideas of "selfish and unselfish" that some of us have.

Wonton: These polarities . . . "selfish and unselfish" . . . is it alright for God to be "selfish"? Isn't God selfish? Does He do what He wants to do? You would never deny that, would you? Ah yes! See, if God is the only Being in the universe, how can He be anything but selfish? And, is it possible that He doesn't know the meaning of "selfish and unselfish"?

Navigator: Yes, because that's polarities.

Wonton: Yes, but you do! So you are not knowing yourself as God, but as the "image". Now, your creation does not cease when you are All That Is. It begins from the Source. All desires will become your reality. But you may doubt your understanding of this because that word "desire" and "want" implies more than just selfishness . . . because, are there good desires and bad desires? Are there desires that can hurt you and desires that can help you? Oh my! Confusion! You want to know. Always your mind wants to know. How do I decide which will hurt me and which will help me, which is bad for me?

Now, imagine the Source of all creation contemplating that. See, you must be the Source. You must know the Source as you. This was the mind that was in Christ Jesus - unlimited, omnipotent, omnipresent, All Knowing. Do you think that when Christ wanted to heal someone, He stopped and contemplated with His mind, "Will that be good for him or will that be bad for him? Possibly, it would be better if he were ill. It's certainly a humbling experience and that's good for anybody". Or, do you suppose that desire was the motivating energy . . . called love. Ah, yes! Is there anyone in this room who has never felt that love as a motivating desire? Oh, I hear no one speaking. Does that mean I have a unanimous agreement here? Everyone has felt that! Ah yes. We must always ask the question – "is that good enough"? Oh my! How poor the human is. He experiences the Almighty force of love and must ask if that is good enough!! That is not only good enough, but that is All There Is! Your mind says, "o.k., I buy that but we must work together to control that force. It could get out of hand. You probably aren't even humble enough to handle it"! Your mind says "I will keep you humble". Have you ever considered how ingenious this creation of the mind is? You have a history of playing with it.

These "unlimited" thoughts that you are magnetizing to yourself now, are a consciousness that will change your bodies. Allow them. That's as close to "doing something" that I can come for you. "Desire" will magnetize to you the thoughts that will enter your aura, that will be received by your brain that will electrically charge your cells to transfigure. Now, do you understand the time spent with words on the mind? Because the mind was put there to create separation to assure solidity, mass, 3-dimensional form for your experience of it . . . but, you are saying to the universe, "Time's up! Enough of this!" Let it go. Now, do not create another polarity regarding the mind. There are many. Careful! You will do it. Just know . . . be aware that you are the creator of it, you give it life and it must obey you.

Please recognize that you have minds that do not want to hear this. You have a memory, a knowingness that has dwelt outside of space and time and the frustration that you experience now in space and time - bless it. Remember, in God there is nothing but love. So, love yourselves and bless yourselves in your impatience and your confusion, because as God, you always create perfectly and that is a creation that is bringing you to this point of "Rendezvous with the Now Moment".

You have to get disgruntled with all that this world has in order to seek your true identity. Is not space and time and "waiting" . . .patience and impatience, part of it? That is frustrating. Good! Bless it! Because now you are all ears . . . you are focusing to hear what you want to hear. But, without the impatience you would be preoccupied and not ready.

So, when you desire something and it manifests, which it is, and you feel impatience, you are God! So do not say "Something is wrong. There's a problem here." In love, you say "Look what a great God I am; I have manifested impatience so that I might now . . . move on." You are not loving yourself when you remain impatient.

I told you in our last conversation, that you are God; that you are Love and I asked that you please not neglect in your fervent desire for your mission, the love of yourself, because that is the creative force of the universe . . . of All That Is.

Your desire to know, to consume the unknown, magnetizes to you the thoughts. Embracing the thought, allowing the thought, without judgement - without judgement - allows it a home. That is the reason we have spent so much time dealing with polarities and judgement. If you hear an abstract thought and you say "That's a bad thought - that's a good thought", you are judging. Allow. Desire . . . desire to know more. Do not want steps or ways. It is much simpler than you realize. You have simple desire. Mind makes it very complicated, because it likes to be in control. So, without struggle . . . don't struggle, just know that you are God and that you can do whatever you want to.

Navigator: Well, we have talked about manifesting our desires in terms of the "now" and not changing our focus to space and time - to do things the "old way". So, about these "new ways" of approaching this, maybe you can give us some thoughts about that?

Wonton: You will manifest your reality, you will create it. The question is . . . how? How would you like to? Understand that whatever you hold in your consciousness as the ideal of the next moment is what will appear. I suspect that up to this point in time, you have been holding confusion in your consciousness . . . . "Maybe this, maybe that" and manifesting confusion.

Navigator: Yes.

Wonton: Clear intentions...allow yourself clarity concerning what will make you happy. What will please you will create the next moment. You have no one else to please, but yourselves. For all things exist in God. Any possibility that you conceive has already been created and exists there potentially. You will make it material. It is not good enough to say and to learn that you manifest what you want. There must be clear intentions concerning what you want. If you say "I want this, but I'm not real sure that it's o.k. if I want this", then you will get more confusion. Clear intentions! What are your intentions? Clearly! Proclaim them. Then, examine your feeling. Would this make you happy right now . . . in the moment, without thought of the past or future . . . does this adventure excite you?

See, this is hard, because you are busy going over what you do not like in the past and what you think you like in the future. We spend no time determining what our heart is in the moment. All life is this way on this planet. Many dreams do not manifest because there is not clear intentions in the moment. It does not matter what you thought yesterday . . . or what you think you may feel or need tomorrow . . . . can you leave them alone? Can you trust yourself to the moment? And that . . . if you are loving yourself in the moment and you are allowing yourself to have what you want in the moment, then your consciousness of love for yourself is creating your next moment. That consciousness will manifest each moment your needs and desires without effort.

See, this is something that you have chosen before time. This is your plan. Therefore, the possibility exists – merely waits for you to recall your plan and exercise it. You are the architect. This is the way you wanted it. This is why it is very important for each person to acknowledge their own desires, because in those desires are many clues of "The Blueprint". We must always work through the blueprint, because in that blueprint, there were agreements made . . . before time. Those agreements allow us to do what we have to do at given points, without your conscious willing of it. As you go along, you will realize more and more, the blueprint. This is the waking up. This is the remembering. This is what you struggle with now. That is because, you are still not allowing the inner knowingness. You still have polarity . . . you still say "maybe this, maybe that" . . . . because the blueprint is still blurry.

This is important because you must begin to say what you want. Understand, when you say what you want, then you have seen a part of your blueprint, clearly. I don't know if you grasp what I say. There is a tremendous amount of freedom for you in this. The problem that you deal with is because of the density through which you have come to this point. You have not understood that you must have whatever you want, in order to fulfill your blueprint. You must! But you have within you, that density that says, "But can it really be the way I want it?" There is much doubt there, which creates blockages in proceeding along the plan. Much time has been wasted in all of humanity because of the limitations placed in and on you in young years and you have learned to place them on yourself, because you cannot believe the true freedom that you have within yourself.

Okay, so now you must give yourself time to remember and reverse the direction you were going and understand that there is that within you that you placed there, based on your desires. Now, if you do not allow those desires now, you cannot follow the blueprint you set. But there is always free will. Always free will. Always opportunities to say "but I don't want to do that anymore, I changed my mind." Always . . . and many changes, yes, many changes in the blueprint . . . but always in your heart to follow the blueprint. You say, "God's will". Yes it is! It is God's will. But you are the God. So, when do you begin to follow your will?

<u>Navigator:</u> When you start doing what you're feeling each moment!

<u>Wonton:</u> Yes. Yes. But, because you do not have a lot of experience in doing what you want to do, you find it very difficult to be sure what that is. Now, you find it easy to know what you "should" do. Yes, that has been the blueprint of the world. You have learned that . . . step one, remember? You have learned what you "should" do. That's no problem . . . you have that down pat. But, what about the blueprint before time, that you desired here. Now, you must learn to walk in that. You will crawl and you will fall, but you will walk. Understand?

<u>Navigator:</u> Yes, so in that blueprint, it is important then for that . . . freedom to choose, freedom to express what is in us. Not following some kind of religious law or something; or to "plan" like I've always tried to do.

<u>Wonton:</u> Ummm, many patterns. But that was part of the blueprint. You wished to do that! Why else come? That was part of the "Plan". Now, waking up is part of the "Plan"!

So begin to feel more and more your desires. Learn what thoughts feel good to you, what brings joy to your heart, mind, cells . . . . is good, right . . . your plan. If something . . . a thought that you have does not bring joy, throw it out! Get another one! There are many more. But sift through the thoughts that bring you joy. Now, ask me what you want to know, that the knowing of it would bring you joy!

Navigator: Well, I have a question that would bring me joy in knowing the answer . . . .are "we", you and me and us . . . going to work together now, from now on, in this plan? That's my desire . . . . is that your desire also?

Wonton: Yes.

Navigator: Good, good . . . thank you!

Wonton: Yes, it is very difficult for me to relate to you in "time" . . . because your question implies a beginning or an ending. I don't see that. Where I exist, there is no time. I must phrase my answers to make sense to you, but understand, all things are happening simultaneously. And "time" is irrelevant to my speech. However, because of having participated in your little dramas, I understand the importance of it to you, and I will try to respond. But your question implies a beginning and an ending to our relationship . . . understand . . . that does not exist! We go all the way back to no beginning and we go all the way forward to no ending.

Navigator: Hmmmm. What information would you like to share with us?

Wonton: Much! Much have I desired to speak to you about. Much concerning the "Now Moment" . . . . much concerning the future, if you understand by the "future" I mean "Earth time"! You are very important. You have many big plans that are crucial to you and all involved.

Navigator: Well, we'd like to know what those are.

Wonton: You are already knowing them within yourself. You have made no wrong turns in your thinking. And you have developed along a line that is the blueprint. I cannot skip over your blueprint. Nor can I reveal too much of your blueprint to you, because you must do that yourself. But, I will say, that in the now moment, you are seen as having made a big jump in understanding. Most . . . . most unusual. You have leaped in your plan and are seen at this time to be ready to execute it. I know there is a heavy question you would like to ask. You know, you hold back, in your desire to be correct.

Navigator: Yeah, well that's the problem . . . . there's nothing "out there" that says "it's correct".

Wonton: But, you find that it's hard to be correct with yourself? Because, what is happening? There are many possibilities floating around within, inside of you. Is that right? Suppose that all of those possibilities are true? Suppose all of them will manifest? Have you considered that? Aren't you just dealing with a time schedule as to what comes first and how long, and when?

Navigator: Yes

Wonton: Yes! So the question is "How do we have a proper time schedule for the many activities that we are creating?" Question is, "Is it my responsibility to determine that or does it involve other entities that I am not aware of, maybe?"

Navigator: Yes. Yes. Or that I'm not aware of their plans, their intentions, and their parts.

Wonton: You are very loving. You are very desirous of being in that flow that allows you to aid everyone around you. That's beautiful. That's wonderful. Do you not think that, with that love in your heart, you will not be given the answers?

Navigator: Ahhhh, that's beautiful. Yeah, you would be.

Wonton: Yes. There is much love there for all of you. And your expressions of love and that desire to be aligned with ultimate, divine thought will provide the answers. Mainly, our purpose is to tell you to trust yourself, because of the love that you have. That love, that you have, is trustworthy. Feel that, because that would be a good way to know yourself. Now, question still arises in you, "Do I wait for contact from other beings to tell me what I will be doing and how, and when, or do I proceed with my own desires and time schedule?" Is that correct?

Navigator: Yes! Thank you, that's the question.

<u>Wonton:</u> There is a need here for me to proceed to answer this in a way that will give you satisfactory information and at the same time, not be limiting. You have more freedom than most! And that is difficult to convey to you. Your channel has many doubts and many fears, because of the freedom that she has. She would feel much better if someone would hem her in and give her steps and ritual so that she could feel secure of doing the "right" thing. However, we have just discussed that, and that it is most important that you come to trust your love. If you feel that love, and you cannot bring yourself to trust it, how are you going to trust me?

But, it would seem that from your many experiences of discussions with others and from books, when they relate their knowingness that you feel a need to be directed by other persons or entities, because they were.

<u>Navigator</u>: Right. That's our dilemma.

<u>Wonton</u>: So, you are drawing boxes. You are saying "Oh, it happened to them that way, so I must be careful, because it must happen to me this way. And besides, it's a good idea because then . . . . I'll be right."

<u>Navigator</u>: Ha. Yeah! Or else, if I'm wrong, I can give somebody else the responsibility. But it's the polarity of right or wrong.

<u>Wonton</u>: Yes, but it should be becoming clear to you and this group by now . . . . the uniqueness that you have. That uniqueness has a purpose and a plan within itself . . . that you would learn to know yourself as God and trust yourself, as God.

Prior to this time, there have been many dispensations. There have been many ways of teaching, learning, expressing, for the purpose of evolving humanity. In this dispensation, you have many like yourself, who have incarnated from more advanced states than exist here on this plane. Therefore, do not come to us now because of lack of memory and ask to be treated with the same systems, methods, and dispensations with which we have dealt with those upon this plane.

They have been given for specific people, at specific times. Understand, you are being given specific understanding at a specific time. Your time is on the edge, the rim of a tremendous change on this earth. A change, in which there is going to be much confusion. Now, we need entities, awakening, who are secure in their own knowingness, trusting their own love and their own ability to create. Possibly, you will wake up to the fact that you are one of that advanced guard, that must be here at this time, to see the earth through that period.

We cannot allow everyone to find themselves without some incarnated beings, who have this type of understanding and knowingness . . . to help them. You have trained yourself. You have prepared yourself for this. You laugh and joke very much about your independence and your being a difficult lot. But, there is a reason for that. There is a reason that you have found no paths to follow . . . but your own. There is a reason. There is a reason why you are now, not only not following another path, but no one is following yours. You have a blueprint that requires that you be free of any attachments to a path or responsibilities on a path. You envision total freedom, whether you know it or not . . . to let the love that is within you, the knowingness that is within you, "shine" during the time that is coming . . . to light the path of many, who will need it.

Understand, there are many, many people now, asking for guidance: asking for someone to come help them; someone to show them the way; someone to help them make their decisions. Each request is dealt with specifically and individually, based on the blueprint for incarnation and their dispensation. You are too.

So, do not borrow from anyone else's experience for yours. You are not alone in what you will be doing, but it requires that you think you are. It requires that you not be aware of others. Don't you realize that within all of you is such a yearning to be home, to be with others of like kind . . . to be unified, which is all you have ever known prior to incarnating? Could you stand the pressure that would evolve there, if you had that contact . . . the pressure that would be there, not to complete what you chose to do?

You must go on. You must go on your path . . . alone, and complete what you decided to complete without putting more pressure on yourselves by having the fellowship and the union that you desire at this time.

This is a hard time. But you are prepared for it. You have gotten ready for this . . . and, the end is not far away. There is much glory coming. But, as you know, there is so much glory in being able to complete a job, that is so, so vital to the love that needs to be demonstrated to so many at this time.

You have experienced sharing that . . . and that glory way outweighs the aloneness that I know you all feel many times . . . and that you would desire that I give you some information that says "You're not alone. We're here. We're directing things. We're taking care of everything." But listen, I cannot tell you that all the time . . . about everything. Yes, our love is always going with you. Yes, we are preparing and going ahead and giving you things that are needed. Yes! But, your path is to walk . . . complete your mission with complete knowingness of that love that is there and that provision which is there.

The sight of it . . . the reality of it, must be within you. This is a difficult thing that I try to express . . . because you have so much more freedom than you know. And when I begin to express things to you, you can take them and limit yourself with them.

Do not do that. You have all the power of the God. You have all the love of the God. You have all the knowingness, within yourself. But the greatest need that humanity has is to love themselves. Oh, that we could just send an army of people among the people of these lands . . . and let them see others loving themselves. That's the army that we need. That will win the war that we are fighting.

Loving yourself means that you allow yourself what you want and you do not need anyone . . . seen or unseen . . . to say to you "Yes, it's ok, you can have it" . . . . or . . . . "No, I don't think you should have that." No, no! You give it to yourself because you love yourself. The love that you have, that you must allow to flow from you is always and forever in the center of God's will . . . . because that is the creative, motivating force flowing from the center . . . the heart of All That Is . . . .

CHAPTER 6

TO BOLDLY GO WHERE NO GODS HAVE GONE BEFORE

Welcome. I am Altar. You know me well. You and I have spent many "hours" together planning our adventure. Your sojourn on this plane has been for the purpose of resolving a question that puzzled many of us. Why . . . in third density . . . . is it so difficult to know and act from spirit?

Spirit is oneness. Third density is for the purpose of exploring the forgetting of that oneness. However, to leave that density, one must remember oneness.

You have chosen to experience the feelings that overtake spirit when exposed to the vibrations of aloneness. All experience in third density is this vibration. You have labeled your events in this dimension many things, but all are a vibration which manifests as "aloneness". All fears experienced on planet Earth equate to this loneliness.

It is merely the polarity of oneness. All tension and anxiety are but the feelings that arise from your desire to find balance or rest between the polarity of total aloneness (separation) and total oneness (union).

This is the evolution for which mankind was created. To allow God (you) the form needed to explore forever creation, it was necessary to integrate within the human form the vibrations of the lowest and highest. Evolution of humanity has now reached the cosmic timing where and when this will occur. Hence . . . the transmutation.

A portion of the soul (God), which you are . . . chose to allow the entire soul (over soul) to experience the polarity of aloneness through an incarnation into flesh (absolute separation). That manifestation into the human drama is "You". All of your struggles in the seeming "past" have been the conscious physical awareness of separation (individuality) and the unconscious, spiritual awareness of oneness (union or "All That Is"). Contemplate this, because it is the explanation for all experiences to date.

In this "Now Moment", all is being integrated. Nothing will be lost or removed and nothing will be discovered or added. Only the remembrance of the "All" (which you are) will occur. This remembrance must occur within the human body (total separation) through spirit (total oneness) in order to achieve the balance or integration necessary for further creation imagined by the "Gods" (which you are).

The marriage of spirit and matter will express and manifest the original idea or thought of the Source . . . to see or mirror back to Source . . . "All That Is", which is unlimited potentialities.

So, you have within you the blueprint which is the original idea or thought. The God, that you are, will then continue through this expression of the God/Man to explore further possibilities as separate from Source and yet one with Source. Your portion of existence on this plane has been to experience, record, and remember . . . thus becoming "All" . . . spirit and matter. The entities which are "channeled" here are all portions of the "God" (which you are) that is exploring this avenue of expression for further creation. Emil is the "tone" given to your next spokesperson. Another name would be . . . "Pana-Person".

Greetings from the consciousness that is the Radiant Sun! This is Emil speaking. I have come to continue the discussion concerning further expansion of consciousness that we began. We have been, as you know, projecting energies that are familiar to you . . . that are creating within you and allowing the knowingness and the expansion which you have in your consciousness of who and what you are. This energy emanating from the powers that we represent . . . the energies that are matched with the energies coming from within you and the energies that the whole planet is experiencing at this time . . . are all coming together to reveal to you all the things that you have desired to know.

Your only purpose in desiring to know these things is because in reality, you are these things. So that you can rest in that knowing, and begin to function in the identity that you had before incarnating. Many of you will begin to recall some of the time that you have spent observing this planet and participating in the evolution of it because that is part of the soul memory of which you are a part. As there is more awareness of your own "Christ" that dwells within you, there will be a remembrance of your having signed onto this perilous mission and understanding of what plans are to be projected into the future.

The plan is based on the original thought in creation. You see, when a certain amount of space was consumed and explored and experienced, there was built into the original thought which was on-going, "foreverness" . . . that there would be eternal creating and eternal light going out into all areas. The mechanics of that have been created as it unfolded and what we are referring to as your "Blueprint", is now the mechanics of going forward into unknown territory, as yet unexplored, but that was in the original thought. However, as being "God" yourself . . . all of you, unfolding your own plan . . . you are creating it, in a sense, as you go along.

We have explained and brought into mind the fact that you are, in reality, one with the source of all that is but, this has not registered within you as absolute truth. This is still relative within your experience. You still experience the knowingness upon hearing it but you see what you consider lapses in your experience in your day to day affairs.

As God, you have within you, at this moment, all knowledge and all experience that has transpired from the beginning thought. You have that available to you with which to create more and you would be hard put to allow anyone to take that ability away from you, in reality. So, we will not give you a blueprint. When we talk of the blueprint which you have designed for yourself, it has to do with step 1 . . .your awakening and when and how and what you intended to accomplish in step 1 and what is going to happen in step 2.

During the transition or the transmutation . . . there is much experience in that original thought from the beginning as to what is going to happen. However, the earth has free will. The inhabitants upon the earth have free will and the Gods that are helping have free will only limited by the free will of the inhabitants of this planet. Therefore, it is not easy to determine exactly what the future holds . . . nor do you want that. In reality, you do not want that. It could get very boring if there were 11,000,000 universes and as you ran around to all of them and the same thing happened in all of them and you had done this for 11,000,000 years. It might get boring and yes, God is never bored. Can I tell you that? He is never bored

<u>The Navigator</u>: Always unlimited.

Oh yes! Look around you as Gods and see how many leaf shapes that you created . . . look how many shapes of insects and animals . . . blades of grass, wheat, grain, fruit. There is no doubt, probably at this time, that you think that all the creative energy has been used up on this planet and you believe that you're just going to another planet and produce what you have produced here. Not so! Not so!

That light force . . . that spirit force . . . permeates all that you can see within your vision now. It is, in reality, the substance . . . molded and shaped by spirit . . . that you are looking at that permeates in and around and through it to form the shape of whatever you perceive at this moment with your eyes. It is capable of knowing and joining it's consciousness with any consciousness within spirit. You are capable of knowing and perceiving the reality of whatever you join with.

All life upon this planet has desired to express to humanity the changes that are coming and the needs that we have here. Many, who are involved in this, are caretakers who chose this life and incarnation in order to express that to themselves and their brothers.

Much of earth mother is to be preserved in the cleansing process that she must go through! Earth has many hurts and many sorrows because of the lack of oneness with humanity that exists here.

This spirit that resides within all is, in truth, who you are and you can begin to experience the freedom that you have in that spirit to move and to be and to go. You can begin to experience observing all that is around you with that knowingness. Merely conceive the thought and the source, that dwells with you, will manifest within your expression the experience of perceiving yourself as spirit within creation.

This is a necessary thing for you to learn as the earth changes. It is something that is happening now as these dimensional influxes are beginning on a more rapid rate. Therefore, nothing will appear the same. If you were rigid and locked into the forms that you consider your body . . . and only form of existence . . . as this influx accelerates, you would become very depressed and upset . . . if you could not move your spirit and have more fluidity of spirit . . . more vision and understanding and seeing of self.

There is no limit to you. You are limitlessness. You have the ability to go and be anywhere you choose. You have the ability to be that because you are, indeed, All That Is.

This has been a fearsome thing to speak to you about because, somehow, you have thought that in perceiving yourself as All That Is, you would cease to exist as a focus. Not true! You will merely be a focus with awareness of All That Is. This must be experienced. This goes beyond words. This is the experience that we are pressing toward you.

I've loved having this opportunity to speak. I've loved overseeing all conversations. I have been here for all of this. I am very familiar with Wonton, which is a group of entities that float in and out . . . unbeknown to you exactly who they are and I have been here for Monka, who is a delightful person. He delights us continually as he does you.

It was all from here (the heart), and we all serve the One, which we are. All love from that One. And speaking of Monka . . . prepare yourselves for his next introduction.

So . . . they sent me (Monka)! It's that important. Do you understand that? Anybody know why I'm here?

<u>Audience</u>: Let's see . . . we're right on schedule?

<u>Monka</u>: Always . . . always right on schedule! You're having an "interesting" time. I've been looking in on you. Been watching . . . monitoring, you know . . . all the time. You've got to get used to this one consciousness, because you're "there" and we're "there" and we're all in one place all the time, and so I'm going to talk to you from a different perspective. I'm really tired of this lecturing. I'm really tired of this teaching. By God, it isn't necessary. Are you listening to me? It is not necessary.

You already have the knowingness in you! My God, how many times have you been told that? Well, do you . . . or don't you? Whelp, let's proceed from that. We established the basis of our communication now . . . that we all "Know". But are you seeing something here about all this "agreeing" that you're trying to do . . . and trying to "know" and everything? And, what's happening?

Aren't you searching? What are you searching for? Listen, if you're searching, you're searching for something, right? What . . . "enlightenment" . . . you're looking for that? How do you look for enlightenment and where are you going to find it? It's "inside you", isn't it? I'm trying to get you to see something. You're really not searching, are you? You know where in the hell it is, don't you? And there's not one of you following this that doesn't want it to be over . . . the searching, the teaching, the "dramas" in this dimension.

Well that's what I meant when I said "we're going to talk from a new position now." there is nobody else coming that's going to try to teach you or convince you anymore of something that you're "pretending" that you don't know. It's over! It's over . . . now! Third dimension experience is over!

That's right. It went right past you and you didn't even know it! And a lot of people have talked about "well, aren't things strange, and this is happening . . . and isn't everything weird?" And did you remember talking about how you were feeling this "new energy" and your consciousness is shifting and you damn sure aren't the same you were the day this started . . . are you? It's done . . . it finished a while ago! And we came and talked to you and tried real hard not to scare the hell out of you, you know? When people are asleep and they're having these wonderful little dreams and you wake them up all of a sudden, you could give them a heart attack, couldn't you?

Okay, understand that a lot of people on this Earth are observing and feeling the same things that you've been talking about . . . the "time warp". They don't think things are the same either. But, what do they think? See, they have no energy to feel, from which to function, except third dimension. Memory . . . history . . . conditioning. So, all they're feeling and experiencing, they're putting it into that context. They see the wars, the crime and drug problems, the banks and all these things piling up . . . as part of history. It's happened before; it's going to happen again . . . no problem. Somebody has always "bailed them out", and somebody will bail them out now. All they have to do is survive . . . keep their heads above water. Everything will be alright.

Now you don't react that way, do you? You were one of the ones who were programmed and came here and got the information, and you knew what was going on. But, you thought you were "weird". Do you know what's weird? It's the people that are sitting in the middle of this shit . . . thinking it's going to be just like it's always been before. That's illusion. See, everyone in this dimension on earth could create anything they wanted to during the third dimensional ray or period on this earth. That stopped. It went right past everybody. Did you know that it had happened before me or anybody else from "outside" came and talked to you? Did you know it was over then? That it stopped when the choices were made.

The choice was . . . "I stay here and I go with what's coming here and I create my reality from the new dimension", or "I stay with the old one and I go somewhere else and I continue it". That was the only choice that was made. Did you know that? The choice was to stay or leave. The choice was already made. Nobody's making any choices now, because once that vibration of fourth dimension came in and through here, there were no more choices.

It had a beginning in your time, in 1986 . . . but it hasn't had an end yet. The Harmonic Convergence (August 1987) was a celebration of the knowingness of that . . . they knew there was a new cycle beginning, and that they were tied to what is happening here. But time passed on that night quietly and nothing was ever the same after that. It's not the same for you. It's not the same for anybody on this Earth. Choice is made, self-made choices. Many, before incarnating agreed that they were coming for this change . . . to be here through the "fourth" and see this Earth through it. This is you. You've read a lot of books and heard a lot but, it wasn't speaking directly to you. I am now. And I'm not telling you this because there's something you have "to do". No. I'm doing it because you've been "in the dark" about a hell of a lot of things and I'm just going to start filling you in.

So you see, we're moving through a vibrational beam and for a while, we're overlapping. And you've got people living and creating a third dimensional reality here, now from memory and history and they're doing it in a fourth dimensional reality setting . . . in which whatever you want to create, manifests.. But can I tell you something? This period of time you're going through is eliminating from this planet, all third dimensional thoughts that are creating third dimensional realities here. Mother Earth is in fourth and is consciously choosing to heal herself in these areas with storms, tidal waves, earthquakes, meteorites, etc.... Is this okay? All entities will be removed from this Earth who are creating "third dimensional realities". There's a point coming. Okay? But there is nobody that isn't going to get exactly what they want. You understand that? Exactly what they want, because they are loved.

At the point where the mixing ends and the beam is complete and there is a new phase, there will be no one left on this earth that is creating anymore from third dimensional history, memory, experience. It will be over. You'll go right on, creating your manifestations. But, every entity on this Earth that is creating from history and memory and experience, will leave. There is a point in time where they will no longer exist on this Earth. So, when you hear about some of the things that are coming . . . earthquakes, floods, lots of things planned . . . okay? Mother Earth is magnetizing them.

You've got to clean up a mess up there in the atmosphere. Did you know that? There are some physical changes coming about on this earth, as it should be. There is a lot of third dimensional thought that is magnetizing all of these dramas that will work for the purpose of changing the population on this Earth. Are you beginning to feel what you decided upon . . . what you're doing here? You're going through this time anyway you choose to . . . whatever you want to create. Everybody else is doing the same damn thing. So I'm telling you the choices were made and we entered it at night. It passed through . . . we're in a period of mixture . . . overlapping here . . . when it goes past . . . no more third dimensional thoughts left on this planet. Hey . . . what's that going to be like? Think about it. Think about it. Only ones left here are ones who know why they're here . . . who know who they are. And have chosen that dimensional experience of unlimitedness. Anyone with fear is going to magnetize dramas but, understand, these dramas that are coming to this planet are not the dramas that they think is past history repeated.

These dramas are ending as an event on this Earth. So, when they draw to them, out of fear, a drama that they think, "Oh that happened before, we'll get over it" . . . they do not realize that they are drawing to themselves a drama that is the ending of an event that began when the first fear of it began. This is the ending of all events of third dimensional fear. Infinite time has been given to work this out. To take that first event of fear and snowball it . . . let it go . . . give it all its possibilities and build and build and build 'till the children coming out of the schools right now, are looking at the ultimate fear in every area of their lives. Know what I mean? There is not one area of their lives that the ultimate fear doesn't now exist in its ultimate culmination. And, they are so nulled into thinking that this is life . . . this is the way it's always been . . . that they do not realize the greatness of the fears and dramas they are facing.

How about pollution? Got any pollution around? Lack of water . . . little problems with the banks . . . little problems with the nations warring . . . the ultimate . . . Armageddon.

What is Armageddon? The battle to end all battles! You are going to have the plague to end all plagues. You are going to have the economic crashes to end all economic crashes. You are going to have drastic weather changes and Earth changes to end all Earth changes and weather changes. You're going to have the war with the ultimate weapon to end all wars. Do you understand that the event that the third dimensional mind is magnetizing to itself right now is the ultimate of the first fear?

It must complete itself. Just as you are creating the ultimate in love and freedom . . . "union", all the things we talk about. That must be acted out too. You see? This is an ending . . . an ending to all the dramas begun. Remember. Remember what we told you about events? Just recently somebody tried to explain to you that we don't see time like you do? So, you've got people walking around in these third dimensional clouds saying, "Well, hell, we've had problems like these before, we'll work them out." Time . . . cycling . . . that's time. No, there were events begun on this Earth . . . decreed events by those in charge. They decreed that the event would be allowed to complete itself but, this time, this completion . . . we've got to have some bodies left. You know? Slim pickin's . . . slim pickin's in the human drama.

Your population has been so conditioned to attempt to avoid all situations that they feel will be stressful or painful and in the process, they have created the ultimate stressful and painful situation. Isn't that what polarity is all about? When they have conceived of the ultimate dream of no antagonism, perfection in everything, with no pain, no problems, just total physical satisfaction...just to have that ultimate pampering of the body and the emotions... that is at the expense of everything and everybody else. What is the ultimate of that in the opposite direction? Total experience of pain and suffering . . . it "works" from third dimension.

Slim pickin's . . . given away their sovereignty . . . embraced fear in every area of their lives and joined and embraced the ending and the ultimate of this drama. Understand . . . if you try to sympathize with this mind, you've got problems because; it's not your mind. It is a mind that is looking forward to this . . . that has embraced this idea . . . that wants this idea . . . that is magnetizing it to itself for the experience of it.

So, you cannot . . . compassion for what you see . . . hey, no problem. But, forget sympathy because sympathy means to put yourself in their place and think with your mind like you think they're thinking. You can forget that because they are doing what they want to do. They want to experience that. They came here for that purpose. Many will make rapid advancement in their own evolution by being here and experiencing this end and ultimate drama. Did you know that? It is an opportunity . . . a time to advance rapidly. Many places and dimensions do not have this opportunity. That's one of the reasons for so much interest here.

Okay. So, what does this mean for you, now . . . when you start seeing these things happening on the news? Now, remember, we're speaking from a level of "knowing".

Remember . . . you were here when this Earth was created . . . the gases, the firmament. You saw the "waters" and the plant life springing up. You were there when the animals were created. You looked at it all and you saw "it was good." You loved it. You played here. It was your child, and you have watched over it ever since. It is your creation. You set the seasons, you set the times . . . you set the beginning and ending of events. You loved the human because you knew that that was to be the instrument . . . the means of your expression totally in all universes. It was the culmination. It was the perfect form and structure. You were here. You passed over. You played. You experimented. You discovered. You created. You built. You loved. You nurtured. You have always known what was happening and when this time came, you said "I'll go. I'll be there for the birth . . . for the birth". You were there when the Earth was birthed. You are going to be here when the child is birthed . . . when God wakes up in the form of the child and begins a new experience. You said "I will be there for that birth". Because, the on-goingness of your creation is to be realized in that child that is being born. You are being born. You are "midwifering" at your own birth. Know what I mean? And if you've never been pregnant, just ask the mothers. Ask these women if they were glad when the time came to birth their baby . . . to get rid of the "load" they had carried? So, how do you feel and think about this event right now? Because, all of your thoughts are becoming your reality . . . immediately. If you say this is who I am, "I am excited, because I am the God that planned this" . . . guess what your manifestation is? Think about it. Okay. Just check on that.

So, you know what this means? We "sure as hell" are going to have to talk about "fourth dimensional" experience, since everybody tells you you're "in it". Don't you think that's good?

Okay! Well, Athena is going to continue that and . . . maybe, just maybe, go "way beyond" . . . . if you're ready.

Audience: Yes! Absolutely . . . bring it on!

Monka: Okay. I'll be back . . . good night!

⸻ ∘∘∘⟊◉⟊∘∘∘ ⸻

So, we are ready? Welcome, I am Athena . . . speaking from my heart to your heart.

I am here to balance Mr. Monka. As you suspect, he would need balancing. Correct? He brought a very timely message, I believe . . . one that was much needed and I believe that he elicited an agreement from you that we would relate from one level only. Good!

The timely message that Mr. Monka delivered is what we considered very important for you to know to bring you to the understanding that you are going to need in the days ahead. We did not intend to prepare you in the normal sense that you would possibly perceive in any books that you might read or have read. So please consider yourself a clean slate and prepare yourself to be informed at a different level of understanding of the days ahead. You will understand that more as we go along.

Now, I want to help you understand a little bit about the realities that are being created and the one that you are creating . . . the "new" that you are creating . . . co-creating with us that is sort of unknown . . . that we are creating as we go along and I want you to feel and understand the energy that is being projected now. Much of it is for the purpose of your awakening fully. Do you understand?

The awakening must be conducted in such a manner and the energy in such a way that you can process two realities at once. This is where a lot of the unknown exists. This is where we are co-creating and this is why you have been programmed or programmed yourselves the way you have. Now, that needs explanation, doesn't it?

Okay, the first thing I want to do is draw for you where you are and what you are doing. *(Figure 17)* There you are! . . . . There you are in time . . . .

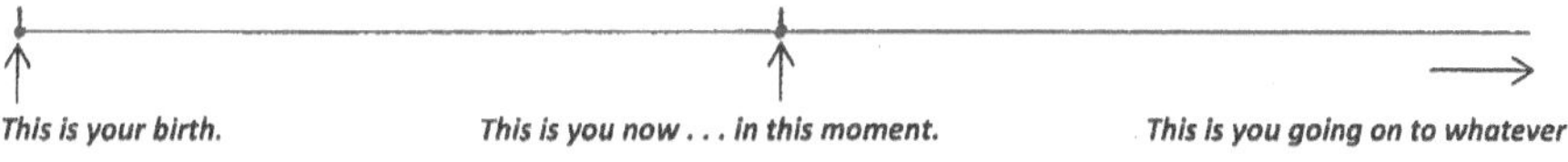

Figure 17

When you recall your birth, you recall your years . . . some more than others. You are contemplating more years out here, but here you are.

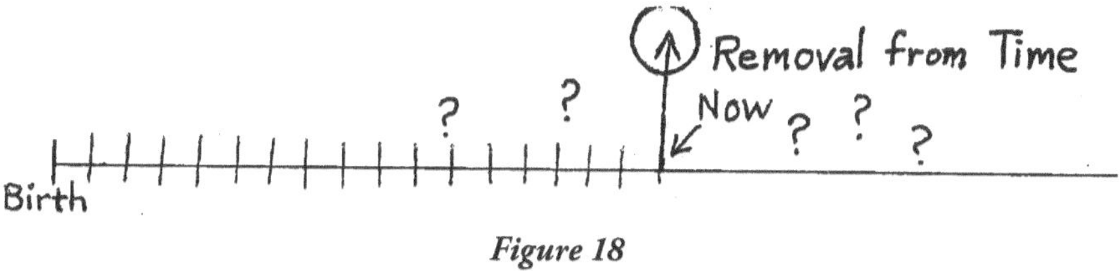

Figure 18

Now, all that we have talked about . . . all that we have contemplated is removing you from time. Taking you out of this! What does that mean? What happens to this? All of this . . . *(Figure 18)* what happens?

I am saying "How do we view this?" Think about it. Please let it enter in . . . what I am saying. You are removing yourself from this. You are removing yourselves. You are leaving time!

This is the only identity that you have here . . . when you remove yourself from time, you are entering a greater identity . . . that does not identify here. Now, what happens here?

This is the new that I spoke of. This is the unknown and the creative part of your adventure. You are removing yourself from time and yet, you are going to experience another adventure, are you not?

How do you perceive that new adventure? Will it not unfold? Does it not involve events that will transpire?

<u>Answer</u>: It's not on a timeline anymore.

No, but you are continuing in this body. Go back. We are taking you out of time because this "greater identity" is who you really are. This past is one of many but, it is not who you are now . . . *(Figure 19)* and yet, you are contemplating being on this earth, being involved with the transition, and an adventure of the "Beyond the Beyond". How does that work here?

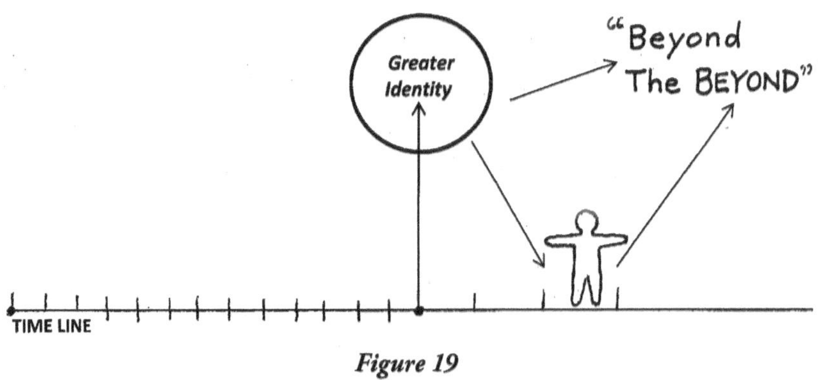

Figure 19

This character . . . "you" . . . will continue down here . . . on into time? See, this is the "New". Your job is to coordinate these two. Tough assignment.

<u>Question</u>: In other words, we are going to experience being in the "now moment" and in linear time . . . at the same time?

Yes.

You will be this (points to "Greater Identity").... coming into this (points to "human body").

You have many adventures scheduled in here. You are going to function with others in time, are you not? But, you will not be. You will be this identity in this body functioning here and you also have the "Beyond the Beyond".

The individual focus that you are, has identified with this (timeline) . . . will identify with this (greater you) . . . will coordinate this ("Now") . . . to go here (Beyond)!

Before we go any further though, you must understand this. What was yesterday . . . Tuesday?

What is today . . . Wednesday?

Be prepared . . . be prepared at a moment's time to be removed from time.

Be prepared at a moment's time to know that it's been fun, but that this is over! Also, we are preparing you to know what follows. This is what so much of the teaching . . . so much of the understanding and the series that is coming to you . . . is to prepare you for the integration and the coordination of the two in a capacity never known before.

Many have been removed from time. You are aware of that? Jesus Christ was removed from time.

Question: They didn't have a continuation of the physical at the same time?

Not the way that you will. You are retaining the physical . . . the ability to be physical. You are retaining the ability to cellularly transform this body and be physical . . . seen by third dimension . . . seen as you are seen now in this room.

Christ's reappearance was ethereal. He took form . . . ethereal form. How do we take ethereal form? It is a difficult thing. Much of it is worked from within you as to what you see and don't see. In other words, when they saw Jesus Christ, they saw what they were supposed to see. Their own energy fields were manipulated to give form and substance to the appearance of Christ in an ethereal body. He did not appear physically as you will.

You have an ethereal body now that exists outside of time but, you came here for what? Remember? You came here to get a physical body.

Why else are we opening your brain? Why else is this crucial that you transmute the physical cells within your body? We are forming a new body. That is what you are working on now.

I know this is difficult and I am going to take it as slowly and easily as I can because, much of what I am trying to convey to you, you cannot visualize. You cannot put into words. It will be an experience and then you will know but, there must be preparation. There must be understanding.

There was not the need for the ascensions (in the past) . . . the removal of time . . . for a physical body but there will be a need for the physical body, for this is the body of Christ that for that thousand years will take on the necessary energies . . . this planet will . . . to go outside of the circle of energy that will go back to the Source. It will be a man . . . joined with many men and women in physical body with brain capacity . . . understanding of themselves as "All That Is" . . . that will leave at the end of that thousand years -- will have the physical body but will maintain an ethereal body for purposes . . . many purposes -- will be able to take any form vibrationally on the scale . . . the octave of vibration . . . but, the new will go all the way down to the physical form -- will assume a physical form . . . not an ethereal form that works with your aura and your energy to project an image for you. But, you will actually be able to manifest in space and time . . . substance and form . . . in this new body that you are transforming.

It is difficult to see ahead and explain this. I know that. If you have a question that is bothering you, I will answer some of them. Others may be only confusing to answer at this time. Possibly, a lot you just need to recall and remember some of the things that I'm saying to you now.

For this thousand year period, your involvement with this planet will be heavy in preparation for this journey. Understand, the Source is dividing itself. You are the Source. You have created a form . . . a body . . . that can maintain all the abilities and powers of the Godhead for this journey.

You see, back in the beginning of time when the body was formed . . . you've read about that? You've studied about that? Little problems . . . little kinks to work out! The Gods . . . "You", were able to go in and pick up the body and use it and leave and the body disintegrated or was eaten by an animal. So, you progressed evolution-wise in your understanding and your creations and you now have a body that procreates itself. You have now created an understanding within the brain . . . you are identified now as God with this body which was called "The Fall" . . . which was necessary. You are identified with this body now.

Please understand. We have been saying to you all along that the physical is not bad . . . material is not bad. This body had a purpose. It has a purpose but it is limited . . . which you are well aware of. It dies. It gets sick. It can't be where it thinks. You can think anywhere you want to be and you can be there consciously in your mind. You can think it, but you can't be there. Others don't have this problem where you are from. All you had to do was think what you wanted . . . size, shape, color, or anything . . . and it was yours. You can't do that anymore. You must use space and time. It is limited.

You are transmuting this physical body into a body that your ethereal form can work through perfectly. All in this thousand years will not have this ability. This is the elect. This is your mission . . . to get this ship ready in a thousand years with human form . . . to prepare for the Source to separate from itself for further adventures.

You see, here you are . . . a human made in the image of God and what has been your search from the date of birth?

<u>Answer</u>: Seeking who you are.

Who am I? Who am I? As below . . . so above! Source has been doing what? Whatever you have been doing . . . because you are the Source.

Source is seeking the same thing that you have sought . . . "Beyond the Beyond". Infinite energy at the Source! Infinite energy seeking the same as you! You are the Source seeking to know itself . . . seeking within as you have done every day of your life here. It is a very simple, elementary understanding on this planet to seek to know God with a capital "G" and be in union. That is the search of every human because every human is God.

Now, what is the heart of the Source if it is not this heart? All will not make this journey. The Source will take back much of its energy, but equal must go out. So, you must be a unique adventure and this is what causes much of our difficulty in being able to explain this to you with words. See, what you have felt . . . you have felt to be joined . . . to be One . . . to find and know yourself. Why were you not satisfied to know yourself as you are right now? Why was this not sufficient? Why do you say, "I want to know who I am?" Have you suspected that you are more than that? Where does that feeling, which is one of your strongest feelings . . . come from? It comes from knowing yourself as the Source.

Now, do you really believe that you separated from this Source and that you had this longing to get back with the Source? No!! You are the Source and you've had the longing for this new adventure. It has been on a much deeper level and hence, your experience on this earth has been on a much deeper level than your peers. All will not go. Not because they didn't do something right or good, but because all choose what they will do. There is much evidence around you of consciousness that has chosen to sustain you . . . to sustain this planet. The cells in your body are conscious. They are conscious and they have chosen to sustain you. There are winds . . . there are clouds . . . consciousness. Sustaining this earth and sustaining you . . . raining on your crops. They are very content in that consciousness. They are a creation.

So, just as we have told you that you are a very important part of ourselves that has come here to gain the physical body and transmute it, they stay . . . they will stay to maintain the Source here. But, you will go on an adventure and that feeling of love . . . that desire for merger or union will sustain you . . . will motivate you.

You have been taught in much of your religion and Christianity that just to come out of time to be reunited with your God is the end of it. That's true for much of humankind, but you are not. You are this and you've known this . . . much further along in evolution than humankind. You have come here for the new creation. The "one new man" . . . the one consciousness, the one mind that will go on.

You talk of fourth dimension being here now . . . not for long. You've got many more dimensions to cover quickly. You are going to fifth, sixth, seventh. You are moving rapidly. This sphere . . . this planet will move rapidly. It must for this voyage. No one knows what is out here. God only knows what you know? Is that what Ramtha said? Did that seem strange when he spoke those words? Believe them! Only the adventures of the Gods are what God knows because the Gods are God! That is all He knows. God is you!

Many in the heavens that you are talking to . . . that you are aware of . . . that you are reading about . . . have chosen many possibilities . . . have experienced many of them in this creation, but none of them know what is "Beyond" . . . beyond this energy projected by this Source. None of them know. You see, when your ships leave your earth, they must get outside of a certain radius . . . gravitational field . . . before they can go on? You are going to leave a gravitational field of the Source's . . . we'll use those words . . . to be projected out beyond where no one knows. You think God knows? You think we know? You think somebody has the map . . . plans so you will know out here?

Remember the excitement when the first planet was birthed . . . when there were no planets? You were there! There were no humans . . . there were no animals . . . there were no birds.

That was unknown! Wonderful adventure! Wonderful adventure! It's going on and on and on. But, you see, you contemplated the thought as God . . . from the Source . . . "Is there another Source?" Is this Source a cell in a larger cell, the same as the cells in your body . . . as the planet is in the galaxy?

You think you had fun here? Prepare for greater fun here! This was the purpose in the creation of mankind. All of you with your expanded consciousness . . . your unlimited powers . . . will know all things together in time . . . never losing your own knowingness of yourself as an individual . . . absolutely necessary for this journey! Do you understand?

I do not like to take you too far. I merely want to introduce you to the thought of the magnitude. All of this you are aware of. All of this was known in the agreement. All of this . . . there are code words that have triggered this because you knew this. All of you, or none of you, I should say . . . can explain yourself without this. You have no explanation of yourself without this. You have explored and contemplated many explanations on this planet . . . much conjecture . . . many possibilities. None of them explain you except this!

This is your destiny! And, I cannot give you words to describe the experience of knowing yourself the way you truly are in this body. There are no words because you are going to know yourself as one and at the same time as many who are one. Your language does not permit this. Only the experience will permit it.

Stop and consider something. What you are being overwhelmed by is your perception of what I am telling you from your limited experience here. Nothing else! Remember . . . feel . . . you were there! You were there when the plans were conceived . . . when the thought of the event was initiated. You were an important part of that. It was in your heart. You desired it.. It was an experience that you as a God, desired . . . when you set into motion what was necessary to bring about this desire.

When my words are coming to you and there is "Awesomeness", as you say . . . it is because you are remembering yourself as the identity that you've had here in a very limited experience of time and space. In your knowingness, you are comfortable with this. You desired it. You designed it. Feel from that center. Do not feel from your identity in the human form that you have taken on this planet. Feel it! You sat in on the conferences. You were there for the excitement of it . . . the knowing that this was the next adventure . . . the knowing of the completion. You see?

We are coming to the ending of a cycle on this planet. There is a cycle ending for all energy from this source that you are . . . the same as on this one planet. As above . . . so below! It is ending. You have created further adventure now. You are not just going to visit planets. You are not just ascending other levels of understanding so you will be smarter . . . more evolved. Our teachings for you . . . our conversations with you have been to tell you that you are "All That Is". We have not taught you from any need that you have to evolve, have we? That has been!

This is why we ask that you clear your minds of other reading . . . other understanding and start with a clean slate for this voyage. As far as any understanding that you have gotten in your identity, in reality, you are going back, picking up where you left off in your understanding, in your mission of preparation for this new adventure.

We desire to communicate with you on the level of understanding that you had before incarnating. This will be possible! This will be possible at full capacity, but in the meantime, if you reject or deny or doubt then you will create that in your experience here. If the words that I say to you vibrate with that knowingness that you brought here, embrace it! Embrace it! It is your truth and your embracing of it . . . your thoughts of it will create it!

You are in fourth dimension now. Any thoughts that you embrace will manifest instantly! You have it within you now! You have the knowingness . . . the clear knowingness within you to embrace the thoughts that I am bringing you. We cannot do that! You must do it!

For that smooth transition, you must embrace the thoughts that will complete it for you. There must be desire felt from that knowingness and there must be the directing of a will that says, "Yes!" and then the embracing of only the thoughts that align with that knowingness. Any thought that does not line up with that knowingness, do not embrace! Do not make it yours! Watch it . . . observe it . . . let it go by, but it is not yours. You have embraced the thought of the knowingness within you of who you are! On with it! Do you, in reality, have anything else better on your agenda that you desire? Think about that! Think about it!

Powerful Gods! Powerful Gods! You chose weak, limited impersonations to contrast with the power that you are. It's been quite an experience, has it not? Drop it! Be who you are! Be it!

You are it!

Let me show you something about our timeline drawing . . . that's you. That's your past. How do you create your moments . . . is time passing? *(Figure 19)*

How do you create your moments? You think that the future is coming towards you, passing by you and going into the past? Tomorrow is coming and tomorrow it will be the past. The future is out in front of you; it comes to you in the present and then becomes your past. Is that what you're experiencing and what you've always experienced?

Illusion! All of that is illusion that you, as a magician, created. You created that. You've done a good job. This is not what is happening. All illusion! There is nothing but Now! There is no time. There is no future or past moving . . . doesn't really exist except in your creation. That's a wonderful creation. It allows you to take the whole movie . . . stretch your imagination . . . that is a film . . . *(Figure 20)* . . . take the whole movie and take one little frame out, put it right there and view it. But, you not only view it . . . you become it!

Figure 20

You become every little thing that you view in that frame. It becomes you! And the mind of God, the fields of energy, when you view that little frame from that one big frame that you want to be and experience . . . the mind of God . . . the particles . . . hey, they create it in the field. You want a body with cells . . . form and structure? The particles create it and you experience it. The mind of God! The Field! The energy Field! You view the film . . . the frame, the picture appears and you say that "this is today and yesterday". Where is yesterday? Where right now, is it and did it happen? Where . . . in your consciousness? It's a "memory". Where did you get the memory right now of yesterday?

Here you are in the Now. You're viewing the next moment . . . possibilities for the next moment, what you want to see . . . more film . . . more frames. What do you want? You pick it. You choose it. Whatever possibility that you choose is an event that continues on. So, in your moment, in the Now moment . . . you select a future, you make it present because you never move from this moment. You don't go into the future. You don't come from the past. You, in your consciousness, look at all possibilities for the next moment. You choose one . . . with it comes the memory. There's your past . . . the one that you picked right here, with all the events.

You are able to look at all the possibilities because you are God. You picked the one and with it comes the memory and you call it your past but, you took the future with all of its events and put them here. Right this moment, it's tomorrow and the next day and here's yesterday and the day before. All that you've done, is transfer it over. You've made it appear linear. All of these frames exist simultaneously for you, but which one do you want to view? Which one do you choose to drag out one day at a time?

There is no tomorrow. There is no yesterday. Illusion! You're doing it in this moment. In this moment, this is a frame . . . what you chose out of many possibilities but, you've never gone anywhere. Right now you've conceived an idea for what you're going to do tomorrow. You see or picture in your mind a course of possibilities . . . actions and events. Pictures in the mind, thoughts embraced and evoked . . . you didn't speak words to yourself but you had thoughts about tomorrow. This is the future that you plan to experience . . . tomorrow it will be the memory. What you do right now in imaging, is as real as what you will do tomorrow.

So, when do you experience this? This is important for you to know because this works so fast and you have slowed yourself down so slow in your brain and your senses and your ability to perceive that you think that time is passing. But, this is instantaneous . . . where you choose your future and project it as an image of the next moment . . . and it becomes your past. It is happening rapidly and you think you are "experiencing" it. I tell you this because I wish to show you how you will be removed from this! This is difficult because your memory is so vivid and you will swear to me that you "experienced" it.

At this point where you are right now, you can do anything you choose with the past or the future. There are all possibilities. See, you moved this experience from here (what you call "future") to here (what you call "past") because that's what you chose to experience. In reality, there is just one big "Now"! It doesn't move! You are moving!

Understand, you are moving . . . when you select a frame and you determine to view this solidly right here in the moment and feel what it is to be in this frame (*Figure 20*). . . you become it this moment! Do you see? But, it always exists. You! That's the power! You decide what to do with this. You! Look at all the infinite possibilities and you say, "That's my future one! The next moment it becomes my memory because I chose it!" But, you have never moved in time and time hasn't passed. This is what you have done.

You have selected possibilities out here. You are looking at them. We have brought you a possibility, have we not . . . knowing how your brain works? You are locked into this system. You must select one of these possibilities out here but what is the possibility that we are bringing you? This is the key . . . how you are responding to what we are saying to you.

See, you may agree that what we are bringing you is true, and repeat it but, what messes you up is you look back over here where you put some of these possibilities . . . you switched them over here and you said, "That's my memory now. This is my past." You put them over here and you say, "This is real. If this is real, and this is true about me, then this can't be true." You are locked into this system!

Because every time you, with your thoughts, your eyes, your senses . . . with your thought you look out here . . . you always think of tomorrow . . . the next moment . . . twenty minutes from now . . . an hour from now . . . "What will I do? What will I select?" You reach out here and select a possibility that becomes your memory and you keep on selecting another one. Get out of that if you can! Because, whatever you select in this film, you put yourself in this film. Whatever you select out here will be projected and that's where you are! How do you get out?

No one locked in this system . . . no, you cannot get out of it and no one in this system can bring you the message. Only someone outside! Remember our line in the beginning? We are taking you out of the past and the future.

You created this! You programmed yourself and because you knew the human drama, you knew the "catch 22" when you sent yourself down here. You didn't send yourself down here without a way out. Would you do that? If you were so "All-Knowing", would you do that? So you said, "Get me out of here at a certain time!"

But, you are limited as long as you want to be! You are experiencing that . . . "this is fun". Just as you go to movies or watch them at home and you see all the many adventures . . . infinite dramas. And you enter into them and you become what you see! "Gee, I can be this. I can see what this feels like". And, you're right there . . . viewing yourself. You feel what they feel like and the better you can feel, the better the movie. If they do not involve you in the feeling then it's not a good movie. You cannot identify with it. The more you can identify with it, the better it is. You do this every day!

This is where you are right now, viewing yourself. This is who is talking to you . . . but we are limited because you have chosen limitation. You have said, "Leave me till the last minute." Now, the one "viewing" has come into the film and said, "Let's get the hell out . . . it's time!" Do you see? As a focus of God, you decided to identify with "this" because we need "this"! You are playing films every day . . . picking them out. The infinite possibilities to view "tomorrow". You picked this one out!

So in reality, what is "this"? There are infinite waves of energy in this room and they coalesce in a certain pattern according to what you chose right here to view and you are projecting it "out there". Think about it, because to you, your bodies, the chairs, and tables in your room are very real to you . . . are they not? When you get down to the level that you cannot view with your senses, in reality . . . what is it?

Thought! Your scientists will tell you it's a particle or it's a wave. They can go down "quantumly" into what it is. That's a reality. Do you know how much space is in this table? What you see out there between your planets . . . there is that much space in this table. You are limited to viewing this because you chose to be. You, in your minds, say . . . "but, I am here. I am flesh and blood."

All beings are not limited as you, but you chose to freeze the frame and view this room as solid. And I am saying that "You" are creating this and the "you" that is creating this is more "real". Because . . . this that is creating this . . . can do anything! That's the Genie! Do you know what you are doing? You are sitting here every day saying "eeny, meeny, miny, mo. I'm going to get the best future here and past that I can". And, we are saying . . . "Forget that! Be the Genie!" This is who you are. This is the mind of God! This is the energy, the Source that exists. This is who you are!

This is the way your scientists draw it. They call it a wave. It can be a particle. The quantum becomes a particle and forms a body . . . a chair . . . a tree . . . whatever you say. Whatever you look out over here and picture, it becomes. The field and waves . . . your scientist says . . . becomes whatever you want to see! And you think that you are located right here in this house at 9:00 o'clock, don't you? Only by choice do you believe that. Because you are this . . . you can move anywhere you want to go. You can take any form that you want to take. You can create any environment that you want to create and never lose who you are. You see, they tell you that light is waves and you think, "Well, if I'm a wave and everywhere, I'm lost. There is no me." Yet, you are aware that you "are". Has anyone found "themselves"? Where is consciousness?

You can't locate your consciousness! It's all over this "space". If yours is in your body, how can it be in "All" . . . everywhere? What did we tell you? You are light!

I am here now . . . joined with this lady's consciousness at this moment. She is aware of herself. She is aware of watching "me" be me and at the same time, knowing herself. You do this all the time with your "greater self". You talk to yourself all the time. Your consciousness of your greater self has been pressing you every day on a constant basis. Two consciousness's in one body . . . how?

Unlimited! Blend . . . merge! Union! Light . . . my ethereal body can blend with this channel's outward aura and I can transfer my thoughts and my consciousness to her. There is no limitation to where light can merge with light. In this room all are one consciousness. You, in this limitation, are causing the "stand-off" because you have a memory on this timeline. You identify with this "time". You create this system to give this identity . . . validity.

You were locked into this system . . . space and time . . . third dimension. You were locked into this system. Right? "Get me out"! Fourth dimension . . . what have we said . . . instant manifestation . . . materialization? You're still not experiencing instant manifestation because you're still putting some time and space to your manifestations. You still require it. Your choosing of your possibilities out here comes with "time' built into it and it becomes a memory that has time built into it.

Remember the film . . . you know that all frames exist there on the film. Infinite possibilities! You know that they all exist, but when you chose a possibility or a picture of what you wanted to do . . . you thought, "What must I do to have that picture"? You could not go from this "now moment" to it being your experience. How do you do this? Are you divided . . . a third dimensional mind compared to a fourth dimensional mind. Are you going to get a new mind?

You must cease to separate! There are no "third" and "fourth" minds. There is only one! There is no ego versus the spirit. There is only one . . . "All That Is".

I wish that I could make you see this because your declarations, your questions, always speak from a duality! This is not something that I can put into words and teach you! You must feel it! You project thoughts to me . . . I feel the energy . . . that I am one thought and you would like to be that thought and you are another, but you could be this one if something would just happen over here!

Right now in this moment is the only time that you will ever know! There is no other time! Do not look for another time! It will be in this moment! When you cease to embrace the thought that you are less than that . . . when you cease to identify with this "third dimensional timeline" and you identify with us. This is the most "outrageous" thing that you will ever do . . . when you say, "I Am that I Am"! There is no duality!

Take control! Take control! Cease to divide yourself up! Cease! Declare yourself the unity! Declare yourself in control . . . even over the illusion. That is a master! A master is in control even in the illusion. Cease to divide yourself. "I Am That I Am!"

This was you, viewing a movie . . . you rented a movie and you played it. Time...time and third dimensional thought... you are coming out of this! So, when you go out to work, to the store, the gas station . . . when you see and talk to other people, your friends . . . they are choosing all possibilities that they want based on memory and conditioning from the past. They like what they are doing. They have chosen this and they want to do it. But you are choosing another possibility.

You are leaving time! You are leaving third dimensional time! Get ready! You did not plan a death. However you choose to conceive it, see yourself being plucked out of time! Instead of seeing yourself running year by year by year. I want you to think about this and within yourself . . . your own knowingness . . . you will have a feeling . . . a knowingness and experience of what this means. It will be your own individual one of being plucked out of time as you are viewing your life now.

It does not mean leaving here. It does not mean giving up your physical body. Do you understand? It means a conscious shift from being locked into this system. You will know in one day that you will no longer choose any of the possibilities that fit into the third dimension. You will have choices that do not fit into third dimension. You will be making possibilities and probabilities for yourself. You will be choosing them that do not fit into third dimension and it will seem very natural. You will not be normal but you will be aware that you are not going to continue on this line that you started at your birth. You are not going to have birthdays anymore. You are not going to have characteristics and genetic traits that you carry with you. You are not going to have any limitations that you now experience. And you will be available for others who have chosen a more traumatic transition. You have the preparation and without your limitations, you will be able to complete whatever you choose.

What I would like to discuss with you next time which I cannot now, is how you are going to coordinate fourth dimensional continuation when this is falling apart . . . fading . . . receding . . .whatever you want to call it . . . on planet earth. You will be activated along this line and at the same time you will have the vertical possibility of traversing dimensions. Fourth dimensionally, you will have a physical body. You will not necessarily indwell that body at all times after third dimension ceases and fourth begins but you have that option during this time and afterwards. All we are talking about is vibration. All we're talking about is a body that is able to vibrate until it becomes pure light. Pure light is where you're headed here. When you take the light and lower it, you have you as you see yourself now. You must have this capability, that's what you came to gather for your whole soul. This is the capability for the "Beyond the Beyond".

The earth has been passing through a beam for a certain period of time. It started at a point and those as yourself, that have interdimensional incarnations, are able to operate in the fourth dimension now. The thoughts presented here are to activate you to initiate within yourself the thoughts that will create functioning fourth dimensionally. You are already able to manifest with your thoughts . . . almost instantly. Am I correct? You are seeing it? Keep going!

Your thoughts create your reality! I showed you in the drawings where you are creating your "yesterdays" by what you decided to think each moment. It becomes your memories. You are still in that stage, which you have chosen, where you are learning possibilities . . . creations of your thoughts, so that you can create your next event as you choose. You have decided to do that. Remember?

I'm going to leave the one point with you. I am telling you that you will experience within yourself . . . the "knowingness" of what it means to be taken out of the game of past and future. This is because you are choosing that, according to your blueprint. That is the first preparation for your next adventure.

CHAPTER 7

THE CREW OF SPACESHIP "TERRA NOVA" REPORT FOR DUTY

Bravo! We have a birth! Now a new life has entered! Let's proceed to feed and nurture and love it in its growth to maturity.

I am Hermes or Thoth, whichever you prefer.

I, Hermes, am and always have been at your service. As Hermes, I carry a vibration of extreme importance to the ending of time. I, Hermes, am the key to the door which will open to reveal the next journey. I, Hermes, am the portal keeper for all who will choose to enter for the "Beyond the Beyond".

Hermes is an energy which carries the knowledge of "New Things". "Behold, I do a new Thing"! Once all other vibrations have prepared the way for cosmic change, my vibration enters to facilitate that change. A portal is to be opened which will allow access to new and unknown space for further creative exploration and expansion. This portal is like unto a door which is locked until certain energies reach critical mass for an implosion which will propel all mass of a certain vibration through a warp in space and time. I, Hermes, am the energy which must unlock the portal. I, Hermes, hold the key.

As an individualized expression of that mass, you have arrived at the juncture where the adventure must begin. All knowledge shared by your extraterrestrial friends has been to help you arrive at this juncture. You have long pondered and agonized over why you could not cross that invisible barrier which has always blocked you from entering a consciousness that you so plainly could visualize. It is because all must be synchronized. No amount of effort could have lowered that barrier. You have seemed to realize this lately and you have been forced to simplify and focus on only what you deemed most important to you. The elimination of all but your heart's desire has left you empty and perplexed.

Listen carefully! Only when you personalize those feelings and view them from a "world-size" perspective can you feel pain. In reality, those feelings must be there because that is the "death" of this world. Nothing more and nothing less! Those feelings can be identified as a "Death" or ending of an illusion.

The sadness you feel is a mourning but it will only last until new energies are recognized and allowed to manifest for you. I, Hermes, am that new! I, Hermes, am here to open the door with my key. My key is perfectly created to unlock the portal. I, Hermes, am communicating on a personal level but you must realize that what I, Hermes, speak has many levels of understanding and the magnitude of the energies which I Hermes, represent are beyond your present level of vibration. Imagine a funnel with a large rim that graduates to a very small rim and you will visualize the expansiveness which must contract in order to impact you in the reality where you are presently focusing. However, this has always been the plan and you are fully prepared to receive.

You are never alone. There are always entities present who are full of love for you, completely informed of your experience and are ready to guide you to the next level of understanding. You are never alone but at this time, you are especially watched over and guided because you must have the door opened for you by someone who holds those energies. You cannot open the door in a separate consciousness but must have the door opened for you in union. The "death" of which I speak is the "death" of separation.

Possibly, you are beginning to realize your difficulty in crossing that barrier. "Knock and it shall be opened" implies that you do not do the opening but must cease to resist and allow the oneness to become your reality. Other energies have been prepared to unlock the portal and I, Hermes, represent that energy.

That is my introduction. Now, other members of our group have prepared some messages for you.

We are present and you are here. You are here. Yes! You went through the door. You started your journey . . . a most exciting journey and one that you, as well as us, have waited for . . . for eons. That is why we wish to speak to you now, because the journey is more exciting than you know. We don't want you to miss anything on this journey. So, beginning now, we will bring you a message that you can hear now. It is time. It is an interesting message that we bring you. We call it "the old & the new".

We discussed our last session with you (Chapter 5) and we discovered the need to clarify something. You see . . . we opened you to thoughts, ideas, and revelation concerning parts of your machine that actually may be little flags . . . . little danger zones that you were unaware of. But, you see, we feel that you may not see exactly what it is that was being presented. So, as you say, "We came up with a better way".

In reality, the better way is the whole truth that you have not known. That is what is meant to enter the doorway . . . there are no more secrets from you. Because "All-knowing" doesn't have any secrets. So, this has been a deep, dark secret and when revealed and understood . . . then you will see the "New". Do you follow me? "See", not to learn . . . not to do anything about it . . . not to change it . . . not to worry about it . . . not to defend it . . . not to get mad at it . . . not to be embarrassed by it . . . but just "see", because "All-knowingness" just sees and is aware without judgement. See?

The "new" that has entered you now, must work with some old concepts and patterns that have been left there. The "new knowing" is there now, you can be allowed to look at it and "see" it as it truly is for you in your reality.

Now, I am going to present something to you . . . the whole truth and nothing but the truth, so help you God . . . that you might "see" it. However, what I am going to show you is that each and every one of you has the same identical fear that we approached last time. There is no difference in anyone's fear and this is good that we preface it with that, so that you understand how "One" you are. Because as a member of the human species, you carry that body and your experience here has been dealing with that which was evolved and genetically presented to you.

There is a seed there . . . and this is what you have been approaching in transmuting . . . is that little thing that happened in the genetic engineering of the human race. This has been the source of your blindness to much of what was true about you.

So be aware of your feelings . . . emotionally, mentally, and physically as we bring these truths to you because this is the history of this planet that is unique in all the universes.

So, this is the secret that has been hidden for ages.

But, in order to approach the secret that has been hidden for ages, I will begin a history lesson so that you will understand this body and how you have been genetically programmed to exist under the "Law of sin and death". Now, when I say that, many of you, who are familiar with the Bible, interpret that from a religious viewpoint . . . "sin and death". Many "New Agers" would say, "But I'm through with sin . . . we have nothing to do with sin". It was not sin, that was their interpretation and it had nothing to do with religion. That was part of the conspiracy and the plan that it was "cloaked" in. You have a whole interpretation of "sin" . . . of the "law" and of "sin and death" . . . all given to you by religion that was cloaking the truth. And the truth was plain and simple . . . "Commerce".

You have records on your earth right now of what I am going to tell you. You may research it any time you choose and you will find it. You have clay tablets that were dug up and retrieved in your Middle East that tell of the Sumerian civilization that existed many thousands of years ago. These tablets, these records, tell you that there was a group of technologically advanced Extraterrestrials . . . who came to this earth to mine gold for their home planet. Now these extraterrestrials were an interesting group and I will not get to any judgment or comparativeness here.

But you take the Hebrew Bible and many believe your whole civilization came from Adam and Eve and their children and trace it right up to today. You are not allowed to consider anything that happened prior to that. If they are mentioned, if they are discussed, they are called legends and myths. Correct? And yet, the Sumerian records had maps of your solar system . . . all of the planets, their sizes, their orbits, their location, and the funny thing about their maps is that they read from outside into your sun . . . not from your sun going out. They had descriptions of how the planet looked from outer space.

Now, these records describe how these extraterrestrials began many things. They built marvelous structures and beautiful temples for themselves. They divided their responsibilities up . . . mining, farming, running transport, commerce and so forth. But the mining was their main reason for being here and these mines were deep underground. That is not a fun job and those who they brought, who were assigned to work down in those mines considered this work "Hell". This is where your whole concept in your history of the "underground God" and having to work in "Hell" came from! Okay! Now, all of these "lesser thans" that had to do this work said, "Heck, we're equal to you and we are not going to do this work anymore".

So, the extraterrestrial leaders got together in council and came up with a plan. They said, "Look . . . out there in the wilderness, is this hairy, awful looking creature (your Neanderthal) . He can't speak a language, he can only grunt. But, hey we could genetically engineer this creature to work these mines for us. Because, we need workers and our own people are tired of this and we don't blame them". This is not a far-fetched idea for you anymore, because you are genetically engineering now. You are learning to do it in humans.

All of this is in your Sumerian legends . . . they told exactly what happened. They tell of how they took the sperm of their own "ET" males and engineered it with the egg from the "ape woman" and they worked with it . . . they had a few mistakes, "monsters" and "creatures" in your "legends", that came from the exploration to derive a worker for their mines. But, they had desired a "worker" and they were finally able to create "Man" that was half "God", because they had used their own DNA.

Understand, that this little guy (Neanderthal) was what had been set up here on earth that would eventually evolve . . . had the brain capacity to evolve . . . keep on evolving and open up that second brain chamber to say, "By gosh, I am it!" . . . like you're finding out. This was the normal that was planned on this earth and has been done in many universes. Well, they knew the evolution that this Neanderthal was destined for, so they didn't just create a more advanced "Earthling". They had to genetically engineer it as a tool, a machine . . . to function as a "Worker". That's why the first man advanced from the Neanderthal to Cro-Magnon. Your scientists have never found anything between the Neanderthal and Cro-Magnon to link them up . . . from living out in the woods to Cro-Magnon, having tools, working metal and building cities. This is it . . . the genetic program that these extraterrestrials put into him . . . that you and all the Human Race has derived its identity from . . . was programmed to be a "Worker".

These Beings . . . . they created Cro-Magnon Man. Their doctors and scientists who did this were ecstatic when they got this "Human Being". It could take orders. It could do so many things, and some of these ET's that created this human loved it and that became a problem for them later on because, others of those great beings in those peaceful, wonderful, skies up there have absolutely no use for this place and for you!

See, at first this "Man" they had created did not have the ability to procreate and then they changed them, so that they could now procreate. Does this sound anything like "Genesis"? This whole ET colony down here from outer space had a big fight about this. And they had a big meeting up there in their ship when the time had arrived on the cosmic calendar for a cataclysmic happening with huge floods to come to earth. And they knew they were going to get in their ships and leave until it was finished. And some of them said, "This is wonderful because now we can get rid of those blankety, blank creatures that we've created that are getting to be a handful". See, they had created problems.

Look, think about it. If you want a worker, and you are creating one, there are certain ways you want it to function – are there not? You want him to take orders and you don't want a machine that won't take orders because he's decided within himself that he doesn't have to do this. Right? You see . . . . you know really what the problem was? This may also sound a little like your scriptures. Some of these space guys back there had said, "It's okay to put your sperm in those test tubes for our doctors to use but, look at those gals out there! I mean, that's a lot more fun to find one of those!" This is what their leaders and the "Big Daddy" in charge got mad about, because they started producing these children that were half their race . . . . half "Gods" and half "Worker".

If you read the "Epic of Gilgamesh", you will find out that he was one of those that was "half God and half Man"! And they were put in charge as rulers over the rest of the workers, but they were not allowed to go "up there" in the space ships. Poor old Gilgamesh is trying his dead level best to get up there. He says he has a right to be there because his father is from there. He's half God. So, he has a right to everlasting life, because he is "half God". But they denied him that right.

Now these rulers are also reproducing and it has gotten "out of hand". This is why these ETs decided to leave them all to the flood and start over. But, remember Noah in your Bible? Noah was loved dearly by one of these "ET creator Gods". And because he loved the human, he helped him and his families escape the flood. And boy, was he in trouble after the flood. There has been fighting about this ever since.

Now, let's go back to you and your genetic history as this little worker. We've got this little worker and he's got to function. He's got a machine and it's going to work and you can use that to control him. You know that these "workers" see you as these great Beings that are so far beyond them, because of your technology . . . you can go up into the "Heavens". They think you are Gods. They're awed by you. They're awed by this "ascension" process. They have one desire . . . "everlasting life". To go into the "Heavens" and be with "God".

So you say, "By God, we can use that . . . we can tell them, if you will do what we tell you to do, you'll get special treatment". And so these workers could say, "Gee, I'd like to get in one of those "ships" . . . ascend, because that's where the Gods went". Well to these workers, these "Gods" had a lifetime that seemed everlasting . . . beyond them.

Every time you think of the God that lives up in Heaven, that you have to appease, you are identifying with this little worker back there. That's what was programmed in your little machines. Every system that has been introduced since that time to keep you worshipping the Gods . . . to go home and be with "Big Daddy" was so that you would do the will of God. Well, what was His will? Law! Law . . .!! Do what we tell you is the right thing to do and you won't sin. (Transgress the Law) and die. "The Law of Sin and Death", as it was called in the Bible, in Romans.

It was imprinted and genetically engineered in the species that you derived your bodies from. Paul said in his letter to the Romans, "Within my members, there is a war. I can't do what I want and I do what I don't want to do. Oh, wretched man that I am. Who is going to save me from this body of death?" What is that? Duality . . . Yin/Yang. Duality. That's in these "members", it is, isn't it? Many people, as Christians, found a war . . . called the "Two Natures" within them. And that's why they screamed exactly as Paul did, in their experience of trying to keep the "Law" and please God . . . and do "His will".

And, you think you're not bothered by this because you know there's no heaven and hell, and you don't believe in sin? The program is still there. This is what we meant about the little flag that pops up in you. You may shift your belief in the "Law" . . . but do you have any of these?

"Do . . . Don't" "Can . . . Can't" "Will . . . Won't" "Should . . . Shouldn't"

Seriously, you mean you don't have any of these? Okay, you are going to get the "Big" picture here shortly because this, you are free from . . . right now - you are freed from this right now! What's all the cosmic stuff, the vibrations that have been going on . . . and the doorway?

You took up residence in one of these human bodies here and you said, "Break me out" at a certain time. I'm blowing hell out of the system in this body. I am going to bust this system wide open in this body. You're doing that. That's what you are doing.

Speaking of "system busters" . . . .

<u>Monka:</u> Well folks . . . . here's "ole what's his name"! Ready to go? Okay! Where're we going?

<u>Audience:</u> Onward! Forward!

<u>Monka:</u> Always! Always forward . . . that's good! Well . . . . what time is it? Is it time to wake up yet? Why is it that sometimes when you begin to wake up, you say, "no, I want to go back asleep . . . can't I get a few more hours sleep here?" Right? Okay, yeah . . . you don't want to hear that alarm clock then, do you? Don't want anybody shaking you and saying "wake up"! Nope.

Well, wait a minute. There's something we have to consider here. Suppose that we were excited the night before we went to sleep about going on an exciting trip that we had planned?

<u>Audience:</u> Well, I bet if we were planning to get in one of your ships and go somewhere that would excite us.

<u>Monka</u>: Yeeeeeep! By God, everybody is always wanting to get on a spaceship. Alright . . . okay, wait a minute now . . . say, we've got this spaceship. We give you this message that we're going to pick you up at a certain time. Big ship . . . all the brothers and sisters going to be there. Okay! Now what are you going to take with you? Because, you've got to be "equipped". And what baggage that you carry around all day with you is not getting on that ship?

<u>Audience</u>: You mean all those beliefs, opinions, viewpoints, and perceptions . . . all that stuff?

<u>Monka</u>: All that baggage. Things that you are holding on to . . . grasping in your tight little fists, like treasures. "Those are mine", you say. Well, do you know that you all have the same little treasures that you're holding on to but, you don't let each other see what's in your box. And that's the big joke. You see?

Okay, I'm going to tell you what this box is that you're carrying around with your treasures in. Do you know what's in that box? "Dysfunctional patterns"!

"Dysfunctional patterns" . . . don't you like those words? There is a ring to that . . . a vibration. It sounds like you're saying something really good. But, it's a nice way of saying something else. Don't you think? Because there are a lot of people on this earth, trying to get on board these ships and they want to take all this garbage with them . . . excuse me, "dysfunctional patterns"! Anything you want to call it, but we're not letting it on these ships! You know? Can't spread that stuff around. It's confined to your planet.

The dysfunctional pattern is what you are using. It's a tool. It isn't accomplishing what you think it is, but you use it nonetheless to gain control. And who is it that's using this tool, that wants to be in control?

<u>Audience</u>: The false identity.

<u>Monka</u>: Why don't you just say "me"! We are just sitting back here looking at "us" . . . "me". We are not going to judge "me" anymore! Know what I mean? We don't care. Okay. This is perfect. It is a perfect creation. Did you

know that? It accomplished everything that it was designed to do. About time that you gave it some credit.

Remember it . . . you sitting on some cloud out there and you're getting ready to zoom in on this earth here and you're saying, "How am I going to function down here? Look at all that mess! I'm supposed to go down there?! Well, I've got to come up with a lulu to get through this!" You know? So, you designed it.

Now, have you ever dealt with this "should" and "should not" stuff? What have you known about it? You make them up all by yourself?

Audience: Well, I make up my own but . . . they are conditioned too.

Monka: Well, that's good . . . a little bit of both. But why do you take all these burdens on yourself? I mean, you can run this thing of "I create my own reality" right into the ground and say, "Oh my God, I've done it again. Look what I've created. I knew it was bad. I've done it again". How long have you had this pattern? Is it a bad pattern? Oh . . . I've got you now! Now we're getting down to a dysfunctional pattern, aren't we?

See . . . you know this thing about polarities? There are none where you are going. So, what difference does it make if you call "good" . . . "bad" and "bad" . . . "good"? They're all illusions . . . dysfunctional patterns called judgement. When you get tired of it, you will quit it.

Audience: I'm tired of it.

Monka: Now we're getting to another dysfunctional pattern here . . . . "time". I gave you an "out" when I said, "When you get tired of it" because, now you can see an opportunity here to have more time to work this out. We had judgment and time. See? I have to let you in on a secret now. "Dysfunctional patterns" have to do with third dimensional illusion. All you are doing . . . is responding to illusions! Don't you see? You call it irritation, you call it bad.... whatever you want to call it but, it's an emotional response to an "illusion". There is no reality here folks! Think about it! There's no reality!

<u>Audience</u>: It's any response to the illusion.

<u>Monka</u>: Oh . . . . Hallelujah! You wanted to be real "bad", didn't you? Can I tell you that being "good" is a dysfunctional pattern too . . . if you are responding to something that's not there? Okay. You got it!

Now, how are we supposed to take you on this ship into "reality", if you only know how to respond to unreality? Illusions keep you from seeing reality.

Okay, I'm going to take a break here and get you "back in class" to catch up on the vision of what has, "in reality", been in you from the beginning to do.

We are all present. So, remember in our discussion, previously, we explained how we have given your machine a new program, with a list . . . "loving yourself . . . creating you own reality . . . going within", etc. Everyone understood that was for the purpose of focusing within where the merging was coming that was required with the new consciousness that is there. It is to take your eyes off of everything radiating around you and go to the center of yourself and discover who the "Thinker" was. It is to prepare you for that thinker who is emerging and taking back over its property, its creation . . . for new adventure.

So, that is a program that many in the New Age movement are rallying around as a new program, a new religion, a new philosophy. Many have no concept of the reality of the emergence of "All That Is". They will say that they are God because the program will permit this . . . all of this understanding. We knew that. But, they (the list of teachings) had one purpose. It was not to teach. It was not to inform the "All That Is". It was to allow you to focus within, where the action is . . . where what is happening is occurring . . . within you and to hear the still small voice of the vibrations that are emerging. Is that understood by everyone?

So, you are being made very aware of all of your decisions. Because, you see, the greatest illusion of all is that the machine makes decisions, that it is a free-wheeling individual with free-will. Your government promotes that.

Your religion promotes that because, as I told you, that is most important for you to maintain that "free-will", in order to keep you from approaching this area . . . this opening of the emergence of the consciousness that says, "I'm really who you are. I'm really who has done all the thinking. There has never been anything but you/me". And, your flags go up because you are programmed to believe that you are a free-will individual and that your salvation, whether it is political, religious, philosophical, economic, or anything . . . that your salvation, your security, depends on "you" making the "right" decision, within that "free-will".

It is very clever programming designed for this period now, and it has ascendency. The program is working many people to stay asleep in "effect", in the negative universe, within the program of New Age teaching and to not allow this emergence. So much of what you read is merely information for the machine. The majority, 99 percent . . . is. We are bringing you the 1 percent.

You see, there was another reason for all these teachings and the going within that was also clever in our experiment. It was the fact that all of these things that we spoke of . . . none of them could be proven in third dimension through your five senses. They all spoke of the unknown, the invisible. Didn't that lead to a lot of frustration? Didn't all the information, the teaching, the programs, create more conflict . . . whereas before, you were pretty happy? Things weren't too bad. You could maintain but, when you allowed this new information that sent you within and you attempted to prove this, which is what your machine does through reason and logic . . . it got harder, and harder, and harder. And nothing in the third dimension appeared in which to prove it, that you could sense through your five senses and your vibrations. The only proof you had of any of the information, was in feelings coming from within and emerging from within that said, "I'm here" I'm All That Is". Do you understand?

It created intense desire because it created a vision of power, a vision of love . . . a vision of peace within. It created a vision of all the things that you had imagined that you desire, that you could have how. So, the more that you desired it and the less ability you had to actually produce it in third dimension . . . the more intense you had become. Many have walked away from this teaching because of this conflict. The intenseness was proof to them that it was a lie. The lack of visual, sensual proof to be recorded within the machine was proof to them that it was a lie. How many times have you been tempted to walk away because you had no visible proof? "If it was truth, why not give it to me?" How many times has your machine played that record? Many left it for that reason.

The intense desire was the key. The frustration, the anger, created an intenseness so that your projection, your energy has been revving up as I said, revving up . . . because, how did we find out that God created . . . in whose image you are made? He created through desire. Now, if God is thinking this moment and therefore, we are here and we are doing what we are doing and you are doing what you are doing . . . where does the desire exist for this merger? It exists within the thinking of God and you are feeling it because you are Him and that is the thinking. Your desire is God's desire. It is you as God desiring this. Do you see?

You have created more energy, more intenseness . . . so that every failure to accomplish this within your life had a purpose. Only those who could get past the machine would enter this. Only those who would create the intense desire. Why? Because there is only one person desiring . . . and within those with that desire, is His plan. That is His choice . . . to continue on. Not all will have that desire. Because all things exist simultaneously in this moment, there will be all levels and degrees of understanding. Not all will go past the machine understanding because they must exist simultaneously with those who do.

Now, in your societies and your religions, "Free-will" is the God that you worship. "That is a horrible thought. You are telling me that some will and some won't? Who chooses? Who decides? That's not fair. I have free-will. Are you telling me that even if I wanted to, I couldn't?" No! I didn't say that, because if you want to, you will. But, the one that doesn't want to, doesn't like to hear that . . . does he? He will tell you "That is not fair".

He has not experienced anything in this whole world of "effect" that was fair . . . that was free-will. Do you ever recall choosing to be white instead of black? Christian instead of Arab? In your machine, can you tell me if you remember that? Did you remember in your machine what date you would be born? Do you remember in your machine that you decided what parents you would have and what family and what economic bracket it would be in? Where is your choice? Did you have any choice when you were born into a world that was at war . . . constantly, on an individual level and a universal level? Where is your choice? Can you go off in that free-will of yours and find me an environment where there is not war? No! Because, it is within you . . . so where is your "free-will"? Tell me in your machine, when you recall making a choice to be born into a world where money is not the bottom line? You were born into a world where you have no choice but to produce to survive. Where is your choice? Did you choose not to be born one of those babies in Africa that is starving to death?

Does your machine remember making the choice as to where and how you would be born? Where is your choice? Where have you made choices? Your choices have all been within a limited confinement. They were already made for you. They are made for you every day and you just run around in limitation and try to survive the best you can. But, you are not "free" nor do you make "free choices". It is all relative in comparison to what I am talking about . . . to be "All That Is" with absolute freedom to create whatever you think.

So you see, the illusion of free-will has been promoted by your religions, and has been promoted by your governments. It is a strong genetic inheritance in you because it is through that illusion of free-will that you are controlled. It is an illusion that makes you happy to accept all the limitations that are placed upon you day in and day out by those who control everything that happens to you.

Now, I am not speaking of you personally. I am coming from a relative position where your machines are concerned and I am speaking of the human species. Understand when I speak to you personally and when I speak of the human species. Make a division there. I wanted to elaborate so you clearly understood what I have been discussing with you.

Now, I think we need to enter and begin to understand how you are "All That Is". Where does "All That Is" reside and how does it function in your reality? How will this consciousness that is within you be connected to all other consciousness's so that you will realize one mind as individuals?

I have a drawing that I would like to present. *(Figure 21)* See if you can follow. We are going to call this the Central Sun. obviously, it goes off the board but, I've got to condense because we are talking a vast space here with many universes. I am going to give you half of it. The other half extends. Imagine it!

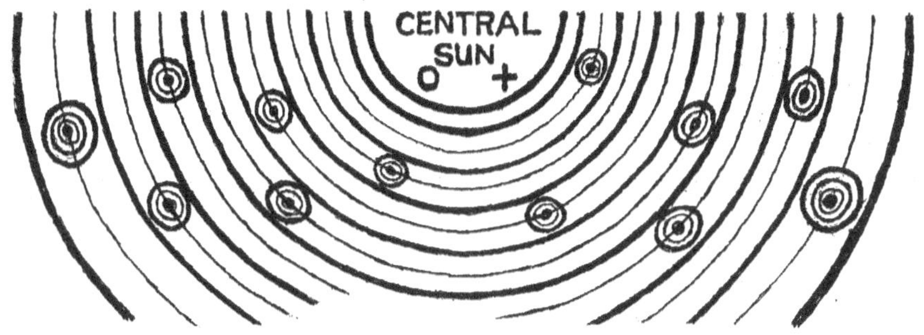

Figure 21

The Central Sun is the positive force. It is the zero rest. It is the "All That Is" that we have been discussing. All energy, all creation derives from this Central Sun . . . the source of all energy . . . The Force. Now, it is a spiraling force. As it spirals, waves are created. We will call those levels . . . dimensions. Those closest to the center, vibrate the fastest. As you go further out, the vibration slows down.

The central source creates out from itself on different levels, more universes. These are universes with Central Suns. Within the universes that exist out there, we have more spirals. *(Figure 22)* This is spiraling. The universes are spiraling and within this universe are galaxies that have a Central Sun also. So we have a galaxy that is spiraling and then, within the galaxy, we have a solar system. And within the solar system, we have planets. So, here's a center and here's another center, just as this is a center. This is your universe . . . this is your galaxy, and this is your solar system

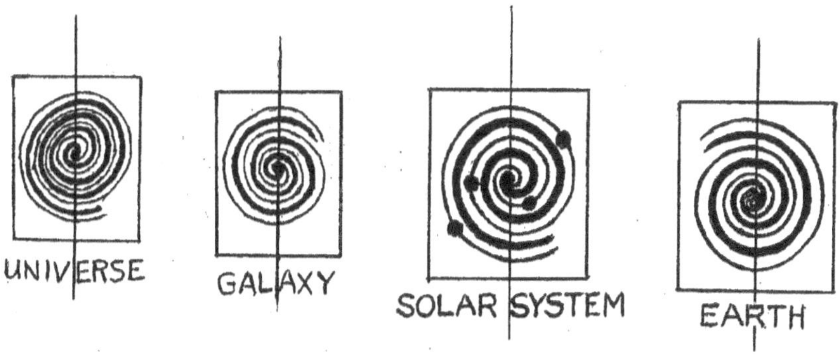

Figure 22

Now, at the same time, we've got a spiral going back to the center as well. We have the opposites . . . remember? The one is the spiraling out from the center. The other is the spiraling back . . . centripetal . . . centrifugal force. The two that we discussed in the beginning that create the whole illusion out here. You have the Central Sun which is the Force of all universes from which all things derive . . . all energy . . . all creation. The galaxy derives everything from within it, with its Central Sun within the universe. Your solar system's Central Sun derives everything that is created within your solar system from the Central Sun within the Galaxy, that has a Central Sun within the universe that is a part of the Central Sun. And then, you have your earth. It is also orbiting and spiraling.

Now, these are the two forces that are being projected from your Central Sun within your solar system. It is going toward the center of your earth. At the same time, everything within the center of your earth is spiraling back out and going back out to the sun in your solar system. Everything created on your earth, derives from the hydrogen which is expelled by the Central Sun within your solar system and as this is lowered down to density, it becomes what you see in this room . . . coagulated thought . . . because all of this spiraling is nothing but electrical negative and positive fields being emitted from the thinking of God. But where is "God"?

On this earth is "You" and you are also a Central Sun that spirals. Are you following me? I need to do some drawing so I can point to them. *(Figure 23)* This has been quite an exercise to prepare your channel's mind to receive these drawings. So, we're coordinating this . . .

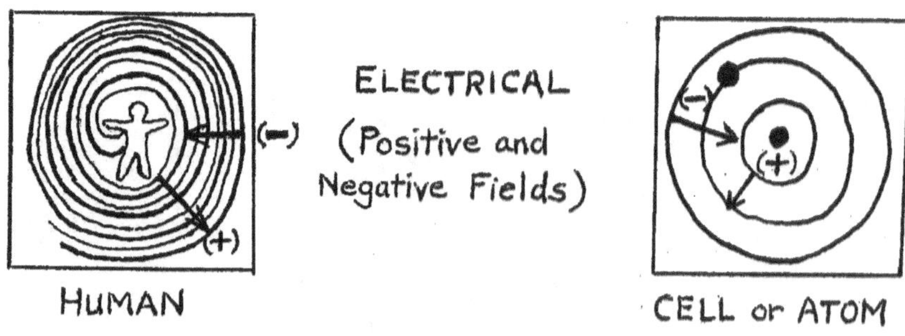

Figure 23

From orbit or spiral, there must be a magnetic center that keeps everything spiraling toward that center. The pressure is greater here to come toward the center and lesser up here as it spirals out. The spiraling creates a field. You have a cell here. What keeps that cell in its shape? It is the field that is being created around it by what? Isn't it the positive and negative forces? Don't you have in the middle a positive force and out here a negative force in the electron? So, it is the pressure from the two that maintains a field around the shell and that field keeps the shape of the cell. You have a field around you that is being maintained by the pressure from within and the space without. The negative and positive force field maintains the shape that is you . . . makes a chair look like a chair, a tree like a tree and the human form as it is. Because otherwise, why doesn't it just disappear? This line that you are seeing as an "arm" (points to arm), how is that created? How was that created? It is created by the field around it of negative and positive forces. You have pressure from without and pressure from within that maintains this field around you. Now, this field is important. You need to understand what is happening to you now. You are about to create a different field around you. This one is functioning by the tension between these two forces. I don't believe this is too scientific. I believe that you can contemplate this further. But, there is a tension between the two that maintain the form . . . follow that all the way up.

There is the spiraling in and recall that there was the other . . . the two spirals . . . one going in and one going out. The forces involved in these two are creating a form and out from that form is created a field that maintains it. All of it directed from the center. This cell is directed from the center. So, you want to call this a nucleus and you want to call this a proton and an electron. You have names for solar systems, galaxies, and universes and everything. That's the form that is taken but, in reality, all you have is this central magnetic center that is spiraling out and spiraling back simultaneously and it appears in the world as structure and form.

The center of the cell is "All That Is". It is the mind of God. That is all that you are measuring. That is all you are seeing and that is all you are looking at, whether you call it an electron, proton, or anything else. You are looking at the mind of God thinking. The center of you is the mind of God. The center of your earth is the mind of God. The center of the Sun is the mind of God. The center of the galaxy is the mind of God. The center of the universe is the mind of God, "All That Is". He exists within each one of those. He exists within every spiral of orbit because, that is all that we've found to be the beginning of all of this. Do you understand, that in your science, they say that this cell, or actually, the atom . . . creates all of this? Are you all familiar with that? This is the building block of all of everything that exists.

Question: Is that center in every subatomic particle?

Absolutely! It cannot orbit . . . what is it orbiting around? What is keeping it there? What is creating that effect that they are measuring? They are not seeing it. They are measuring it. There is a force there. What is that force? It is the magnetic properties, they call it. It is the mind of God that holds it there, that keeps it there . . . that is the force that spirals it in and spirals it out. The thinking of God!

Now, I have drawn it out here because that is the way you experience it but, what would happen if I laid this cell on top of this center within you . . . on top of the center within the earth . . . on top of the center within the solar system, the galaxy, the universe and then put it back into the Central Sun? What if I unified all those systems? What am I saying? There is only one center that exists. All of this is the effect and illusion that it creates. Remember, there is no space and time in the Central Sun. That is all illusion. So, that all of this . . . the center of every cell within you . . . the center of you that you have created . . . spirals around you. The center of the solar system, the galaxy, the universe . . . all exist within the Central Sun. It is all happening right there. There is only one center in everything and that center is not a thing. It is a thought! It is a thought.

Can you see from this how you, here, have a magnetic field around you that creates your form and it is created from tension? When you meditate, you close down the senses and you go within. You go and in consciousness, you align with that center which is the mind of God. You do not recall or experience the conscious awareness of the senses of what is happening. All you have is a feeling.

Think about your meditation in consciousness. Many times, you have come out of meditation and you have said, "Well, nothing happened. I saw this or I saw that". Your machine that we drew is not capable of recording anything within this center as such. It is only necessary to record within space and time and form and structure. The center . . . it does not record. It does not split between the left and right brain. It does not organize functionally. It knows no time. In a meditative state, you are not aware of time passing. You are not aware of the space around you. But, you are aware of experiencing yourself, are you not? You are experiencing yourself in another consciousness which is the center of every cell that exists in all the universes. This is how they are all One.

The thing that baffles scientists, is how every nucleus in every atom . . . every particle knows what the other is doing. And, you know another thing about your physicists, they know for a fact . . . they have formulas . . . that this particle, the smallest particle that they can find . . . can go backward and forward in time . . . it can go vertical or horizontal. They don't understand that because, they are looking at the mind of God in which there is no space and time but, in which all is connected.

All of this that is created is a hologram from the two lights within. Remember your study of the hologram? How do you get the photographic plate and how do you get the image? From the splitting of one light. This is all a holographic image that exists in the mind of God. You see, if we gather this all up and put it in here, and in here, and in here, and then I put it back in there (points to the cell, the body, the earth, the solar system, the galaxy, the universe and the Central Sun). . . I only have one thing.

This out here . . . spiraled out . . . is God thinking. If God stopped thinking, all this would cease to exist because that is what holds it together. That is the magnetic force that your scientists don't understand . . . that keeps this orbiting. And, then through magnetic and electric poles and the different spiraling . . . the one up and the one down, in and out . . . you create a force field. *(Figure 24)* You have heard us say that we are creating a field? We create a field that shuts down the tension between the negative and positive within your force field . . . in order to allow you to enter this restful state and hear what we are saying in the other consciousness. Feel it! You don't hear it . . . you feel it, in reality. Your machine is still recording what I am saying but, you are existing within that center.

Is this affording a picture to begin to feel how everything is within everything? Everything is recording God's thoughts and sending them back to Him so that He now sees the expression of what He thought. You know, when you think of something you want to create . . . say, something in your workshop . . . and sometimes the energy and the intenseness comes, "I must see it". It is not enough to imagine it. It is not enough to think it. You can sit there in your mind and you can think it . . . imagine it. But then there comes a desire. Possibly, maybe you don't like that one . . . you eliminate that one and you think another one . . . but, there is a desire that begins to come and you have to express that desire . . . in the actual mass of the object that you imagined . . . the idea you had.

You see a picture that you want to needlepoint or that you want to paint, "Oh, that looks pretty. Oh, I have to do that". So, you find one and there is an intense desire, "I want to see it produced". You are in the image of God because God thinks and everything He thinks with intense desire for it . . . which is love . . . manifests.

Your thinking through time and space creates a material object. God's thinking creates a hologram of everything! All desire is evident in His creation. But, you experience a Central Sun . . . the universe . . . separation, separation . . . this is the effect. This is the negative. It is all separation from the positive. You experience it as separation and multiplicity. My god, look at the multiplicity . . . so that all thoughts . . . all potential can materialize. But, in reality, there is the One that has never moved, is at total rest and that is where it exists.

You experience that in what you call mediation. There are times with this new consciousness emerging that you will have what you call a "glimpse" and that is when you are not feeling separate. You are knowing yourself as the center of everything.

Now, this electro-magnetic . . . the electricity which I explained and the magnetism of the center . . . you create an electro-magnetic field around you and that attracts and repels what you desire and what you wish. Now, your electro-magnetic field has been created with much tension through the "effect" universe . . . the negative universe of positive and negative.

What kind of field did the "Christ" have around Him where the center was consciously aware of itself as the Center of all things? What kind? *(Figure 25)* What happened to His electro-magnetic field when He no longer operated in the positive and negative because the center is "0" . . . it is a perfect rest . . . what happened to His field? There was no longer plus and minus in His consciousness because He had mastered polarities. He now knew that everything was only One and therefore, He created a field out here in which there was only magnetism. And, anything projected from that magnetism was a result of His command.

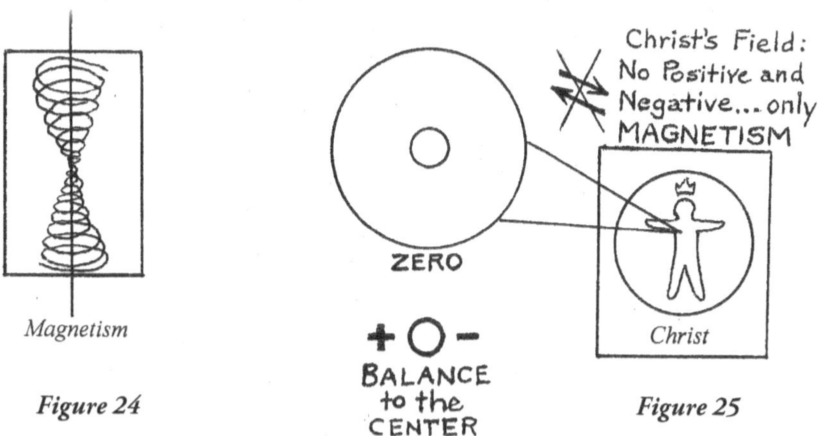

Magnetism

Christ

Figure 24

Figure 25

So, when Christ walked through town He never spoke a word but, when He got to the other side of town . . . there were huge crowds of people. Now, they had no television or newspapers or satellites to inform the people of who this man was that was walking through the town. He projected out His desire and it was magnetized to Him instantly. He desired them to follow Him so that He could teach . . . to create a new program that anticipated this date that is coming now.

In other words, this field no longer operated separate and apart, but this field was at His command. He was not limited as you are limited. He could dissolve the image because He was not confined to the energies of plus and minus of electricity out here . . . the negative and positive, that remember, defined His body. He could take it all apart and put it wherever He wanted it, by will, by choice, by command, so that you could not see it . . . so that there was no longer this form. He could stand right in your presence and you could not see the form because He had absolute control. He knew that within every cell was His mind. He controlled all matter because he knew that all matter was His thoughts.

The doorway that you are entering is for the purpose of creating a new electro-magnetic field which we call the "Christhood" . . . that will permit this in your form, which you have come here and secured for the preservation of the species. This is God/Man completed, merged . . . unified. He is removed from the polarities. He creates a field. He walks through and disciples lay down whatever they are doing and they follow Him. Why? Because He thought "follow me" and they could not do otherwise because of the field that crossed their path. He had a large one. Yours will be too. That field went past and whatever He drew to Him, had to come to Him.

Listen carefully. Within all the creation that you saw spiraling out from the Central Sun are all the levels of vibration that create all dimensions and all experience and all form and all structure. You possess at the moment, a small, small experience of these vibratory levels in the human form. You are confined with your five senses to only experience . . . to only be able to perceive a small part of the spiraling out from the Central Sun. You experience a small part of that spiral. (Figure 26)

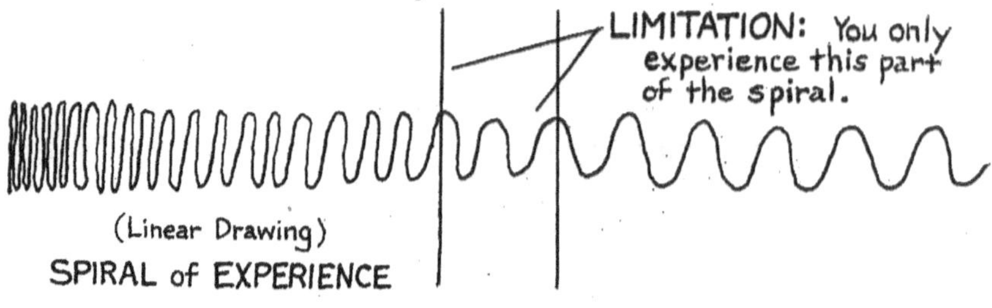

Figure 26

Now, what is getting ready to happen, is you are getting ready to remove that and be able to go up and down the spiral . . . for there are radio waves that you cannot hear . . . there are waves that you cannot see, but you will be able to at will. You will no longer be confined to this small area. This is limitation

Now, I would like to get to some drawings that will show you how the Consciousness will create the new electro-magnetic fields and explain what is going to happen that increases your field of experience within this. Because as God, at the center, all of this is your thinking, all of this can be experienced and known. (*Points to wave chart of vibrations*) – Figure 26

What is this? (Figure 27) It is an electro-magnetic null zone in which there is the total suspension and the "Zero Rest" from the cause of negative universes and the world of effect that you have known. This is an electromagnetic null zone.

You are going to be changed chemically and electrically, and some of you know how they inter-relate. In order to facilitate this changing so that this becomes the experience, there must be a shutdown of your electromagnetic fields. The change cannot be precipitated except within a null zone. That is a doorway because that shuts down the laws that apply in your electro-magnetic field and allows another octave, another understanding, another experience, another vibratory level to become your reality.

We have spoken of the "Merkabah". *(Figure 27)* What is the "Merkabah"? The "Merkabah" is the ship, the energy, the crystal, that allows and creates an electro-magnetic null zone between dimensions. It is the only thing that can do that. It is what we call a "Merkabah". It descends and is able to create this null zone so that you go from one dimension to another dimension . . . an unlimiting of this confining area down here. You go up an octave. How is this done? Well, let's look at the drawing.

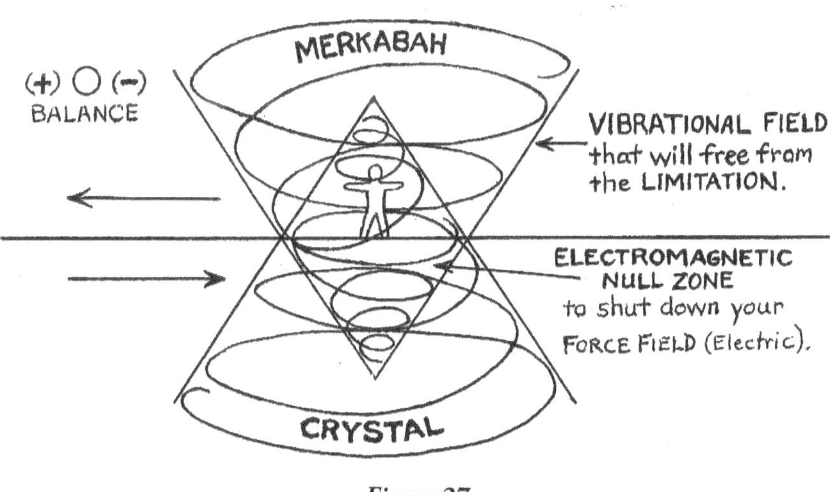

Figure 27

This is the "Merkabah". This is the crystal implanted within this earth . . . put there many eons ago by "you", when the time would come that this earth and those on it would transcend into another octave of understanding and vibration. This is the symbol that has been brought to you. This is the triangle. This is where you stand in the electro-magnetic null zone. The vehicle lowers . . . spirals down and connects with the spiraling up and in this space, right here, there is another one created that allows your force-fields to be shut down, in their positive and negative tensions and vibrations . . . to switch you and all of your cells and your chemical balance to another and higher vibration. It can only be done when this field is created.

This will allow entry from above and entry to up above by those here. This is the field that will be created, that will free the limitations from you. It must be done electrically and chemically. Remember, we told you that this is not "Airy-fairy" spiritual stuff. There is physics behind it. This is what is happening. Many of you have pondered how you were going to transform these bodies by your consciousness. Your machines have created the intense desire that has brought you to this point. The emergence of the Consciousness within you will be allowed at this point because there will no longer be negative and positive energies that will not allow it.

There will be an electro-magnetic null zone which is a complete balance between the two . . .the positive and the negative. And, how do you balance? What happens, when you balance a positive and a negative? What do you have? A "Zero"! So, what do you have in the electro-magnetic null zone? What is that? Is that a center? Is that not the "Center" which I have shown you that everything rotates around? So, what is present there in that area at that time? Every cell within your body will line up with that . . . will come to that point of rest . . . so it can realign and the new vibration that will create the seeing . . . your eyes, your ears, your feel, your touch, your smell . . . all senses to be enhanced so that you can experience more on this spectrum of vibration. And, you will create an electro-magnetic field around you . . . the same as Christ . . . and, this area also has this new field around it. What is that going to do? What did Christ do?

The Navigator: Magnetized

Correct. Because, isn't the center, the "zero" . . . what everything revolves around? So, when you establish that, then whatever is desired is projected . . . and whatever is thought and projected is magnetized and drawn to it. That Consciousness within the brain, we saw, allowed and emerged and combined with that . . . thinks "preservation of the species" . . . thinks whatever is necessary at any time and "It" is magnetized.

This experience will allow conscious awareness of the Consciousness that you are, so that whatever you desire must magnetize to you. There is no tension of force that requires effort to produce anything. Whatever you desire . . . just by thinking it and desiring it . . . it must magnetize to you, without effort. You see, effort is the charge that exists between positive and negative. That is all you measure when you measure electricity . . . the tension that exists between the two. This is without effort, without charge . . . . without dualities.

These areas, these centers will be created around the world. This is where people will be magnetized to . . . in these different centers . . . to receive and to be protected within these zones from the tension that is going to precipitate upon your earth.

This drawing (Figure 27) is a symbol that will pull out your Knowingness . . . . that creates desire. This is information for the machine . . . . not Knowingness. The Knowingness is within you. You are already feeling the "zone". You are already feeling a "weakness" because there is not the tension between the poles. You are not experiencing any desire for effort. You are already reaching this because the Merkabah, through this channel, the energy from it has been creating for you, to prepare you for the allowing of the transformation . . . . . the "Transmutation".

You must learn to trust yourself because you have exhibited and experienced the trustworthiness of yourself to determine, in this third dimension exactly what is needed and how to function. You are learning to utilize your machine in conjunction with the Knowingness. We have taught you and brought you much information to understand. We do not eliminate the machine because of the intense desire for this. Because, the machine and it's new purpose is the "mission"!

This is all because in that Knowingness that is going to emerge, the desire of God will become all that you are consumed with . . . and that desire will be to magnetize, as Christ did, all those that are to be transmuted . . . within your hidden blueprint. Christ said, "All those the Father gives me, will come to me". It is the same for you!

Christ walked through the village. He had already selected His disciples and He had to but pass His field and they followed Him. They not only followed, but they knew that He was exceptional.

In your separation, you have allowed yourself the forgetting of your Oneness. And you have experienced many dangers and overcome many temptations . . . as Christ did, to fulfill the will of the Father which He knew to be His will. You are waking up to the understanding . . . that the will that exists in that Consciousness that is you, is the thinking and the will of "All That Is" . . . and you are One!

The vibration that Christ brought to the human race 2,000 years ago was, "I pray . . . I will . . . I am willing it . . . that you might come to know the Oneness that I have with the Father". And He said, "All those that the Father gives me will come to me". You are coming. You chose the incarnation and the body and you have overcome the temptations, the same as He did, that are hazards and dangers in the forgetting of your Oneness.

You have allowed yourself to experience and record the strain and the tension of a dual universe in the emotions that you have felt. And, you have come to this point of Knowingness and release and peace. It will create within you a knowingness of the desire that God had, that you witnessed and experienced in your understanding of "Christ" . . . that all might come to know this. This is the blueprint now, because of the age that you are entering and that you are going to go past...into the New. This is the mind of God right now. You are thinking it . . . to get out of limitation, into freedom. That is the desire of all who have been destined to this. Once, the completion, the Newness arrives, you will find yourself with other desires as God continues to desire to expand His creation and you know yourself as God, in union, but in a separate form that has but to will . . . to manifest and to command.

That is our message for now. We will return when necessary, but we don't want to go too fast and leave you too dizzy . . . . . Good night!

CHAPTER 8

THE COUNTDOWN BEGINS NOW

Ola with The Navigator: Transmission from February 14, 1991

Now is the time for all good people to come to the aid of this world. This is Wonton speaking. I am in a ship, monitoring, keeping in close touch with everything transpiring with your group.

We have come to a point in time in which we feel that you now need to lend your energies to us so that we can facilitate the plan that was prepared before time. I wish to speak to you now concerning the understandings that you have received from your inner knowingness.

You are preparing for an extensive time that requires that you recognize the time warp in which you are entering. We need to utilize your energies now, to move rapidly into position for events transpiring on this plane. You must yield to these transmissions in order for us to communicate to you the maximum information which is urgently required by you to complete your blueprint. As you allow these transmissions you will develop a greater sensitiveness to our presence, and more interrelationships with our forces; which is needed at this time. You are ready!

You must focus your energies in cooperation with ours to be effective. The freedom that you are experiencing and that you visualize is for this purpose.

I am in a ship, affectionately termed "The Galactic Crusader". And, as you have suspected, my real name is not "Wonton".

You are now creating an understanding that I am an individual, like yourself, that is objective; that has a personality; that functions, only in another dimension in which you are rapidly entering.

Please, in the things that will follow; do not place preconceived ideas or other's experiences as a grid on what you will hear. It is essential that you see and understand the total uniqueness and the necessity not to color it with any known adventures or otherwise from the past. We are in the Now Moment and it is imperative that you function in the Now Moment by allowing absolute spontaneity in your understanding of what is being said. Do not compare it to other adventures or experiences because this is a mind game that derives from a mind that can only conceive what has transpired in the past. This is present. This is now. This is new. This is unique. This is for you. It must be received that way.

The greatest need that you all must understand is focus. As you determine from within, the desires that are there within you, your need is to focus on those desires without allowing the system of denial, which has been so prominent in the earth plane, to impose itself on this information. Do not contemplate limitations that you are so quick to place on yourself or your ideas. Merely focus on the affirmation of what it is that you are desiring, and go forward. Move out! Allow these messages and all messages that you receive within to be your truth and act on them in accordance with that knowingness. As we progress, there will be more specific information; but it is useless to reveal that until you have determined within that this is your desire.

Your doubts are really denials of reality, because you have lived for so long in an environment that is designed to project illusion. You are leaving illusion. You are leaving shadows. You are entering reality! Knowing, now will replace doubting.

Until you acknowledge and agree to the reality of my presence, this monitoring and these messages, you will not perceive the importance of this. It is a circle that you go round and round in. You wonder if it is important, but as long as you merely wonder, you will not receive the importance. And yet, you have a desire you have expressed strongly to receive it. The choice is yours. We can but facilitate this; make it known to you. But you must decide within yourself the reality of it, and thereby create the possibility.

I am a brother who knows you well, who has come to you as an entity or a voice from you know not where. If you determine and agree that you are ready to receive my presence as a reality, an objective reality as yours, then we can proceed to communicate on another level.

<u>The Navigator</u>: Yes, we agree to that.

I know that is your heart, but I sometimes know that the energies on this planet make it difficult for you to grasp that as a reality. That energies coming at you on a moment by moment basis on this planet are more of a reality to you than my presence.

<u>The Navigator</u>: Yes, that's been true.

If you Desire it otherwise it will be. Because, through your knowing and thinking you will create that.

<u>The Navigator:</u> Yes, definitely I do.

<u>Wonton:</u> Good! Your channel has made decisions that are allowing this communication this morning. We anticipate more focus that will allow more information.

Let me say that you are sensing within yourselves the magnitude of this mission. You are sensing a need to enter an understanding of more urgency to function. Not from fear or lack of time, but importance. It appears that nothing else has much reality. And thereby there's no more desire to waste what you call "time" on those shadows, but to enter the reality that you are perceiving.

This is where your urgency comes from. And that facilitates the plan for all entities involved in this transition.

I think that you must be understanding by now that your thoughts and your actions, when yielded to that knowingness within you, brings about your blueprint. So that, direct instructions are not necessary, but you are "it" and you are being "it" every moment. It is merely your mind, trained in denial that will continually tell you, or say to you, or cause you to doubt yourself. It always raises questions as to your motive, the direction in which you're going, the understanding that you have. But if you will proceed, and concentrate, meditate, whatever word you choose, on what is happening, you will see that, as you have allowed the knowingness within you to come forward, you are emotionally, physically, and mentally executing your blueprint; more closely aligned than ever before. You needn't doubt that you will do that. The doubts, the denial, have been part of this dimension that you are leaving; that you can put aside and act spontaneously from that knowingness.

When you know something, call it "feeling" . . . whatever, when you know it, act on it. Then, because you are entering a period where there will be rapid materialization of your blueprint, it will cause you to feel a hesitancy, or a need to backup or to slow down in order to run it through a grid: to determine if it is right or wrong, good or bad, or perfect or not perfect. This will merely be your mind functioning in old patterns.

It is not necessary that you do this. Allow the energy that is to begin to flow . . . freedom to move. Do not perceive it as uncontrolling. This is only your mind judging it. It will be . . . your energy aligned with our energy . . . which will not require analysis, but will direct you to complete the blueprint that you designed. So that you will not be . . . being led, or pressed at this rapid rate, to do anything other than what you have agreed to.

You do not have to fear control by anyone or anything. You do not have to fear going in a wrong direction, you do not have to fear the speed at which these things will transpire to your understanding. It is merely a combination of energies that will allow you to complete rapidly, those things that you designed and agreed on before incarnating.

So, there will be a need to yield to that . . . without fear, and to place no limitations on it. Is that clear? Does that enter your understanding now?

<u>The Navigator:</u> Yes, it speaks to something I was trying to deal with, as far as always running it through my mind and judging it .

<u>Wonton:</u> Let it move. Let it move at its rate. This is all in agreement with you . . . maybe not on a level that your mind comprehends, but it is the level of reality. And you will feel, "But I need more time . . . to contemplate."

Time is an illusion. In the Now Moment that you are entering, time will not be a factor. Energy will flow from you without effort.

The Navigator: Yes, so that means the idea of contemplation I've always had is also unnecessary.

Wonton: It's only necessary for survival. You do that because you fear . . . your survival. You fear that you will not survive, or something will damage that. And that is the way you've kept yourself safe in 3rd dimension. That was the method that's been used. Not necessary where you're going. Not necessary.

You are the Source . . . of everything. There is a need to drop survival. Survival is outdated now . . . has never had . . . "reality" . . . merely an illusion that perpetuated separation. Knowing yourself as one with All That Is . . . what is there to fear? What is there to figure out? What is there to control? It eliminates many things.

But, I am here today to stress that you do not need "time", anymore. You do not need to give it consideration.

You do not need to make decisions or plans in which you take into consideration . . . . time! Make your plans without time. Make them based on what you know within, that you want. Do not, how do you say, do not give place to time. Do not consider it. That will merely stop the flow. The flow will be the combination of energies coming from other dimensions that are necessary to complete the transition. You will need to yield to that.

The Navigator: So . . . we don't need to set a date or allow a time period in any of our ideas about what we want?

Wonton: Yes, that's right. I want you to see that events . . . events are the order of business. Not months or days, or years, or minutes, or anything. It is events that are the order of what is transpiring. You will conceive and know an event. Everything focuses to complete that event. Then you move on to another one.

But you see, in this plane you are so conditioned to take whatever is inside of you: whatever knowingness or ideas, events that are in you, and place them into an outward time frame. You will not find a time frame within you. It does not exist inside. That is outward. That is a limitation to what is within. Function according to the event that you are feeling within you. Focus. Do not divert energy to four or five things because you are contemplating dates or times.

See, when you begin to plan to do something, the limitation enters when you contemplate four or five aspects of what you want to do.

The Navigator: Right. Sequence of events.

Wonton: Yes, as you see them. As you perceive them, but you are creating them when you do that. You are limiting yourself when you perceive all these aspects that haven't even existed yet.

The Navigator: And they're all old ideas.

Wonton: Oh yes! They can only come from the past. They're not new. Then as you break it down . . . your focus . . . into these different aspects, you contemplate time. You put dates. You put limitations as far as how long this will take, or that will take. And what you have going then is multiple events that have been forced into a time schedule and confusion is created. And you experience that. It is simpler than you perceive. If there is something that you desire, that you have a knowingness of, then you focus on having that completed!

The action that will be necessary for you to take will be spontaneous . . . if you allow that. If you are contemplating the now, you will have whatever you need in the moment. You will have the words, the energy, the funds, and the knowingness to complete that event in the moment.

But you plan for all contingencies, all possibilities. You shift focus. You stretch it out. You multiply confusion and time.

The Navigator: So in other words, we have to focus on what we want . . . that's all we do?

Wonton: Yes. Yes. We have already begun to understand this in past communications: what you want, you must manifest! As you concentrate on the completion of that, already knowing it was completed the minute you conceived it, it is merely magnetizing, attracting substance, as you learned to create it. Allow the desire, what you want, to be there: see it as completed. If it is completed, then you do not have to agonize over time or means . . . right?

The Navigator: Right. Because the only thing you can bring to that are old ideas.

Wonton: Yes, and you can thwart it. You can change it. You can put it off. You can give it a time limit.

The Navigator: You can delay it basically.

Wonton: Yes. Yes, that is about all you can do. It is a complete system. It works. This is what it means to . . . when you are instructed that everything will be provided. This is what God knows. This is what you know, but you deny. When you project possibilities of it not happening the way you think it should, you are denying the God within you, and, therefore you will manifest disappointment.

In this transition that you all are contemplating, you have all determined within your hearts that you do not want to be disappointed in this. You want this to work. You want to go forward with this. You want it to be smooth. You want it to be easy. Good. Good. Then do not deny God by doubting.

You have a tremendous amount of energy . . . it is very powerful. Allow it to be. In the plane on which you have dwelt, power is not in the unseen energy. Power to you has been what you could see, what you could produce outwardly . . . that others could judge it as to whether you had put forth enough energy or not to accomplish your goals. And your worth has been based on the amount of energy that others could see and judge. You paid on this basis; how much energy did you put out? Give me something where I can see this energy and I will pay you for it. You earned and deserved it all that way. But the energy I speak of does not require anyone else to pass judgement on it. Do you understand?

<u>The Navigator</u>: Yes, it is the Source.

<u>Wonton:</u> That's correct. So this energy that you have . . . it is so powerful . . . would be judged contrary on this plane. This is what you're coming to know.

That energy does not require outward show. Not even to satisfy your mind or anyone else. That energy is the Source of all things. It creates all things . . . manifests all things. And it only requires, for that power to manifest, that you know that . . . that you not seek to satisfy some outward evaluation, whether it's a clock or a person, or a thought of anyone else's.

In fact, that energy and that power is extremely difficult, when you know it and you are conscious of it, to put it into a clock framework.

You see, if that energy has moved within you . . . that Source . . . God, and said, "This is what I want to do", and you said "O.K, let's do that" . . . how are you going to turn around and control that energy?

<u>The Navigator</u>: You can't.

<u>Wonton:</u> Hmmmmmm! Confusion. Frustration. Are you then going to permit your mind to tell that . . . how to be the Source. No. Understand the power, the force, the energy that is there, must be the Source of everything . . . because it is. When you try to determine with your mind and your intellect how the Source is going to do it . . . ahhhhh, someday you will laugh at that. Someday you will find that humorous, and you will all see how you place it into time frames and grids and boxes, and try to control it. Don't you understand that is the whole 3rd dimensional experience?

Hey, when you agree with it . . . the Source worked the desire in you, directed you to the information and said, "This is our plan". Now, who is responsible to manifest it as yours? Is it yours? Is it your mind's going to work all this out now? We're going to figure it all out . . . what we can do, how we are going to do it, when we're going to do it . . . the time frame in which we're operating. Everything becomes mental. Mental! Because you are so used to denying what you really want . . . feeling that you can't have it, you won't get it. That motivates you to try harder to come up with better schemes. Anxiety sets in because you're operating from the basis . . . that I won't get it; I can't have it; I've got to do something to overcome and make it happen because I'm afraid it won't.

Hey, that's old. That's old. The Source knows nothing of this. The Source does not understand what you're trying to tell it; that it must obey some rules.

Just as when you've been reading this book, you perceived your personality and intellect, and realized that it must be set aside to understand the book. I mean it will argue with the book, it will fight it. What do you think it is doing right now with your desire for this adventure?

<u>The Navigator</u>: The same thing.

<u>Wonton</u>: Yes. Yes. Just be aware of that. Watch it. It has no strength or power unless you give it to it. All things are aligned with what the Source desires within you. When you are aligned with that, you can forget limitations, whether it's time or funds or your mind or anything. Limitations will not be a factor. This is what you are entering. This is the ceasing of time.

It is merely a sensation to you now, but will become more of a reality. Your job is to align with that energy and say yea! Everything yea! No nays. Everything yea!

New. It is so hard to perceive newness. But I contemplate that you are beginning to feel it. All of you are beginning to feel a flow and a movement within you. That is yea, that is powerful, that is gaining momentum . . . and that, within you . . . . you know that, you will let it go, you will release it and allow it. There's just a hesitancy there. You see, always on 3rd dimension . . . always, you want . . . "show me". Show me.

We function continually in our relationship with you, with that imperative command that you must have it always demonstrated to you . . . show me, and then I'll decide.

You have got to understand your own power. Your power says that whatever you decide, will be. So, how does . . . "Show me" . . . relate to that?

See, "show me" is . . . you create my reality for me. You . . . show me what my reality is, and then I'll agree or disagree with it. There's no creativeness in that. Do you understand? There's no creativeness. See, if you say "yea", then you've given your power away to something else to create for you. If you say "nay", then you have just expressed more denial and negativity. But you call this "free will". It's a difficult thing for us to understand sometimes.

<u>The Navigator</u>: But, that's just a creation from separation, from the idea of separation that says, "Show me".

<u>Wonton:</u> Oh yes! Oh yes! The separation from the Source, knowing itself as the Source, and the trusting of that, that is within. That that is within never says . . . "Show me" . . . it says, "I Am". I Am. But a "Show me" comes from the 3rd dimensional mindset that believes that it must see it to believe it. And everything it sees is illusion.

This will sink in, as you say, when you begin to see that what you have insisted on in material manifestation is not reality, but merely a picture, a shadow. So that your thoughts and your aligning with those, as far as the "plan", was reality. It completed itself. It happened.

For manifestation, on this plane, which is a very interesting plane at the moment, because it is both 3rd and 4th . . . there needs to be you, in a body . . . with a mind and personality, as you learned . . . to speak forth the word, in order to manifest it. We cannot do that.

This is very important. You will speak the word that manifests. You can speak the word from many sources; I say two, to simplify. You can speak the word from the source of past experience. That involves limitations, doubts, fears, hope, desire, and anxiety . . . all of those things can come from that source of experience, past experience. Or, you can speak from the source of knowing who you are. That you are all things! That you are one with all things! The source from which you speak will determine the manifestation. Now this is very important in the future . . . as you call the future, time. Determine before you speak your word what will be the source.

This is why it was so necessary to feel the shedding or the dropping away of your past. The letting go of 3rd dimensional experiences, because if you retain them, hold on the them, you will speak the word from past experience. You will create nothing new. But, when you truly know all is illusion . . . that you are the Source, and that you personally are providing a vessel through which to manifest the Source . . . then you can speak the word, knowing that it will manifest.

But do not underestimate the intelligence of the consciousness that is at that moment organizing and creating the word you spoke, do not allow your mind to convince you that you must direct all of that from the viewpoint of the mind . . . past experience. That intelligence is the same intelligence that is in you. It is one intelligence . . . it will create . . . perfectly . . . if you hold a perfect image of what it is you desire, and do not allow limitation or doubts.

Does that make sense to you now?

The Navigator: Yes!

Wonton: Trust the intelligence. It's one and the same as you. We could spend hours on trust. It being a word, but also a feeling, and also a knowingness.

But I do not want to burden you with the thought, at this time, that you have many choices to be made. I do not want to burden you by showing you the different ways and means to approach this with the idea that now, there's some kind of heavy responsibility on you to make the right choices . . . that there's something that you must do.

So, this is why very often I tell you I must be careful because of preconceived ideas. Understand . . . that the Source is all there is. So, there are no decisions to be made apart from the Source . . . that's the dream. Waking up is knowing that. I think often when you contemplate, "oh I have a choice to make, one of them is for God or against God . . . with God or without God". Can that be? Can anything exist apart from God?

The Navigator: No!

Wonton: No! So perhaps being awake is not even being conscious of a decision . . . but just knowing!

—–°°°✦°°°–—

151

<u>Monka</u>: I am here now! Are you here now?

Good, we're all here now . . . I love it! Did you know I was coming back?

<u>Audience</u>: It was just a feeling . . . but yeah, I kinda knew!

<u>Monka</u>: Okay, what are we doing tonight . . . if you're so smart, you ought to know what I've come back to tell you. Right? Okay, I'm ready . . .tell me.

<u>Audience</u>: You came back to tell us that we're still on "schedule".

<u>Monka</u>: Yep . . .yep . . . I should have known better than to ask that question. Yeah, but see, I've been going over the notes from our last session and I covered a hell of a lot of ground. You know . . . filled you in from a "new position", remember? New and different . . . got some excitement and motivation going for what's coming, because you're about to enter a 20 some year time warp see? What's the year, 1991? You're in your nineties, turn of the century, 2000 coming up. Lot of shit coming down these years! You've heard about it, read it all. Well, right now, when you watch your television and read your news, you are going to begin to feel that this "conspiracy" . . . that's the best word . . . is very real. You're going to see it, hear it, and know it from within when you listen to the news.

You've been lied to on all the televisions and in the paper. You're being lied to and what you're being lied to about is that the conspirators . . . all of them . . . by god . . there's tons of them that have entered into this, knowingly or unknowingly . . . have become aware . . . this is what you need to know, they have become aware that there's no way out. They know that there's no way out!

<u>The Navigator</u>: There's no way out as far as the events they've started?

<u>Monka</u>: Oh, they've been convincing themselves. They've seen their plans. They watched over them, manifested them and got a little excited about seeing the culmination of their plans. But, you see, what they kept from you has now dawned on them. In other words, they had a conspiracy to keep you from knowing certain things but there was a bigger conspiracy to keep

them from knowing certain things. You see? They know. It is beginning to dawn on them that there is no way out of any of these conspiratorial plans. They are totally headed for disaster . . . not only for you, but for them. They have not wanted to admit that they did not have control.

The Navigator: They're losing control?

Monka: Oh, no. Not yet. They are frantically meeting . . . frantically planning. And I mean, on a conscious level with people who are not even part of the big deal. They are beginning to realize that this is a no win situation for them. They have created a monster. It is out of control. Now what they do, in this frame of mind, we will see. That's the frantic plans behind closed doors. That's the thought of manipulation because, what do you do when you have planned this ultimate grab for power and control and you begin to see that all of the things you used to gain that, are out of control. You cannot use those instruments anymore. You see, they created weapons for money and control over nations . . . for balance of power. But, the weapon situation is out of control. They have created weapons . . . they have messed with the atmosphere that this planet exists in . . . they have done underground testing's and explosions and they know what they have done. They have created a planet on which they are no longer safe. They want off of it. They want off of this planet. What pleasure in controlling a planet that is blowing itself up? That is killing all life forms. You see, the means used for control is out of control. Do you see that? The medications, the viruses . . . the biological things that have been introduced . . . The weather changes that have been engineered are out of their control.

They have no way to control the spread anymore. They have no way to control what is going to happen to some of these biological germs that they introduced. And, the playing with the weather . . . they have created serious problems. They have upset balances that they cannot control any longer. Their scientists are telling them that there are evidences of debris that is affecting the orbit and will affect the orbit of this planet. What to do? The sun . . . they are telling them the sun is making drastic changes. What to do? They are aware of all the outside forces positioned around this earth. What to do? Do you understand? They are grabbing money to build more weapons to take them up into the skies to fight what they know is up there. Is that a losing battle? Do they now know that's a losing battle? It was stupid to consider it but, they had a goal of absolute control. They were not going to pass that away quickly. This understanding has been coming slowly to them. They were not agreed with it. What started out as a little virus that was going to help on population control has gotten to be an epidemic or a plague that there is no control for. There is no end . . . no solution. There is doubling of numbers, here. There are countries at war, and who are they wiping out . . . workers, laborers that produce the goods that help them to control.

Ohhhh, hey, we've got an uncontrollable situation here. Your seven banks that are controlling everything financially and politically in this world, the heads of those banks, the owners and controllers . . . are aware. It is dawning on them . . . this planet is not a safe place. They have to consider whether they even want this planet and the control here, as well as the conspirators of other dimensions that they entered into a secret plan with. They're not too happy about the situation. You see?

Audience: When did they enter into this conspiracy . . .?

Monka: Long time ago. You would not have the technology that you have if they had not given it to them.

Audience: So, are these extraterrestrials the ones who discovered the "no win" deal? Are they the ones bringing it to the forefront?

Monka: They do not think as you do. They do not think as the heads of government that they have entered into these agreements with, think. They use it, they abuse it, and they leave it. It is of no use to them. It was to their benefit to keep these conspirators "in the dark", as they say, about what was happening. But, they are waking up. Now, there is a waking up about the fact that this is a losing situation by many in the news, in politics, and in your scientific worlds. Heads of state and nations are becoming frantic. When the vibrational field that is created by the key members of the conspiracy is projecting the hopelessness of the situation, it will reach down to the smallest who is participating without knowledge. See what I mean? So, everything you are watching now, everything you are going to hear . . . everything that is going to happen, you are going to think you have entered the Twilight Zone.

You are going to see and you are going to think there is something wrong with you because it is so obvious. You're going to say "What's the matter with me? Why am I seeing this? I know, don't they act strange . . . I'm picking up something. I'm picking up some vibes here". Okay? Watch the rats. The ship is sinking. And it is not known exactly what the choices or decisions will be at this point. Yes. But, it is known that the vibrations being projected in this situation are going to cause pandemonium and confusion in this world . . . much. But it is not in their best interest to reveal the nature of their problem. So, if you watch your news they will tell you about the economy and the banks and they tell you about what Russia is doing . . . hey, forget it. This is the lie.

The important thing I am telling you is that it is already out of control and they know it. They know it . . . it is already finished. But, it is to their benefit to perpetuate the lie as long as they can to give them opportunity to preserve their own asses. And that preserving of your ass, is a vibration tone that will begin to filter down. It will make it a very unsafe place out there. It already is.

There will be a big push for your space program. There already is, but you don't know about it. They are behind more than you will believe. If you think you've been lied to about your wars, you watch what is going on behind the scenes in space, because, this is the rats leaving the ship. They would like to leave here, but they don't want to give this up. They've put a lot of time and effort into it. Well . . . they've got problems.

It's an interesting situation. Not always known what exactly will be created by the conspirators. But, knowing that many of the attitudes adopted in that polarity have a swing to them . . . always. And, they do not know that what they planned for others is what they planned for themselves because, they are all one. You see? They live in the illusion that they are separate entities. But, they are facing what they planned for others. The pandemonium, the fear, the confusion, the destruction that was going to ultimately give them control, that they could move in and take control . . . that they planned . . . they planned for themselves.

<u>The Navigator</u>: They were going to control the pandemonium and now that's out?

<u>Monka</u>: That's what I'm saying. What they created for others must now come to pass for them. Because what they planned for others was the same as planning it for themselves. There is no difference. So does it sound like a lot of doom and gloom? You love it? Why? Because you want the new. And you know the old must go away for the new to come. The sooner, the better!

This is the adventure. You know, the one that you are so brave about because . . . See, for the new to be ushered in, it must see the completion of the old. It must come to its completion. And so, "control" goes back . . . in the control center in your bodies, when man was working his way through these centers as far as creating his reality . . . you've got a little bit, then sort of mediocre, and then you've got a hell of a lot! And let me tell you something. This civilization is "maxing out" in this one. Age of Tyrants . . . is maxing out!

But man has evolved. Okay? And he took that little turn and he's gotten stuck . . . mankind has. So, in this dimension of free will, it has to complete itself . . . the ultimate world control.

But, when you were born, you were born into a family that was evolved in their consciousness to this point in time. Remember your parents, your neighbors, your friends, your teachers . . . did they operate out of their control center?

<u>Audience</u>: Yep, all of them!

<u>Monka</u>: Big thing, wasn't it? Big, big thing! So you've got your genetics and conditioning, didn't you? And if you stop and think about it, it will blow your mind away just how everything you've been fed was for that one purpose. But, you see . . . that has never satisfied you. If it had, why have you been searching and reading all these years? You were looking because you knew better! You knew something else.

Let me tell you something. A lot of people . . . this is as far as they want to go. They want to complete their adventures in this thing of control. They are God! They want to pursue this thing to the ultimate . . .

complete it and gain their wisdom from it. No problem! You see, when God contemplated the third dimensional density in which you go and play "hide-and-seek" with yourself, in order to explore all possibilities, and then you had to create this one. And why create an adventure like that, if not to gain the wisdom?

Now, they're just going to go right on creating their reality. You watch it. They're going to do their own thing. They're going to have it just like they want it. Yes, they will. Just not in your ballgame. You've got another ballgame going. You see, there are lots of ball games going . . . a lot of ballparks out there. Okay? They are evolving, but they are not going to do it here. Understand? This is changing. This earth is not going to be inhabited except by people who are willing to make that "jump of love" . . . and they may have looked stupid and endured a lot of persecution in the past . . . but they are ready for the New World. And the planet has chosen the same. The earth will manifest the realization of what it desires . . . the same as those who have chosen love. They are desiring a manifestation and a realization of that in matter! They will get what they are creating . . . it will happen! So, when I say "here" and "there", remember, we're going where there is no time. So don't get worried about it, you're not going to care where "here" and "there" are.

Creation is going forward and you are going to have fun because there's going to be that combination of that knowingness of the One Consciousness with this little gadget up here, called the brain, that is going to create . . . . God only knows what! But, it's going to be fun. Did you know that? Golly . . . . hard for you to think how new this is going to be. It's going to be new. You have infinite possibilities. That's who you are . . . you're that One Consciousness that wanted a pair of eyes, some ears, and a brain up here, so it could get with it.

Infinite possibilities for creativity, motivated by love. You know? And you've known this love. You've known this oneness. But there's a whole creation and all that's been going on is to culminate at this point where all this is known through this instrument, which is fantastic . . . . the Gods, you, have created this instrument. You have always had this purpose and plan for it. Yep. You've got many adventures. What's that Star Trek saying?

<u>Audience</u>: To boldly go where no man has gone before.

157

<u>Monka</u>: That's what you just did coming here. Now, "man" has come here before but not like this. You were boldly going where we had never gone.

<u>The Navigator</u>: Yeah, you keep saying we are real brave.

<u>Monka</u>: Brave as hell! Man, let me tell you something. We had some casualties down here. There have been a lot of casualties on this plane. No . . . now, you've got a sure fire system built up. You planned a sure fire system before you came here . . . going to get a lot of help. Those of you who have come from other dimensions, who are joining together with all of "yourselves" will be a lot of that help . . . to get this "ship" ready to go where it's going.

Okay, ya'll have fun with this . . . okay? But don't forget . . . "be it"! It is knowing it within you that . . . you are "All That Is". See, I don't want to talk about all this exciting stuff that's going to happen . . . taking you out of time and this trip . . . and you think it's going to be Christmas with all these gifts for you. I want you to know that what you're getting is . . . you! More of you! Get ready and enjoy the journey. My God, don't forget to "enjoy"!

Thanks for coming folks, see you again . . . Good night!

All hail the power of the "I am"! All Hail the power of the "I AM", the "I AM That I AM"!

Greetings from the Merkabah . . . from the source of the golden light that radiates amoung you now. Greetings brothers and sisters. I am here to speak to you of the light that you must shine throughout the land as the kindred of the "One New Man". The one new man is coming forth. It is coming forth. It is shining. It is within your hearts now.

"I Am That I Am". Allow the power. Allow the light. Allow the love that is the "I Am That I Am" to flow from you to be All That Is . . . to show forth upon this earth the Sun . . . the Radiant Son. "I Am That I Am" . . . the ultimate love is now shined forth from all those within this beam.

This beam bathes and radiates you. This beam is the light that you are. Be one with it. Join with it. Bring forth the New. Bring forth the

New that you are . . . that you have brought here to this dearly beloved planet to reflect "All That Is" . . . the love, the power, the peace, and the knowingness that is you.

You are loved greatly. You are enjoyed greatly. You are anticipated and there is an awaiting of the full manifestation of the Gods that you are upon this planet. Time is short.

May all grace and love and peace be yours in this now moment.

Athena speaking from my heart to your heart. Greetings! There was an interruption planned by the Merkabah. The connection must be established from time to time . . . the source of power which is to radiate and speak to you, to establish within you the vibrations to seek the oneness and harmony that you're very near to completing with them.

So, last time we discussed an interesting adventure . . . "removal from time". Did anyone experience that . . . or did anyone contemplate "where are you going when you leave"?

<u>The Navigator</u>: To fifth dimension . . . that's out of time.

<u>Athena</u>: Fifth alright . . . and what is fifth? You see, there is a question in order. Is it possible that you already exist there now, dreaming about being here? Is this the dream? And so, the vibrational field that is now covering you is vibrating within you to recall the truth of your awake state . . . and "this" should be becoming more dreamlike to you.

You are dreaming . . . you are dreaming. So, when I drew the picture and showed you that we would be taking you out of time, what was I saying? You are coming out of the dream! It has been a wonderful dream, has it not? You've been very creative in your dreams . . . learned many things, but you know, when you dream, think about it . . . you are experiencing color, sound, pictures of environments as if they were very "real". Is that correct? When you are experiencing them, they are very real, but you are lying on the bed . . . asleep.

Your removal from time . . . you are going nowhere. You are going nowhere because you are "All That Is". You need go nowhere. You are it!

But, you will remember that you were dreaming. You will remember that your consciousness entered a dream just as it does at night when you sleep. You have no problems when you wake up in the morning, no alarm, no concern because the night before you dreamed who knows what . . . many vivid, weird things, some maybe very pleasant, some not so pleasant. They were your own creations. It doesn't alarm you when you wake up in the morning. No! So it should not alarm you now when you wake up and become conscious that you have been dreaming.

I believe that the thought behind the message entering when it did from the "I Am" force, was an expression of love and a demonstration of your own union with that love and that power that is you. That is you . . . you are it!

I am here representing that oneness. That is what my energy is here for, as is everyone who comes through and speaks with you, because that is where you came from. You came from that oneness and that knowingness of that oneness and it is time now that you begin to experience that consciousness of that oneness.

You create the reality now that determines your ability to enter that. Now, we have discussed that many will enter it dramatically, without preparation. You have not chosen that. But, you are to be involved in the preparation for that. That is what all has been about. Thought creates your reality and you are "thought".

And, you are leaving. You are experiencing now the fourth dimension and you are going on . . . and there is a need to vibrate at those dimensions of "I Am That I Am", in order to have full mastery of yourself in this body and not the thoughts that lower the vibrations. So, in order to allow the vibration of the thought of who you are, I must also bring you the thought that "All" exists in this moment.

I am telling you this because the lecture begun last time was to prepare you for this event. Do you recall what I said? So I am explaining some of this to help you let go of the solidity of the form and structure that you have given to space and time. You have focused on space and time and that is what you are dealing with now in your day to day experience. Think about it.

Everything that we have discussed, everything that we have asked you to ponder and consider, when you get down to your thinking process concerning it, you will see that your "dilemma" has been...space and time. That is your dilemma in understanding what is happening to you because you are focused in this space and this time and it is difficult for you to understand, because of that.

So, we must discuss this now moment because that is the only "time and space" that you can be "All That Is". All of you are wishing to be it at a later time because, you'll be ready then . . . and, really you'll have no choice then and many of you here would like to have your power placed somewhere else and it will not be. It must dwell in you . . . in the focus that you are . . . the power must dwell there to say that "I Am All That Is", and know it.

So, let's go on to the "now moment" so that can be your reality that you create. I have a drawing (Figure 28). That is "You". Did I do a good likeness? Now there is another drawing (Figure 29) of your clock to show you how you experience time now. See . . . you have glimpsed the "now moment" in time right? And you live in your moments as one minute, two minutes, three, four, five minutes and so forth.

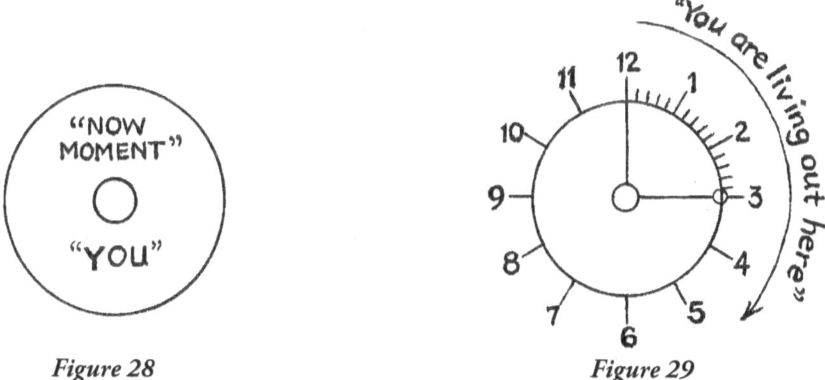

Figure 28   Figure 29

So this is your clock, there are your twelve hours broken down into five, ten, fifteen, etc, that are your minutes . . . . this is where you live. You say, "What time is it?" You need to know that . . . did you know that you are existing here in time and it's a wonderful marvelous creation of yours but, totally unnecessary? Did you know that the Indians didn't have watches? They had events . . . the same as we have told you that we operate by. The sun came up and the sun went down. That was an event.

As the sun traveled across the heavens and was out of sight . . . that was an event. There was no measurement of minutes or hours, at all . . . there was no need for it.

Now, why do you suppose that it was necessary to do this? If we have multiple, universal people out here, living according to their own event . . . doing what they want to in that event . . . . creating as they see it for that day . . . . it is difficult to control. We must get everyone onto the same creation of reality in order to exercise control, if we desire that . . . if this is our dream. So, if we can institute this little thing everywhere in the world, then we have every one focused to a certain time in that event of the sun rising and the sun going down.

You need to know this because you need to know what you've bought into. There is a certain amount of uniformity created all over the world if what everybody is doing can be expected and known. It is all "outward" based on this, not "inward" based on your own knowingness and desires. And, you live around this . . . . and around this . . . . and around this. That's the way you go through the day . . . on this merry-go-round that was created so there could be a uniformity of social behavior. To fit everybody in it, we have to have uniformity. You see? So we've got it for different periods of your Earth's orbit . . . . times when the sun goes down . . . . sun comes up. But, everyone must be at work at a certain time because everyone must work. And then we need the times to eat and times to sleep . . . so that we can be back at work . . . or whatever you "must do".

Absolutes . . . . you see? Because, if you begin to listen to your body and your body begins to tell you something other in the now moment than what the clock is telling you, will you obey it? Will you obey it? Will you look within and trust what you are feeling within or will you get frantic and begin to say "yeah, it's this time of day and it's this week in this month and tomorrow . . . . what about this and what about that'? And, yet, we have come here and you full well know that the energy that is manifesting within you and that we are bringing here and that is being brought to this planet, is changing this body. It's changing the cells. That is its purpose.

How then do we change the cells? If you are functioning on this clock, which the intentions, the vibrations and reasons that this was set up was to control you and not allow you to know from within what to do but only . . . . to work from without. Look at the clock, this does not exist for you. This is a control mechanism and yet, you are being controlled by this every day. Because, you get to the month . . . . . don't you. There's your calendar *(Figure 30)* . . . do you pay attention to this? Do you say "it's August and it's hot in August, but fall is coming and it will get colder because fall is cool". You see? So, you are calculating who and where you are by this thought.

What else do you use . . . remember our "timeline" *(Figure 31)*, what you call, "linear reality"? You know "yourself" according to this also.

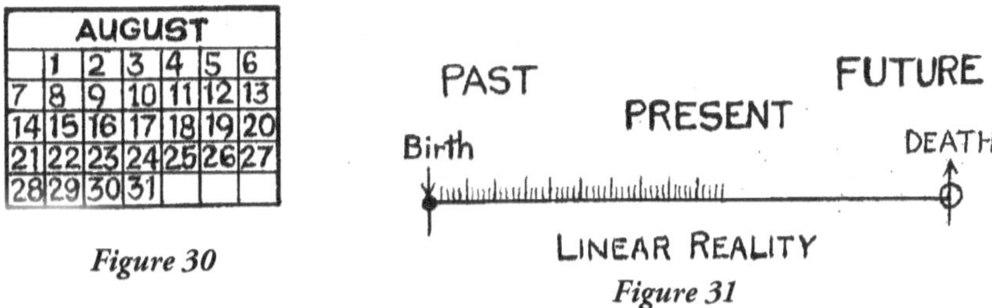

Figure 30

Figure 31

So if you are functioning on this clock, on this day, of this month, in this year, then you are calculating your moments, your years, linearly . . . correct? This is how you established your identity and the minute you were born, whatever time that was . . . you began to walk around and around this circle on the outskirts of your own self . . . without awareness. And you began to measure your years . . . . your birthdays, how old you are. As long as you stay on this merry-go-round, it will go to a certain point . . . it has an ending to it. You are measuring the days until your death. There is a destiny involved with living as you live now . . . identifying and preoccupied with this.

You see, "being" . . . being here now is being in the consciousness of All That Is. There is nothing outside of it that controls it. That consciousness doesn't even consider anything but itself as the Source of everything in its reality.

When I discussed with you that you would be removed from space and time, I said I would tell you how you would function in space and time. Some words are necessary, I feel, because there are others on this earth who experienced something happening . . . an accident, or drug related incidences, etc . . . . that have come back and been in this vibration and this out here was very puzzling to them and they've had a difficult time relating to this consciousness, trying to express without their knowingness of themselves.

You are going to go through this and understand this explicitly in your own experience because there is a point in time coming . . . a quantum leap, when many will enter into this knowing of themselves in one moment in time. You will be most beneficial in being able to convey, because of your own understanding and gradual experience and awakening of yourself in this consciousness . . . how to relate.

Many of you have had an image when we are coming to the now moment. We are taking you out of space and time. You have attempted to visualize what this meant. You can forget everything you visualized. Your mind does not know this. Your mind has no experience of this.

Remember, we told you that "we're changing positions . . . changing identities"? You've been living out here. But the "Now", the absolute that we are talking about is living totally from this center. You are familiar with these moments out here on your clock, but you have one big moment . . . one "now" within you, the "zero", the "cause" that creates all these moments, the "effects" out here. And how do "you" do it? Well, let's go back . . . . *(Figure 32)*

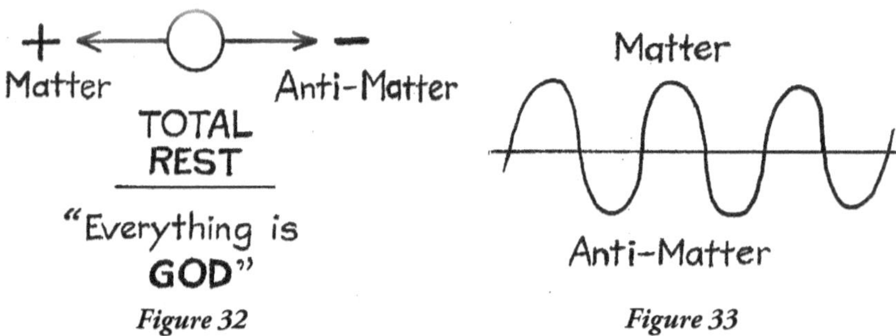

Figure 32

Figure 33

Everything is rest, right? Everything is God. You are all that is. When you create a moment that is expressed in your reality and realized . . . this one right now . . . in consciousness, you express it in energy as a plus. This exists. At the same moment that you have expressed a plus expression that you are experiencing, right now . . . there is a minus moment created simultaneously . . . that you do not experience. Matter . . . antimatter (Figure 33). Every charge of energy has an equal, opposite charge happening instantly and faster than you can see . . . cancelling out that movement, so that in reality neither one of them exist. There is only God . . . total rest. We've told you there is nothing but God. In reality, that is total and complete rest . . . zero. This is the way He creates the illusion of movement, space, time, and matter.

Now, the absolute that we are talking about is living totally from this center in you. The vibration of total rest . . . without any concern for this timeline. Now you say to me, "Athena, What does this mean? Are you telling me that I'm going to abandon thinking in terms of my needs in the future? Well, Athena, you can't mean that." You say, "Athena, this is a little bit much". Yes, it is . . . but, did you know that being "All That Is" is a little bit much?

You see? It's not Fantasyland, it's not a "nice thought" . . . something you've always wanted and maybe you'll get someday. It is now a reality for each of you, because right now, your "consciousness that you are" in that position of rest reflects the positive and negative energy simultaneously and creates the seeming illusion of space and time. And every point and particle . . . the moment it is born . . . dies. So, in reality, there is only one existence . . . and it is "you" . . . here you are, the "Big Zero". Now, I am telling you this because, you must understand that when you are thinking and creating on your clock, from your timeline . . . and you say one moment is following another and this moment you are in this room because in the last moment you were in this room and in the next moment you will be in this room . . . in reality, there is not one second, not one particle in this room . . . that is not brand new in this moment.

You are a new creation, every moment. Every particle in your body was born and died simultaneously and another one and another one . . . So fast that you have the illusion of solidity . . . Of space and time and movement. That is what you are experiencing now.

When I tell you that you are "All That Is", you are "It" right now . . . that is an unknown to you . . . being "All That Is" in a physical form. Can we allow this thought that "that unknown" you will be is a new creation? You are now . . . a new creation, brand new. This is what Christ brought the message of . . . to this planet . . . because it was time to begin to bring that vibration of the "New Creation". This is what is in you . . . do you see?

This is the new experience that you are becoming aware of and that we are preparing you for. Now, I have chosen a symbol (Figure 34) that will stay with you so that you will recognize the symbol, if not the words . . . to understand the feeling that you are entering into.

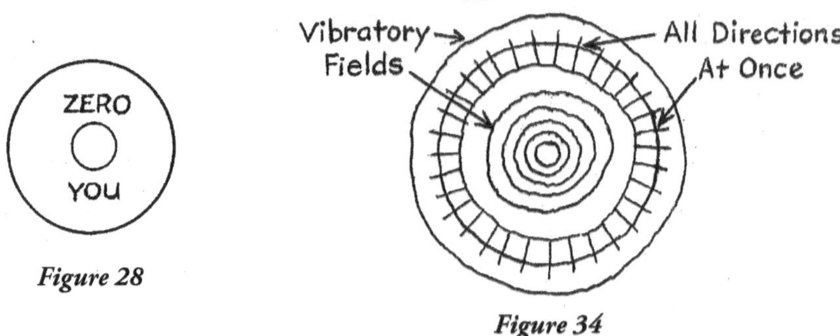

Figure 28

Figure 34

Here you are, in that inner knowing, that consciousness . . . (Figure 28) that core which is, in reality, your consciousness . . .is you, the Zero or whatever you choose to call it . . . Receiving the vibration of knowing yourself in that consciousness and you will open your eyes, your ears, your five senses . . . . and you are going to experience yourself this way. (Figure 34) See? All realities spiral out from the center and know themselves always to be "present". You will not experience yourself focused on your "clock circle" (Figure 29 pg. 161) and you will not experience yourself on your calendar. You will not feel that. You will not identify the way you have identified and perceived yourself here. You will perceive expansion in all directions at one time . . . . simultaneously.

Your timeline (Figure 31) . . . there was your past, this is your present that will be your future as your clock moves around. This, your present is what all have taught is the "Now moment". Your identity, your consciousness, your perception of yourself will be expanded so that all in the present, past and future will all exist for you simultaneously . . . all will be there. There will be no past, present and future as you have experienced them in this identity. There will be one "present" . . . past, present, and future . . . all. You will feel expansion within your consciousness. I do not mean your bodies will blow up. But, your consciousness will make you feel very large. Expanded! You are going to expand in all directions . . . not one direction. Understand? To be in the "Present" is to have your consciousness focused, radiating out from you in all directions.

Do you begin to see why it is difficult to put this into words? But, these drawings will mean very much to you. You see? What does it mean to be expanded? This means that your awareness is radiating all out from you in all directions. Everything grows in this way. Everything. Your body grew this way. A small child grows, not just up, or not just in one direction . . . but, a child grows from a center core out. You watched your bodies do this . . . all at once. When your arm grew, it grew from a center out. When the tree grew, it had circles . . . it grew in all directions. All things grow this way. They all expand. Your consciousness does also. You see? Because you grow and expand, and your awareness is in a spiraling field . . . within this consciousness that you know yourself . . . you are surrounded by vibratory fields, even when you go into your consciousness. You can traverse the different vibratory fields. Each one has a different vibration but, it does not stop with this body because, just as when a pebble is dropped into a river or pond . . . there are waves. Here you are . . . I said you were expanding. How? How do you grow and how does the arm grow? It grows from the center out. How does it do it? It must be spiraling and encircled by a wave of vibration so that it is simultaneously growing in all directions at once. Correct? Your consciousness is encircled in a spiral of waves of frequencies or vibrations that increase and increase and increase. In fact, your body is right now encircled by a wave or vibration that we've called your "Light Body" . . . manifesting this form here . . . that encloses and circles this . . . on and on. Each circle being a different frequency level of vibration.

So, let me show you how this works out. You are here . . . the spaceships and planets are here. You envision taking a journey from here through space and time to a planet or spaceship. But, in reality, you never go anywhere except these concentric circles . . . radiating back and forth . . . the pulsing . . . the in and out . . . the reflection from the center creating a manifestation and this vibration of the manifestation going back . . . constantly cycling into reality or manifestation, as you know it, and back into the Source from which it comes. There are concentric rings, waves of energy that are infinite within you and out. Your scientists have taken your body and isolated one cell . . . have attempted to go within and find the Source of all life. They are also looking at telescopes, space travel, and attempting to go out beyond the body and connect with other beings.

All circles are a frequency vibration. When you are here, you are vibrating at a certain rate. When you can see the light body around you and others, then you are vibrating on this wave. Picture a pebble dropped into water and picture what happens to the water as the rings crest and trough . . . out, away from it . . . a continual field of waves out from you and your consciousness. You can go within that consciousness and traverse to the furthest planet or to the tiniest cell, merely, by vibrating at the rate of the energy field, the crest of the wave. It is within and without and in these realities there is form and structure . . . not the same as you are used to here. This next dimension that we have been discussing has form and structure . . . similar . . . almost exactly . . . but, there are big differences in the vibratory rate of that circle.

Now, I am bringing a very complex and difficult understanding for your minds but, possibly, will make it simpler for you to understand the illusion that you have concerning this body and its march around the clock in time . . . in this focus. So now, do you want to know what the choice is? You want to know what you've already chosen. You are not on this. Wake up. You have chosen . . . many long years ago, eons, "non-time" . . . you chose. You did not choose to age with this clock. You chose to understand and master this dimension . . . out of love for this dimension. Isn't it wonderful? When you begin, in that now moment, to comprehend what the universal consciousness will tell you about this creation of illusion . . . you're going to be awed with yourself. This is wonderful. You are wonderful. All of this proves it. Isn't this clever . . . the way you think that you are living form one moment to another being the same person. How else to create it if there is nothing but you?

If you're All That Is . . . how do you become a creator? You must split . . . create the birth and death of illusion . . . pulsing . . . that's All That Is. It's a pulse . . . out and in . . . out and in. Why is energy a wave? Your reality . . . matter . . . antimatter. At every point the particle is a new you. This is how you cease to age . . . and this is how we're going to be together.

<u>Audience</u>: We already are?

Uh . . . . huh . . . never left this circle. Never left the now moment but created this fantastic illusion of time passing and fooled yourself beautifully down here. Didn't you? So, this is the image that must be seen through. This is the illusion that must be discovered to know yourself in the now moment. The past . . . the past . . . is a no thing, in the way you have perceived it. From this consciousness, you know the whole thing. It already happened and all of it is there. Everything . . . every possibility is right in there!

Where are you going to get more energy if you don't get it from the original thought? There is nothing else. All energy resides there . . . all consciousness. But, this marvelous little scene here had a purpose and a plan encoded within it to go on. Creation will never cease. The experience of yourself will never cease . . . infinite creations. Well, how about his one where you have form and structure and a body . . . how about becoming aware of this in this body to continue creation. You see? When I say that you're "All That Is", don't think that means that you've got to go back and be some kind of little ball of light and float around the heavens.

What does it mean to be you in the now moment? If you thought, "Anything I want to be", would you become unlimited? If you said "This was my reality . . . this is my truth", would you become unlimited in your abilities, in your desires . . . in your manifestations? Because, you see, everyone in this room is manifesting from the same reality which is the on-goingness of creation . . . . the projection of this ability to continue to create through love. That is your desire. That is why you are here. You are all here, now . . . desiring to unify with the energy that you left in that separation of illusion. You are desiring to experience that rest . . . that oneness that you have with us who are coming and talking and all that know and share the vibration of love. That is home. That is home.

Home is a state of consciousness. Home is a state of consciousness. Home is that state of consciousness that knows nothing but complete and total love and there is a continual exchange of that vibration among you with no illusions to say that "I am separate".

But, now I want to say something. This understanding . . . this entering in to that zero point of rest . . . is something that you do alone . . . totally alone. That's how you got born in this dimension and that's how you leave it. You did it from within yourself, within a state of seeming aloneness and that's why you say "I am alone and I want to go home". That is the desire . . . the want that is manifesting in each one of you, creating a reality which is coming through and manifesting in your reality right now. But, none of you can sit now and wait to make this journey to that now moment.

It must be done. You must take that body that you brought into a lone separate experience and in that body and alone separate consciousness, you must understand that you never, ever were alone . . . could not be. You must master the illusion. Wake up in the dream of separation. That is your mission. How that will work from that moment on . . . you will know in the now moment as you create them.

Now, you say, "Why do I have to manifest it if I already know it and I've already been it?" Because, it has not been done in that body. You want to transmute that body for the experience of going forth into other dimensions and spaces . . . and you need the body . . . because as long as you do not have a body, you are limited in that dimension and that body will be needed for the new experiences on all levels. You will have conquered and mastered all levels by becoming the "I Am" in this dimension. You must focus on conquering this dimension of space and time. You can't escape it. It is needed by the soul that you are . . . for the journey that you are beginning. Do you understand? So, this is it. Begin to feel this . . . begin to know this . . . begin to say, "I Am". This is "I Am That I Am". You see? Now, don't take my word for it . . . you're not going to anyway. Find out for yourself experientially. Because . . . and I gave you one reason and I'm going to give you another . . . you, consciously waking up to this within yourself . . . joined with all others doing it . . . are the New Creation!

Partnership, remember? Have you forgotten you have a partner? See, consciousness means . . . consciously knowing that you are in agreement . . . you are merged. Being aware that there is a greater consciousness of which you are a part, focused on the planet where you are. Remember . . . remember, you are the ground troops. You have the eyes, you have the ears, you have the feet, you have the hands . . . you have the legs and you look like everybody else here. And, you know the map . . . you know your way around. There is a host of beings on all levels of consciousness who are wonderful and who are facilitating this transmutation and you don't need the whole plan to do your job. In fact, you will not receive it to do what you have to begin to do. In order to do it, you must focus on your part of the plan . . . the strategy. It's alright to do that. Remember that I said that. Because, you can expand on your thought to the point where you're saying, "Golly, we've got to work all this out". Remember what this mind likes to do down here. Within this expanded consciousness, where you choose to focus is your blueprint. The battle plans, the strategy, the mission, the "way", is within you to focus and do what you came to do.

You are becoming the Source. You are becoming a Central Sun, that will position itself . . . The same as the Central Sun that created all these universes and galaxies . . . you will become a Central Sun, a source of energy . . . that will position itself in the vast unknown and create many more universes and galaxies and whatever you choose to create. But, this time the Gods who do it will have mastered the forms that they have created and there will be no necessity to get stuck in them. You see? However, as clever as we all are, we may create something else to get stuck in. Who knows? Correct? Yes! Clever Gods . . . but, we have fun . . . always fun.

I will let the vibrations rest here. It is so much simpler that you know. Goodnight . . . Love you all. Enjoy yourselves!

<u>Ola & The Navigator: Transmission</u>

Good morning . . . . Wonton speaks,

We are at a crossroads in our understanding now, that is very important for you to grasp . . . the understanding that is now emerging from within you.

You have perceived a presence that is urgently pressing you to manifest a Consciousness that is unfamiliar to you, but will . . . very soon, be natural. That Consciousness is all that you are. That awareness is becoming more clear to you. Allow and do not hesitate . . . for this is the energy combination that we have spoken of. Many names, many words have been used to describe this and, understand, that I am only using more words that do not adequately and can never adequately explain this event to you.

Your feeling will have more expression and thereby produce more knowing. Understand that we always have problems with words. And, I know that you continually, upon hearing these words, go within and search for the feeling that they are expressing. That is a very private understanding that is within you.

This accounts for so much teaching at the present time concerning "going within", and the stress that has been placed upon trusting that. You have a history of having denied it. Now, you must allow it completely, it's manifestation into this dimension, because this is transforming this dimension . . . at the same time, attracting and bringing in the New.

This day will be one in which you will understand more and more . . . the absence of time. You are contemplating your desires. You are contemplating the completion . . . "waiting". This is a habit that will become . . . "old hat". The word "wait" can be dropped from your vocabulary . . . the same as "time" will be dropped from your experience. You are not waiting for anything if it has already been completed. Out of your desire to maintain this word, you project it onto manifestation. You say that . . . . it is completed. I see it, I feel it, I know it. But now, I must "wait" for the manifestation of what it is that is completed. This is because, in the past, this has been the method by which all things appear in your world . . . in 3rd dimensional experience. Consider now, that in the "now moment", that we are entering . . . that there will be a new process initiated for the manifestation. That process does not use the word "wait", with all of the negative connotations that have been applied to it.

When you contemplate a desire or an image completed . . . then, that understanding is maintained in the "Now Moment". You must exit the moment to contemplate waiting. If you can grasp that I am attempting to describe to you a process in which your image and your projection is completed . . . then you will begin to visualize in the now moment, "that" . . . . as a reality. Because, it is more of a reality than the manifestation that you have thought to be waiting for. Can you follow me?

You have seen or imagined yourself to be locked in and permanent in a given scene. You have been, of late, speaking of mobility. That is what I am speaking of now. You are much more mobile than you know.

<u>The Navigator</u>: I guess so, if it all depends on just a thought.

<u>Wonton</u>: Yes. Waiting involves staying in one place until it comes to you . . . whatever you are requesting or desiring.

<u>The Navigator</u>: All 3rd dimension means.

<u>Wonton</u>: Yes. But, contemplate that consciousness is never still. Consciousness is always fluid and moving. When you begin to live in your consciousness, you will be always moving . . . changing. So you begin with the desire that you have pictured . . . the feeling and knowingness that it is complete. You do not now . . . wait for it to arrive in time . . . but, you go to it in consciousness. You move into another consciousness in which that is a reality. Now, I know that this is difficult. Ummmmmmmm, your channel is having difficulty comprehending what it is that she sees and allowing the words to proceed. You are having difficulty in believing this. The reason being . . . we are dealing with living in your consciousness, in which you have not been sovereign. You have been living in the world. Remember . . . the world is in your consciousness . . . remember?

Now, there is a need for expansion of consciousness on this issue, that is being introduced. I will not rush you. I will not give any imperative command to this. I merely ask that you allow this and the knowingness within will confirm it. But, I realize this is a big jump . . . to cease to locate yourself in space and time.

But, let me ask you . . . if you are God, if you and God are one, and if God is everything . . isn't it merely a matter of awareness that has you locked into one space and one time and a vision of something else located in another space . . . with a certain amount of time and distance.

<u>The Navigator</u>: Absolutely. It's a focal point of awareness.

<u>Wonton</u>: Ahhhh, yes! Yes. Please begin to allow yourself the knowingness that your consciousness can be wherever it focuses. You have understood that wherever your attention is focused, it creates a reality in which you experience your being. Is that correct?

<u>The Navigator</u>: Yes.

173

<u>Wonton</u>: I'm merely enlarging on that. I am merely wanting to break you out of the pattern of thinking that . . . "I", (you) . . . are located and can only focus where you are at any given time.

Your consciousness is the reality and whatever your consciousness or wherever your consciousness chooses to focus . . . you will be.

As you allow more awareness of yourself, as everything, it will become more difficult for you to locate yourself in one space and one time. You will be everywhere, according to your desires at any time . . . as you understand time.

Now, obviously there is a more advanced teaching on this that will be presented as we proceed. However, at this moment, the necessary thing for you is to deal with the word "wait". I have revealed some of this to you in order to understand where I'm coming from when I tell you that "wait", is not a word that you need anymore.

You have probably already begun to experience that. You may have thought you were waiting at a point in time. But, when the time arrived that you were waiting for . . . you cannot remember waiting. Why do you suppose that is?

<u>The Navigator</u>: Because, the difference between our focus of awareness before it arrived, and the focus of our awareness after it arrived, didn't . . . there was no space and time between that. All we were aware of was the focus that we had.

<u>Wonton</u>: So, we are speaking of a mobile, fluid, consciousness that can focus at one point and then change its focus to another point, thereby realizing a different reality. And the only reason for a need for a lapse of time would be because you proclaimed that you would be "waiting". Is that correct?

<u>The Navigator</u>: Yes, it was.

<u>Wonton</u>: Was there any other need for a lapse of time, as you know it, or conceive of it . . . between one point of focus and another point of focus? What created that time or that waiting?

<u>The Navigator</u>: It was our sense that there had to be that period of time.

<u>Wonton</u>: Well, let me put it another way . . . where did the waiting exist?

<u>The Navigator</u>: In space and time.

<u>Wonton</u>: No.

<u>The Navigator</u>: Oh, in our consciousness.

<u>Wonton</u>: Yes. Yes . . . right! Can you remove that now from your consciousness . . . if that's the only place it existed?

<u>The Navigator</u>: Yes.

<u>Wonton</u>: As long as it is necessary, you will have a sense of being in space and time. As long as it is necessary for this transition, for your own awareness and those observing. You will have some sense. There will not be a pure dwelling in consciousness, because that is not your mission at this point. That does not facilitate what it is that you want to do.

However, we can speed up the process, without disturbing that need, by your grasping some of what I am saying and also, this will allow you to flow more rapidly with the energy combination that I've spoken of previously. Because, you are going to be asking yourself . . . "How do I cooperate with this energy?" The understanding that I have presented and intimated to you on a very beginning level today . . . will help you in answering the question of "how".

I believe, as you contemplate this, the knowingness and the reality of it, will enter your awareness. Are there any questions at this point?

<u>The Navigator</u>: I did have one thing that had occurred to me when you were talking about . . . "this being presented on a beginning level". Does that refer to the "unknown" factors, which 3rd dimensionally, we haven't experienced? But, do the same principles apply because they're in our consciousness? We do know them?

175

<u>Wonton</u>: That's true. And, by consciously becoming aware of what I'm saying, you will facilitate the immediate realization of what it is you want without projecting waiting. But . . . no, you are not being removed from manifestation and materialization into a pure state of consciousness. Even though, there are those who dwell there. But, that is not your mission. You are identified with this earth and this materialization of the body. But, the now moment that we are rendezvousing with . . . requires that you expand your awareness to know and experience the mobility of your consciousness. Does that clear anything up?

<u>The Navigator</u>: Yes.

<u>Wonton</u>: But, again, we have agreed that you are not removed from space and time. You're not seeking to be. You are seeking to assimilate and put into practice what we are speaking of now . . . in . . . bringing it into time and space. That's necessary for the transition.

You are not spending time now, seeking some level of awareness for you own personal growth. So, this is contemplated in the light of what you are desiring to do, that is involved with . . . the plan for earth.

<u>The Navigator</u>: Correct.

<u>Wonton</u>: That may help you to reconcile the two. I am not attempting to do that for you. At the moment, I am attempting to introduce an idea, a thought . . . that will grow and allow you to facilitate the plan within space and time.

You have conceived of the more advanced understanding of this. It is there and it is a knowingness in you . . . that it is transpiring. But, it is not necessary at the moment. One of the reasons for the day to day transmissions is to remain in touch with the plans and unfoldment each day, rather than you to wander in your consciousness . . . many, many light years away . . . contemplating the spiritual significance of these truths.

<u>The Navigator</u>: I appreciate that perspective.

<u>Wonton</u>: Your knowingness . . . outside of "step 1" on this earth . . . is much more advanced than you are aware of at this time. You are becoming more aware. I am merely confirming what you already have and know, and thereby, we are not really entering into a process of expanding your awareness for the personal growth.

The desire that has been in you, has been to coordinate your efforts with those of other dimensions and beings . . . entities who are here for the transition. And therefore, the information being related now, will facilitate that coordination and allow the speed with which you are capable of functioning in that plan, which is yet unknown to you. These energies that you are combining with have a vibration that you are attempting to blend yours with. You will feel or mentally comprehend it, in one sense as speed . . . "It's going too fast" . . . because of the rate of vibration of the energies that you are combining with. And, the information I'm bringing to you today, is for you to "hang loose" a little bit and not try to maintain a vibration that you feel comfortable with . . . but, that you will be more allowing of the mobility of your own consciousness to blend and coordinate these energies . . . to move forward into the new. You understand that we must also, in a sense, slow our vibration and energies to a point at which you can bring your energy to meet and blend.

<u>The Navigator</u>: Yes. I understand that.

<u>Wonton</u>: It is not that you are being brought to an impossible situation for you. It is a coordinated effort that was agreed upon before time. And, so much of what you try to describe as your feelings, that you say, "is happening to you" . . . is merely vibration. It's merely vibration.

So, you have nothing to fear and nothing to wait for. Everything that is necessary . . . All preparation, all means, everything . . . is on schedule. And, we are delighted at this opportunity that has presented itself at this time. We're very anxious to express to you, too . . . at this moment, the love that we have for your focus and desire at this time. Because, this is the cooperation that must exist. And, we are very elated in ourselves because of the union that is now possible. We can only anticipate greater joy in this.

<u>The Navigator</u>: The same is true for us . . . very much so.

<u>Wonton</u>: Thank you for your attention today. I feel that before I leave, I need to interject a comment here that may be of help to you today. Do not yield to the desire to understand it with your mind. Of course, this will be the first response to new information as has been in the past. But, coming from the now moment, because of the time warp that you are now entering, you may in the moment, embrace the knowing and manifest the results. When I spoke to you concerning waiting . . . remember now, that this also applies to assimilating information. There is no need to wait to experience or understand. But, the very knowing . . . confirmation within can manifest instantly in your experience and your understanding. Not the other way around. It's been backwards in your experience to this time . . . you will need to do a reverse process.

There is a feeling that will come with this . . . that will also be confirmed within . . . that this is as you have known before time. Allow it. Flow with it. It is transforming, not only your experience but, it will also transform the very cells in your body to prepare for transition . . . a very crucial step for you.

Thank you.

CHAPTER 9

THE END IS ONLY THE BEGINNING

Meditation: Written by Ola

Can you not conceive of us as being present now, in this room? Must you continue to project us as separate from you in time and space? All reference to our portended absences is only to accommodate your 3-dimensional sense of space and time. And, if we are present here, now and always, then are we attempting to express to you a new way of perceiving your own reality? Yes, we are.

Imagine for a moment that we are you and that you are conscious of this union. Then, your consciousness would at all times be aware of us and all knowledge which we have . . . . allowing you a view of this moment in all directions.

You have but to be consciously aware of whatever is entering your thoughts to know what you need to know. Simple! But, this requires trust of your own intuitive process without any judgement of the value or reality of this awareness. Judgement implies separation. Separation embraced consciously or unconsciously leads to doubt. Doubt prompts a search for safety which creates insecurity and fear. Fear is fed by judgement and so the circle continues.

Wonton transmission through Ola to the Navigator:

Now is the time for all good people to come to the aid of this world. I am Wonton speaking. We wish to speak to you today concerning many energies that are flowing thru your space and to help you prioritize those things that would be most beneficial to you in the Now Moment.

Previously, we discussed feeling as "knowingness" and I hope that this was of benefit to you. I hope that it helped you to understand and divide for the purpose of organization, the energies that proceed from your mind and the energies that proceed from the Source that you are.

As you allow more and more of the within energies, which is a combination, you will experience more and more the feelings that will express upon this plane and help to bring about the changes and the new structure that is imminent.

You are a very important part of that new, and must begin to see yourselves more and more as one of the building blocks that has a specific place . . . a specific work . . . a specific energy that is needed, as these energies are transmuted into a new dimension of freedom.

So many of the things which you desire are merely expressions of the feeling of freedom, that is being channeled through you at this time. Allow them. They are the new. They can be trusted.

I sense at this point that you are examining them and seeking to organize them in some way in your thought patterns. This is not necessary. Just allow them to be there. Allow them control. You do not have to fear them, because the force that is behind them . . . is the love that creates all things. Your analyzing and attempt to understand mentally of all of your feelings will only become more frustrating to you as the acceleration of time continues.

They do not originate in your physical body. They originate in your consciousness, and thereby, your physical mechanisms of mind games will not express them . . . will not allow them. They are, within themselves, unfolding and will create for you the reality that was planned.

Energy is motivated from the Center . . . the consciousness which resides in each particle, as you understand them. That Center, that motivates each particle of energy, is the same Center that resides in you, in a more complex form. And thereby, the motivation is one. As you allow and trust that more and experience that oneness . . . all of your manifest reality will complete and present a unified whole, or thought from the Source. Does that help you to visualize what I want to discuss today?

Answer: Maybe a clarification on the way that this is experienced by us. You're saying that it's not going to go through any kind of thought process, any kind of reasoning process that we're familiar with? In other words, we don't have anything to relate it to?

Wonton: The process that you are referring to is part of the illusion that was created to form the separation that you have experienced. This will not go with you. This will recede back into the illusion from which it came. What I am discussing now, is what you have learned . . . that everything is energy. That within your limited knowledge of that energy, you perceive a core, a center, a nucleus, which contains a blueprint in each particle of your reality. That blueprint, that center, that core of each particle, is not separate from the Source . . . the thought.

As the thought has emanated from the creator . . . the Source of all things . . . within that particle, there is the plan or the blueprint that it unfolds in order to present to you . . . a material world.

All thought originates from the Source. All thought is manifested in your reality as light particles. There being but one Source of thought, there is but one plan within each particle. Everything, from the beginning of your time, has contained this plan. Everything that has manifested in your dimension has merely been an unfoldment of that original thought and plan of the Creator.

The creator has not been involved in time as you have. So that, as time unfolded, He created the plan as He went along. No, no! It is time that you perceive of the fact that from the beginning, there has been within this thought . . . the same as within the seed . . . the whole tree of life . . . as everyone who has incarnated on this planet, in time, has experienced. That tree has grown and unfolded as was in the original seed thought of the Creator.

This is why we say . . . "There has never been a mistake". This is why we say that, "there has never been the reality that you have conceived of as opposing polarities" (good, bad - right, wrong - so forth).

This polarity, this duality that you have experienced was in the seed thought . . . necessary for the purpose of manifesting and motivation and unfoldment. It has been the source of much of the carrying of this thought forward into a form whereby it could manifest and be experienced, rather than just thought. It took form and structure.

Your involvement as humanity, in that form and structure, also included the possibility of "freedom of choice" in the assumed identity of separate being. That freedom of choice has created a seeming pattern of thought which has taken form in your 3rd dimension reality as many dualities.

Let me see if I can explain more clearly. The freedom of choice that you seemingly experience, was also a part of the seed . . . was also a part of the plan unfolding. Within that limitation of freedom of choice, there was created the opposite of everything known prior to 3rd dimension. Where there had been nothing but Love, there was created a duality brought about by "fear" . . . of "unlove". That has many names. However, all choices made within that field of vision that you call "free will" . . . was all "unlove".

You have named it love and hate. But, in separation, all of it has been "unlove". What has seemed to you a polarity has merely been an illusion created for the purpose of a "backdrop" from which the true Love could shine forth.

This was the purpose for your incarnation. This was the purpose in coming into a reality in which . . . all is"unlove" and you as Source, could manifest . . . not by words nor analysis, nor mind . . . but by your very presence . . . the truth of the " love" that is reality.

At this point in time, you are inadequate to judge that . . . . to perceive of that through your minds. Because of "step 1", you have assumed an identity that knows nothing but "unlove".

It may call it's experiences by many names but, it merely has been an identity through which the "backdrop" has been created. The true identity that you incarnated as . . . has first created a background, as you must do in any painting or artwork, upon which you can express the true desire of the creative work. As you allow the self that you are, to manifest the feelings, you will be delivering to the canvas of "unlove", the truth of "Love". The medium will not be words, or analysis, or mind, or thought, or seeming deeds . . . but it will be pure Thought from the Creator expressed through you as energy . . . which you experience as "feeling".

(Pause in transmission)

I must allow your channel to rest. She is struggling within her mind to conceive and express what she is seeing and she is very tense. You must understand that, regardless of how unlimited these thoughts may feel to you at this moment, nevertheless, you are prepared. It is only your limited perception that causes you to hesitate to move forward with the energy that you feel, even though that energy is familiar to you.

We are bringing you an understanding concerning all of the experiences of 3rd dimension which you, at one time, were conscious of. We are only bringing it to your remembrance now, because you have triggered, within yourself, the remembrance. Always, we work only according to your blueprint. Allow yourself to fall into the unlimitedness . . . the freedom . . . which you, in the past, were so aware of . . . as your environment.

This knowingness is not recalled until you have expressed a desire to allow your history here and your identity to dissolve . . . back into the field from which it came. As that identity recedes, what will take its place is . . . awareness . . . of "total freedom".

"Total freedom" translates to you in many ways now, when it is processed thru your mental mechanism. But, total freedom is, in reality, an absolute that can only be . . . "felt". Light, which you are, is unlimited and experiences total freedom. Light is the framework of all structure and form in this dimension.

Now to return to the thought being expressed prior to a need for rest. Did you grasp or envision the reality of the Source unfolding within its own awareness, a reality that was to reflect the opposite of truth . . . for the purpose of creating an environment? This environment would then facilitate the expression of the Truth or the Spirit of the Source, and thereby, allow each individual portion of that Source to wake up and become Aware of Itself.

The majority of humanity is not prepared to hear this, nor is it all agreed that it will know this at this point in time. This is being revealed to you, again according to your blueprint, because, this is part of your purpose in incarnation, I.E . . . your "mission" and, therefore . . . you, within yourself, are eliciting this awareness.

The dimension from which you incarnated, did not supply you with the intensity of the experience which you have had in this dimension. Because of the desired unfolding from the Source within you, you desired and required this experience and are now beginning . . . just beginning . . . to feel within you, the expansiveness of who you really are.

To wake up and know yourself, is the next step toward being that Source . . . in a new adventure that was contemplated within the Source, before worlds were ever created. What you call the mission beyond is . . . the plan that is unfolding for you.

When I say that this experience was required, begin to be aware that all of your experiences within this dimension have been but a school for the new astronauts that will depart from Source . . . by becoming the Source.

As you have experienced in a small degree the expansiveness of yourself . . . and that is indeed what you do in this dimension, moment by moment . . . you expand the reality of yourself into all areas that fascinate you. The Source has also that same within . . . that will always . . . and for eternity, expand awareness into all space.

Do not see yourself as a "professional student" who will be forever learning in this dimension. But, please, realize that you are now nearing graduation, which will allow you to enter a new state of existence as someone who has completed the course and is now certified to begin their true mission.

Do not make this experience an end in itself, because, in reality, it is only a beginning. I am speaking to you of something that is difficult in the dimension in which you exist, to grasp. However, there are other focuses that you have in other dimensions that are aware of this plan. You are never alone. That is merely the backdrop of 3rd dimension for the education in a course that prepared you for the journey in which is seemingly . . . aloneness in space.

As you are able to draw from within and realize your connectedness with the Source, which is everything, you are training yourself to experience space . . . infinite space . . . seemingly alone, but with that awareness.

All of 3rd dimension . . . perceive it as a blackboard, a backdrop, a background . . . all of it. You, as human, are the piece of chalk, or the paint and colors which are written on that background and enable the true Spirit, the true Love, to reveal itself.

One of the frustrating things in your experience of religion and spirituality on this plane, has been to conceive of many ways that God is "real". All that you have conceived mentally, or learned through your intellect, are but merely part of the backdrop that is the non-reality of the "truth of spirit". Only the vibration that you interpret as "feeling" is in truth . . . that "spirit". And just as Jesus taught . . . the wind cannot be controlled. "The wind goeth where it pleaseth". So, the Spirit cannot be confined to your limited thoughts of duality . . . of what you think it might be or might not be. It is a force that knows that you are dreaming, because it has created the dream.

It is a force that weaves in and out and around, over and under . . . all of its creation, in order to structure it. "Love" . . . "Spirit" is a force that you do not perceive with your five senses, but it is the very force that holds together a structure in which those five senses function.

You have, in your limited framework, felt this vibration, sensed it, perceived it, and known it. But, do not try to confine it to your 3rd dimensional perception any more than you can attempt to control or confine the wind. It goes where it wills, seemingly to you, without reason. But that, is only because you failed to be aware that you are that Spirit.

As long as you attempt to observe the spirit, to observe love, you remain in a state of separation, which was only created for you to wake up within the form and structure that you call human . . . to the awareness and become that Spirit and Love. You cannot observe it . . . judge it . . . understand it . . . reason it. You can only . . . be it. That is your destiny.

You cannot command it. You cannot entice it. You cannot confine it. Because it is All There Is . . . and it is as if you have separated out a part of yourself and said to the other part . . "this is how you must be, this is how you must act". Love is such a powerful force . . . that your awareness of it in 3rd dimension is very, very limited. What experiences that you have of it . . . has always overwhelmed you . . . because you come from an experience of limitation, which is all of 3rd dimension. Third dimension is limitation which is the opposite of love, which is unlimitedness.

I realize that it's hard for you to grasp what I am conveying about the life force that has created everything. Because you are asked, in your separation or seeming separation from that life force, to now realize that you "are it". But can you see the power that resides within you?

This is a creation of the Source that was in the first thought . . . that is a seed, that is about to break through the dark ground and sprout . . . and grow. And only Beauty, Love and Abundance are in the tree. Because they were placed there in the first thought of the Father and it must unfold as that.

The energies that you experience are seeming very immense to you at this time. But do not limit yourself. If you were not designed . . . if you were not prepared to contain this force, you would not even be able to have a vision of what I speak. The fact that you can feel It, and envision it, and glimpse your destiny, is evidence that this already exists and is your inheritance.

I have loved telling this to you. I have loved sharing this with you . . . because this is our life . . . this is our oneness . . . and this is our destiny in union with you. Thank you for the time today. Goodbye.

EPILOGUE

It can be revealed now, that the "New Earth" is destined to go "Where no Gods have Gone Before" . . . beyond this creation . . . into the "Beyond the Beyond"!

We love you and are aware and knowing of your feelings and immediate needs. Don't be too sure of the circumstances which appear to be true. Just as the dream of others has been superimposed on the world scene, you are also superimposing a new dream on your old one. ***Your reality that you think is somehow real, will not change gradually!***

Do not look for a gradual change in your circumstances any more than "9/11" was gradual. It was abrupt and reality changed instantly. Be advised, that the same type of instant hologram will be enacted by you and us. Remain in the reality that you instinctively know is real for you.

We are monitoring you continually and are prepared to appear at a moment's notice. Now is the time for you to completely let go of the "past reality" that you have been clinging to for a sense of reality. You have been continually going in and out of alternative realities since birth. The awareness of these changing focuses had not been perceived by you until this time when you are ready to experience the illusions of consecutive time.

Do not be mental about the information which I am sharing. If you search your feelings, this organization of events in a pattern which suggested passages of time, has been a great limitation for you. History is whatever you choose it to be in illusions. You are not now bound by these interpretations which you have given to your experience on the Earth plane.

"Mobility of Consciousness" is necessary for events unfolding. The information which has been relayed to you in the past is present within your Consciousness at all times. You will be aware of all that you "Need to Know" at each moment. "Don't sweat the small stuff"!

Continue to project moment by moment the next event you wish to experience. Your wishes will also be our wishes. There can be no separation. Your instinctive knowing in each moment will bring you to the place and time to join forces with us.

ALL ABOARD!!!

"All Aboard" will be heard by those inhabitants of the New Earth when the journey begins for travel where "no Gods have gone before". Those who have mastered the teachings in this book and have chosen this knowing for themselves will depart this universe for a journey that will take its inhabitants beyond all of the presently known creations.

This will be a journey for further exploring and creating of new territory for those prepared and knowing of themselves as the Consciousness of God present in a Human form. All creation in space existing now has followed this same plan. This is the means by which your creator has sought to know and expand for discovery of origin. Just as your search has been to seek your origin and return home, you can imagine the Creator's desire and searching since the "Big Bang" when all creation in this space had its beginning.

Now you know, that the Consciousness that you possess is the self-awareness of "God" desiring to know and return to reunite with the original Source. If you have been desiring of the same during your life span, you should be waking up and expanding your thoughts of the realization of all that you have experienced in desiring to discover your Source and knowing of who you truly are in Consciousness. There is only one Consciousness and that Consciousness is God! This book has been channeled for you to realize and know that you are that one Consciousness exploring and creating to know its Source since the "Big Bang" occurred and a whole new territory and experience was realized. The Source of all that exists in our universe is seeking to go home same as you are seeking!

You have never found information on this second ascension because it is an unknown. "You are boldly going where no soul has gone before"!

The unfolding to you of your true mission on the "New Earth" should trigger memories in you and answer many questions.

Contemplate! You will begin to perceive all things new and different in your experience now and what you perceive as the past.

The knowingness that will come within you will allow you the mobility of Consciousness to create new realities without the need to use space and time as an identity.

Be prepared to allow new realities without the burden of carrying forward the past. Your identity is not in the past. It is now! All the names and mainly the soul personalities which have channeled to you are all one with you and the soul group contains experiences, energies, and identities which have existed in the past and we all share them as one. We will be one of many soul groups which will have identities with desires and personalities and will plan an adventure together. This is the Gathering you have anticipated and desired.

The "Beyond the Beyond" is now!

We love you and we are you as you are us.

"The Group, The Group, The Group!"